PALLAHAXI TIDE

Other books by Michael G. Coney

King of the Sceptre'd Isle
Fang, the Gnome

PALLAHAXI TIDE

Michael G. Coney

PORCÉPIC BOOKS
VICTORIA

This edition is published by Press Porcépic Limited, 4252
Commerce Circle, Victoria, B.C., V8Z 4M2, with the as-
sistance of the Canada Council.

Canadian Cataloguing in Publication Data

Coney, Michael G.   1932-
  Pallahaxi tide

(Tesseract books)
Previously published under title: Hello summer, good-
bye in the UK.
ISBN 0-88878-293-4

I. Title. II.Title: Hello summer, goodbye. III. Series.
PS8555.053P34 1990   C813 '.54   C90-091488-2
PR9199.3.C68P34 1990

ONE

I OFTEN THINK of that day in Alika when my father, my mother and myself hurried to and fro, assembling a pile of possessions on the front porch in preparation for our holiday in Pallahaxi. Although I had barely reached puberty, I had learned enough of the ways of adults to keep out of the way during this annual event which always constituted, for some reason, a panic situation. My mother scuttled around with quick movements and vacant eyes, constantly asking the whereabouts of vital items then answering her own questions. My father, tall and dignified, stalked up and down the cellar steps with cans of distil for his prize possession, the self-propelled motorcart. Whenever my parents caught sight of me, there was no love in their eyes.

So I kept out of their way, while nevertheless making sure that my own possessions were not forgotten. I had already secreted in the pile my slingball, my Circlets board, my model grume-skimmer and my fishing net, unassembled. During a furtive visit to the motor-cart I slipped my cage of pet drivets behind the back seat. At that moment my father emerged from the house with yet another can in his hand, scowling.

"If you want to make yourself useful, you might fill the tank." He set the can beside the cart and handed me a brass funnel. "Don't spill it. It's valuable stuff, these days."

He was referring to the shortage resulting from the war. It seemed to me that he hardly ever referred to anything else. As he strode back into the house, I unscrewed the cap, sniffing at the heady aroma of distil. The stuff had always fascinated me; it seemed incredible to my juvenile mind that a liquid, particularly a liquid bearing a close resemblance to water, should be capable of *burning*. Once, at the suggestion of a friend, I had tried drinking it. The basis of distil, this friend had told me, is similar to that of beer and wine and all those other exciting, forbidden drinks served at inns.

So I crept down to the cellar one night, hugging a hot brick to keep the fear away, and opened a can, and drank. Judging from the way the distil burned my mouth and throat as it went down, I was not surprised that it was capable of propelling a steam engine. But I couldn't believe people gained pleasure from drinking it. Sick and dizzy, I spent some time groaning against the outside wall while the cold crept into my spine; my shivering was due as much to fear as sickness. It was winter and the cold planet Rax watched me like an evil eye; in Alika, the icy nights of winter can be terrifying.

But I always associated Pallahaxi with summer and warmth, and that was where we were going that day. I shoved the spout of the funnel into the tank of the motorcart and tilted the can, and the distil gobbled out. Across the road, three small girls watched, dirty mouths hanging open with awe and envy at the sight of the magnificent vehicle. I set the empty can down with a flourish and took up another. One of the kids threw a stone which clanged against the polished paintwork, then they all ran off down the road, yelling.

Beyond the houses opposite I could see the tall spires of Parliament Buildings, where the Regent presided over the House of Members, and where my father worked in a dingy little office as Secretary to the Minister of Public Affairs. My father is a Parl and the motor-cart bore a crest to that effect—hence the kids' resentment. I could sympathize with them over that—but it seemed a shame to vent spite on the cart, rather than on my father.

I turned to look at our house. It was a large structure in local yellow stone; my mother flitted past a window on some obscure mission of panic. A few sentient flowers groped for elusive insects in the garden, and I remember wondering why the yard looked so neglected this year. Spreadweed was everywhere, proliferating cancerously and strangling the last of the bluepods with emerald garottes. There was something relentless in the visible creep of that weed and I shivered suddenly, thinking that by the time we returned from our holiday it would have taken over the house and would creep from the wainscot at night, throttling us in our sleep.

"Drove!"

My father towered over me, holding out another can. As I looked up at him guiltily he shrugged, his expression odd. "Never mind, Drove." He too was regarding the house. "I'll carry on here. You go and collect your things."

Back in my room I took a quick look around. I'd always found that I needed to take very few belongings to Pallahaxi; it was a different world there, and there were different things to do. I heard mother scuttling about in the next room.

On the window-sill stood the glass jar containing my ice-goblin. I had nearly forgotten it. I examined it closely, imagining I saw a faint film of crystals on the surface of the thick liquid. I looked around, found a stick, and poked the ice-goblin gingerly. Nothing happened.

During the previous winter, when the distant sun

fled tiny across the sky and Rax was visible as a fearful cold stone at night, there had been a craze among the neighbourhood kids for ice-goblins. Like most such enthusiasms it was not clear exactly how it started, but suddenly everyone had their glass jars full of saturated solutions, each day dropping in a little more of the strange crystals which came from the flat marshy lands of the coast where the ice-devils lived.

"I hope you're not thinking of taking that awful thing with you," mother exclaimed as I emerged from my room carrying the goblin.

"Well, I can't leave him, can I? He's almost ready." Sensing the fear in her voice I elaborated. "I started him at the same time as Joelo down the street, and Joelo's goblin came alive two days ago, and nearly had his finger off. Look!" I jiggled the jar under her nose and she backed away.

"Take that freezing thing away from me!" she cried, and I stared at her in astonishment. I'd never heard my mother swear before. I heard my father coming and put the goblin quickly on a nearby table, turning away and busying myself in the corner with a pile of clothes.

"What's going on here? Was that you screaming, Fayette?"

"Oh... Oh, it's all right. Drove frightened me for a moment, that's all. It's nothing, really, Burt."

I felt my father's hand on my shoulder and turned reluctantly to face him. His cold eyes stared into mine. "Let's get this straight, Drove. You want to come to Pallahaxi, then you behave yourself, right? I've got enough to think about without you playing the fool. Go and carry the things out to the cart."

I always used to think it unfair that my father was capable of imposing his will on me by force. By the age of puberty a person's intelligence is fully developed and from that time on he begins to go downhill. So it was with my father, I told myself resentfully as I loaded the motorcart. The pompous old fool, aware of his inability to defeat me intellectually, resorts to threats. In a sense, I had won the small battle.

The trouble was that father was not aware of the fact. He moved to and fro from the various rooms to the porch, ignoring me as I struggled to keep pace—ineffectually, for the pile of boxes continued to grow. I gained some small satisfaction by dropping his things heavily into the luggage space in the cart, while placing my own stuff carefully on the spare seat. I found myself wondering why I liked to frighten my mother from time to time, and decided it was because, subconsciously, I resented her stupidity. She used her superstitions like weapons, brandishing them in argument like clubs of incontrovertible fact.

We are all terrified of cold—such a fear is natural and no doubt evolved as a means of warning us against the night and the winter and the things cold can do to you. But mother's fear of cold is unreasoning and, quite possibly, hereditary. Whenever I press her on the subject she purses her lips and says: "That is a thing I'd rather you didn't ask me, *ever*, Drove." In a way, this little speech is perfect, in content, in intonation, in the hurt, mysterious expression on her face. It is pure, exalted theatre.

What she means is that they put her sister away. It is a simple thing and it happens to a lot of people, but my mother has succeeded in investing the affair with tragedy and drama. Nobody suffered more over the Aunt Zu business than I, yet I have almost been able to forget the terror which possessed me at the time, and see the funny side of it.

I always thought Aunt Zu had a thing for my father; anyway she persuaded him to lend her the motorcart—which was an achievement beyond anything my mother had accomplished. Aunt Zu, who was unmarried, wanted to show me off to some distant relatives; it was a long drive in her lox-drawn buggy so, quite simply, she borrowed the motorcart. It was winter.

We were about half-way back, in totally uninhabited country, when we ran out of distil and the motorcart hissed to a shambling halt.

"Oh dear," said Aunt Zu mildly. "We shall have to walk, Drove. I hope your little legs are strong enough." I remember the exact words she used.

So we began to walk. I knew we would never make it home before dark, and I knew that with the dark would come the cold, and we were not dressed for it. I was intelligent enough—despite the way she talked down to me—to weigh up the possibilities and realize that she was right, that we couldn't stay with the motorcart. Despite father's exalted Government position even he could not afford an enclosed vehicle such as that used by the Regent.

"Oh dear," said Aunt Zu some time later as the sun disappeared and the sinister orb of Rax glittered on the horizon, "it's getting cold."

We passed a group of feeding lorin, sitting amongst the branches as they munched noisily and I remember thinking to myself that if I became really cold—terrified cold—I could snuggle up to one, burrowing into the long hair. Lorin are harmless, friendly creatures and around Alika they are chiefly used as companions for the lox. On cold days the lox can become torpid and semi-paralyzed with fear and the presence of the lorin has a soothing effect. Some say it is a form of telepathy. I looked longingly at the lorin that evening, envying their silky fur and their air of indolent good nature. Although young, I knew what life was all about, and I knew enough to be frightened of Aunt Zu just a little...

Rax had risen above the trees, reflecting counterfeit light with no warmth. "I wish I'd remembered to bring my fur coat," murmured Aunt Zu.

"We could cuddle up to the lorin," I suggested nervously.

"Whatever gave you the idea that I would countenance approaching such an animal?" snapped Aunt Zu, fear feeding her temper. "Do you think me no better than a lox?"

"Sorry."

"Why arc you walking on so fast? You must be warm in that coat. My clothes are so thin."

I should have been as frightened as she; we were a long way from home and despite my coat the cold was beginning to bite like fangs. I stuffed my hands into my pockets and hurried on, not speaking. As a child I was more primitive and at the back of my mind was still the thought of the lorin; if all else failed—including Aunt Zu —the animals would look after me.

They always did...

"Lend me your scarf to wrap my hands in, Drove. I don't have pockets."

I paused, unwinding the woollen scarf from my neck. I handed it to her, still without speaking. I didn't want to give her a hook to hang her terror on. As we topped a hill I could see lights far in the distance; too far. The winter wind whipped against my bare legs and the blood ran icy towards my heart. I could hear Aunt Zu mumbling.

"Phu... Phu..." she prayed to the sun-god. "Phu, I'm cold. Warm me, warm me... help me."

There were low hedges beside the road composed of spiky, insensate plants. Knowing our fear, sensing it in their strange way, lorin stood close by the far side, their shaggy heads a pale blur in the raxlight as they watched us inquisitively and waited for the cold to crack the civilization away from our shuddering bodies.

"I must have your coat, Drove. I'm older than you, and I can't stand the cold so well."

"Please, let's go to the lorin, Aunt Zu."

"Drove, I've told you before! I refuse to go near those disgusting brutes. Give me your coat, you disobedient little boy!" Her hands were on me like claws.

"Let me go!" I struggled, but she was much bigger than I, wiry and strong. She stood behind me, tugging and jerking at the coat, and I could feel the rigidness and terror of her.

"I'll speak to your father about you, you little beast. He'll know how to deal with you—I'm sure I don't. Now give—me—that—coat!" She punctuated her words with fierce jerks and suddenly I was standing in my underthings, the warmth evaporating away from me. Aunt Zu babbled to herself as she knotted the sleeves around her shoulders; I saw the light from Rax flash in her eyes and she was regarding me cunningly. "Just give me your pants and I won't tell your father, Drove."

I was running but I could hear her close behind, and hear the whining screech of her breath as she gasped and shouted at the same time. Then suddenly the hard iciness of the road hit me and she was on top of me, tearing at my clothes and screaming an incomprehensible babble of terror. In my fear I had drifted into a dreamlike state and soon I was hardly aware that I was naked, hardly aware of her receding footsteps. While I lay there I felt the lorin take hold of me, and dimly knew the reason for the warmth in my mind. Then they were carrying me, enfolding me, soothing me with their murmurings which I half understood.

As I fell asleep, the image of Aunt Zu bounding and screeching along the raxlit road faded from my mind.

The lorin had taken me home the next day, delivering me naked to the doorstep in the warmth of the sun Phu, then fading about their duties. As I came to my senses I saw a few of them; one straddled a lox, urging the beast into motion between the shafts of a night-soil cart; another squatted in a field, fertilizing the crops. A third swung from the branches of a nearby obo tree, munching winternuts. I opened the door and went into the house. My mother bathed me a lot that day; she said I stank. It was a long time later that I heard they'd locked Aunt Zu away.

Later I remembered the night-soil cart; it is a vehicle one rarely sees; and I asked mother why we didn't spread the dung on the fields instead of dumping it in the town pit. I mentioned the fact that we encouraged the lorin to excrete among the crops.

"Don't be disgusting, Drove," she admonished me. "You know perfectly well that's an entirely different matter. And by the way, I'd rather you kept away from the lorin."

To return to the day of our departure for Pallahaxi. In due course all our belongings were loaded into the motorcart which now smelled intriguingly of distil. It is my father's policy to drain the tank after using the vehicle, ever since he discovered it empty one morning and surmised that the lorin had drunk the contents. The vehicle is used rarely; it spends most of its time standing outside the house mutely identifying my father's position by means of the Erto flag emblazoned on its flank.

I slipped back to the house intending to say goodbye to my room, but was waylaid by mother. She was spreading bread with winternut paste; a pot of cocha juice stood on the table.

"Drove, I want you to have something to eat before we go. You haven't been eating well lately."

"Listen, mother," I said patiently, "I'm not hungry. We never have the things I like, anyway."

She took this as criticism of her housekeeping abilities. "How can I be expected to feed everyone on the money I get, with all this rationing? You've no idea what it's like. There's nothing in the stores; nothing at all. Maybe you ought to do the shopping yourself some day, young man, instead of moping about the house all the holidays. Then you'd know what it's like."

"I only said I wasn't hungry, mother."

"Food is fuel for the body, Drove." Father was standing by the doorway. "Just as distil is fuel for the motorcart. Without fuel in the form of food your body will not run. You will get cold and die. In my position with the Government we are able to obtain food which others, less fortunate than ourselves, must do without. You should realize how lucky you are."

In a few short words my father was thus able to drive me insane with rage, while denying me the possibility of any reprisal. I wondered if he had the perception to know what he was doing. I wondered if he knew how much I disliked being told simple facts which I knew already, listening to educational comparisons of bodies and machines during the holidays and, above all, being told that I am lucky. I simmered quietly while we ate a dish of fried fish and dryfruit.

My mother had been giving me speculative glances from time to time and I thought that she was aware of

PALLAHAXI TIDE

my mood, but I should have known better. After the final glance—which could almost be described as crafty—she addressed father.

"I wonder if we'll see anything of that little girl again this summer, let's see, what was her name, Burt?"

Father answered absently. "Daughter of the Cannery President, Konch? Goldenlips? or some such name. Fine girl. Fine girl."

"No, no, Burt. A *little* girl, she and Drove were such friends. Such a pity, her father was an innkeeper."

"Oh? Then I don't think I remember."

I mumbled something and left the table quickly before mother could get around to her original intention, which was to ask me the name of the girl and to watch my face closely as I told her. I ran up the stairs to my room.

The girl was not little—she was slightly smaller than myself and the same age, and her name—which I shall never forget so long as I live—was Pallahaxi-Browneyes.

I stood at the window of my room and watched a group of kids playing around the public heater on the other side of the street, and thought of Browneyes. I wondered what she had been doing all winter in her magical town of Pallahaxi, and whether she had thought of me at all. I wondered if she would remember me, when we met again. Childhood days pass slowly and a lot happens in a year and, despite my mother's remarks, Browneyes and I had hardly known each other. We had only got around to speaking to each other in the last couple of days of the holiday; that's how shy kids can be, at that age.

But no day had passed since when I hadn't seen her face in my mind's eye; the cute dimples in her cheeks when she smiled—which was often—the wide shiny

17

brownness of her eyes when she was sad—which was once, when we said goodbye and my parents looked on with indulgent relief. She was the daughter of an inn-keeper and she lived in a house where people *drank*, and I know my parents were glad the holiday was over.

The last thing I took from my room was a small green bracelet. Browneyes had dropped it one day and I'd picked it up but I hadn't returned it. It would serve as a simple re-introduction, because I still felt shy about meeting her again. I slipped the trinket into my pocket and went down the stairs to rejoin my parents who were ready to go. As I passed through the kitchen I noticed a glass jar, empty. I picked it up and examined it closely, and smelt it.

Mother had thrown my ice-goblin away.

TWO

THE FINAL PREPARATIONS were carried out in silence. Father lit the burners in ceremonial fashion while I, still smarting from the underhand way in which my ice-goblin had been disposed of, watched from the required distance and hoped the thing would blow up in his face. There was the usual muffled 'poof' as the evaporated distil ignited, and before long steam drifted from among the rods and cylinders and a stewing sound from the boiler announced that the motorcart was ready. We climbed in; father and mother side by side in the front seat, myself behind, next to the boiler. The friendly warmth soothed my temper; it is impossible for anybody to feel moody for long in the back seat of a motorcart. Soon we were passing through the back streets of Alika;

people watched us in silence with none of the friendly waving I remembered from previous years.

"Freezing Parls!" a little girl with no arms shouted.

We passed the final public heater, a small thing of vertical tubes leaking a tiny feather of steam, then we were in open country. Father and mother were talking to each other but I could not hear what they said; the pistons were hissing and thumping right behind me. I leaned forward.

"Is that where they found Aunt Zu?" I shouted.

Of course I knew they had found her there; people talk. It seemed that a search party had been sent out, a small number of brave spirits fortified with heavy furs and hot bricks and, I should imagine, stomachs full of distil. They had found Aunt Zu just a hundred paces from the safety of the public heater. She had been hugging an anemone tree, trying to climb its slippery trunk to crawl into the dubious haven of its stomach in search of warmth. She was, they said, screaming continuously and her fingers had dug so deeply into the resilient flesh of the tree that they had to be levered apart with sticks. She was naked, so my informant told me ghoulishly; by this time the story was circulating around school. The tree had snatched the clothes from her back and eaten them, but Aunt Zu was too heavy to be lifted and too weak to climb.

"I would rather you did not refer to your aunt, Drove," mother said. "There are some things it is better to forget. Look, isn't that a lovely view?"

Hills rolled away before us like the slow waves of the sea when the grume is at its height. Here and there were cultivated fields of root crops but mostly the land was open range where lox grazed peacefully in the continuous sun of early summer. Everything was fresh and green after the long winter and the streams and rivers still flowed; later on they would dry up with the heat. Nearby a team of four lox dragged a heavy plow through the soil; two lorin walked upright between them, occasionally patting their smooth flanks and no doubt giving mental encouragement. A farmer sat atop the plow on a precarious seat, uttering meaningless farming cries. Like many people who spend their life under the sun Phu he was mutated, his favour taking the form of an extra arm on his right side. In the hand he brandished a whip.

We passed occasional small villages, taking in water from time to time at cottages where farmwives eyed us sullenly from low doorways and children could be seen lurking within. Here the mutations were many and father complimented one man on his multifingered hands.

The man continued to work the pump, water gushing in rhythmic spurts. "Phu looked kindly on me, I reckon," he panted. "This is hard country. A man needs all the help he can get." His fingers danced among the machinery of the motorcart, checking a pin here, tightening a nut there. He pushed an old leather funnel into the watertank and tilted the bucket carefully.

"I suppose things get short here, with the war..." ventured father with surprising diffidence. For once he was out of his element, here in this primitive country. Through the open door of the hovel I caught sight of a lorin, actually sitting in a chair.

"What war?" asked the man.

I thought about this remark as we continued our journey into the barren lands of the equatorial regions and the sun circled closer and closer to the horizon. Travelling, I had lost track of time, and with the continuous sunlight of early summer one standard day followed another with only periodic tiredness to acquaint me of their passage. It seemed that the only elements of existence were the desert, the occasional ground-drivet, the seat beneath me, and the chugging of the steam engine.

Then there was a diversion; we met a fish truck broken down at the roadside. The crew of two sat dejectedly beside their stricken vehicle. In the manner of their kind, a few lorin had materialized from the empty desert and sat with the men in pointless mimicry.

My father mumbled something to mother and I have no doubt that he was considering driving straight on by, but he braked at the last moment and stopped several paces past the truck. There was a dreadful stench of fish.

"I can take you as far as Bexton Post," father called over his shoulder as the two men hurried up. "You can get a message out from there. You'll have to ride on the fuel bunker, there's no room inside."

The men grunted thanks, swung themselves on behind me, and we were moving again. "Hello there, sonny," one of them shouted through the maze of flashing rods.

"What went wrong with the truck?" I yelled back. I resented them invading my privacy and thought the question might annoy the man.

He grinned ruefully and stepped around the running board, seating himself firmly beside me and forcing me to edge closer to the boiler. I stared ahead, furious with myself for having invited conversation. For once my parents had been proved right. This is a class of person it does not pay to encourage.

"Freezing thing's freezing well clogged up," he explained earthily. "No distil, y'see." He glanced at the cans on the fuel bunker. "Except for some lucky freezers.

We had the truck converted for woodburning—that way you have to build a freezing great fire under the boiler and you have to remember to keep throwing on logs. Well, we remembered that all right; it was the cannery was at fault. They forgot to give us brushes to clean out the tubes—like long thin flues they are. And now they're all clogged up with freezing soot and the truck won't go."

"Listen, there's no need to swear like that."

"Cocky little freezer, aren't you? Your dad's some sort of Parl, I reckon, is he? Must be, to run a motorcart like this." His eyes kept straying to the cans and his presence had become overpowering, menacing. My parents sat in front, side by side, oblivious, discussing shortages.

"Father holds an important position," I said firmly to hide the fear within. The phraseology was not mine—I was repeating words I'd heard my mother use on many occasions. For the first time it occurred to me that I was unsure of their meaning. I visualized a group of pinnacles, snowy-like mountain peaks in winter. Father sat atop the tallest, while his underlings perched on subordinate peaks. The general public huddled in the valleys, awed by the majesty of it all.

"I'm sure he does, lad. Sits at the same desk every day, I'll bet—except once a year when he takes you all on holiday to the coast to watch the grume, and you stay at a hotel called Seaview."

"If you must know, father has a holiday cottage at Pallahaxi."

"I suppose he would have." He smiled at me with blackened teeth, his eyes remaining cold. "Now, let me ask you something. What do you think I do?"

"You drive a fish truck."

"And that's all there is to it? No, boy. I see the world.

Or at least—" he corrected himself "—I see the land of Erto, all of it, not just the little bit between Alika and Pallahaxi. I've driven the whole coast from the old cannery at Pallahaxi right around to Horlox in the North and Ibana in the south where Erto meets with Asta and the border guards are—or were, before the freezing war made it so you didn't know where the border is. And I've driven the old border road both north and south in the shadow of the Great Central Range where the sun Phu is like a furnace in the sky and no two animals look alike—and no two men, either. You know your geography, boy?"

I knew what I'd been taught, and I knew this was not the right time to air my knowledge; this gross fellow would contradict everything I said. It is difficult for a person like me, one who has not travelled much, to visualize the globe, the planet on which we live. I'd been taught to think of it all as a ball held in a hand. The ball is the world, the hand is the single continental mass. This mass is divided into two by the first set of knuckles, representing the Great Central Range and the boundary between Erto and Asta. One half (the back of the hand) is Asta, the other half (the fingers) represents the deeply indented land of Erto. This hand-continent wraps almost around the globe, leaving three oceans: the huge polar oceans and the long, narrow ocean joining the two, through which the grume flows in summer. I can visualize this, just and only just.

The fish-trucker was talking on. "I've been caught in snow and ice, all out of fuel and only the little heat left in the boiler to keep warm by; the cold eating in at the gaps in my clothes enough to drive another man mad, and I've come through it. I've driven through the wetlands and had the truck sink up to its axles and an ice-devil snatch at the wheels, and my foot too—and I've organized lorin and harnessed lox and dragged the truck free. I've been attacked by grummets on the coast road and beaten them off with a shovel until the land all around was white with feathers and red with blood, and those that were left took off screaming. Now, what do you think of that, boy?"

"I think you're pretty much as conceited as my father is," I said sourly.

Suddenly he laughed, a giant roar of genuine amusement which sent his disgusting fishy breath rolling around my face. "And you're right, boy; you've hit it right on the head. It's what a man thinks of himself that matters—not what others think of him. I'm sure your father's a good man in his own way, for all that he's a Parl. Well, now. Are we friends?" He shoved his hand under my nose and I noticed for the first time that he possessed only two fingers on each hand; giant pincers starting at the wrist. His hand would never have served as an example of continental mass. I shook the strange object, more from interest than friendship.

By now his companion, no doubt feeling out of things, had thrust his narrow head perilously through the whirling machinery between us and was joining in the conversation, a connecting rod flashing an inch from his throat. Only a man with as long a neck as he could have accomplished this feat.

So the journey continued and I began to enjoy the company of my strange travelling companions. The large man beside me introduced himself as Pallahaxi-Grope and his friend as Juba-Lofty; and between them they contrived to spin yarns of the road until the houses appeared before us and the darting birds in the sky signified that we had reached Bexton Post. I don't like being taken for a fool and I hoped they hadn't thought I'd believed all they told me. I said so.

Grope squeezed my shoulder in his bifurcated grip as the motorcart slowed down. "It's the meaning behind the story that counts, Drove boy. A story is told for a purpose, and the way it's told has a purpose too. The truth or otherwise of a story is immaterial. Remember that."

They shook hands again, thanked my father for the ride, then walked off in the direction of the message post, a small white hut with newspigeon dung.

I had not been looking forward to our arrival at Bexton Post. Before we left Alika there had been rumours of a clampdown on travelling due to the war, and I was half expecting to find there was a message for us saying we had to turn back. I was relieved that father ignored the message post, instead making his way along the single, dusty main street in the direction of the town's only eating place, while the newspigeons clattered overhead.

Bexton Post is a small town, hardly more than a cluster of dwellings and stores which owe their existence to the message post and the fact of the town's position at the edge of the Yellow Mountains which separate the desert from the fertile coastal plain. The hills ahead were bare and brown and sculptured by erosion, but beyond them lay grazing lands, rivers and towns. I could hardly wait to see something green again.

The township was busy at this hour. People thronged the streets, peering into windows which displayed newspapers, dried and canned food and weirdly-shaped examples of lorin art; while they waited for the steambuses which were shortly due to depart. The main purpose of these vehicles was to transport the pigeons to the next message posts in the communications networks, but they doubled as passenger vehicles for the sake of economy. Father bought a newspaper: in this outlandish spot it took the form of a series of news releases pinned together, rather than a paper as we in Alika understand it. THE BEXTON MERCURY, the flysheet announced grandly STRAIGHT FROM THE PIGEONS LEG. We entered a stuva bar and sat down to a poor meal of thin broth, vegetables and dryfruit. Water was rationed; at first I thought we weren't getting any, but I saw father show his card to the waiter; a strange furry little man, but pleasant.

Father was reading the paper; he uttered an exclamation of annoyance.

"There's nothing in here about the opening of the new cannery!"

"Maybe it was in yesterday's paper, Burt," said mother anxiously, glancing around. I sympathized with her; father had a knack of attracting attention. Everyone in the stuva bar seemed to be looking at us.

"Mestler's not going to like this. The release should have been today. Why do we always have these foul-ups; that's what I'd like to know? Rax!" He fell mercifully silent, staring into his water.

"Forget it, dear. This is a holiday." murmured mother soothingly.

I felt compelled to make a comment; encouraged, I think, by my father's despondency. "I don't see that it matters. It doesn't make any difference if people are told about it or not."

Father's eyes had accumulated little creases around them and the muscles were pulsing at the corners of his jaw. "Are you suggesting that I, and Parliament, do not know our own business best, Drove?"

This was exactly what I was suggesting, although it was not what I'd said. Father's intelligence was waning, he was older and set in his ways of thinking, he was used to leaning on the dignity of his position; in short, he had lost the power of reasoned argument. I had him where I wanted and now I could proceed, coolly and logically, to defeat him.

But I had reckoned without mother. "That was a *nice* meal," she said firmly, picking up the paper from where my father had thrown it in his suppressed rage. "Oh, look at this. I see our forces have taken Gorba. How nice."

"But that's only what they say there, mother," I said desperately. "So far as we know, Gorba might be nowhere near the line of battle. It might not even exist. I've never heard of it."

"Oh, but I have." Mother was smiling indulgently at her too clever son. "I went there with my parents once, when I was a little girl. It was lovely. It's on a river; a very old town with a *lovely* Phu temple in the quaintest green brick..."

She reminisced in this vein for some time, effectively dulling the edge of the argument while father recovered his equanimity and I became merely bored. It never occurred to me to doubt the truth of what she was saying; I had already forgotten the point of my own argument. Soon father was reading again, satisfying his compulsive need to keep abreast of current affairs, as befitted one who held an important position with the Government.

They can't stop you thinking. I found myself remembering the time I had placed a paper in front of father which was three days old—in substitution for the current issue. He read it all with deep interest; the law reports, the political platforms, the latest news from the front. It was not until he reached the sports page that he became aware of a certain staleness in what he so eagerly devoured. I saw the flicker of a frown cross his face as he scanned the slingball results, which deepened into puzzlement as he turned to the front page again and, at last, looked at the date. I was then a little disappointed in his reaction. There was no bellow of rage and frustration, no scrumpling of the offending paper into a ball and hurling it into the fire, no tirade of despair and desolation over those precious moments wasted which could never be replaced and, significantly, no admission of the meaninglessness of current events or vows never again to accept as fact the printed word. Instead he shrugged, put the paper down, and gazed absently out of the window. Soon, his eyes closed and he slept.

Nevertheless I found it comforting to remember that moment, as we got to our feet and stood waiting in the Bexton stuva bar while father haggled over the price of the meal.

The continuous daylight gradually dimmed to twilight as we descended the hills and ran on to the coastal plain. The attitude of the people changed too; here we saw more smiling faces, more signs of genuine friendliness when we stopped for food or water. It was as though the easy life of the coast had created an easy breed of man; they went about their way slowly in the soft twilight while the sun circled just below the horizon and threw a curtain of crimson half-way up the sky.

It was colder, of course; but summer was not far away and the chill was only temporary. Wisps of steam rose from the public heaters in the villages and old men sat with their backs against the pipes, nodding their heads in respect as we went by and they caught sight of the insignia on the side of the motorcart. Lox, singly or in tandem, dragged carts of produce from the fertile fields to the sorting centres; here there was no sign of scarcity. Lorin swung from the yellowball trees, dropping the sweet fruit accurately into tubs below. In other fields the summer crops were already showing through, green and lush.

Rivers paralleled the road for long periods and we filled the motorcart at these whenever possible; even in these pleasant parts it was noticeable that people's eyes dwelt longer on the distil cans than was seemly. Now there were few cans left; just enough, father told us with obvious pride in the accuracy of his calculations, to get us to Pallahaxi.

Eventually we reached the coast and the fishing villages, and now the rim of the sun appeared on the horizon for longer periods as we bumped along the clifftop roads and watched the ocean splashed with blood. Seeing the waves scattering into pink spray against the rocks, hearing the rushing and booming, it was difficult to imagine the change which would be wrought in late summer, with the coming of the grume. The ocean is timeless, yet even the ocean is subject to seasons.

Later the road wound inland again, following a wide estuary where the deep-hulled boats moved with trailing nets. A small town had grown about the bridge at the crossing; here we stopped for water for the last time, climbing the estuary banks with buckets, tipping the brackish water into the tank of the motorcart and moving on. People paused in their work to wave as we went.

At last we passed a long-remembered landmark; an ancient stone fortification on a hillside, then soon we were running through the narrow street and a familiar harbour lay before us, alive with boats and seabirds, hanging nets and floating debris and busy men and the smell of fish and salt. We had reached Pallahaxi.

Three

PALLAHAXI IS BUILT around a rocky inlet, the houses mostly of local stone, rise steeply from the harbour to clifftop level except on the landward side, where the inlet becomes a valley. With the passage of time the small fishing village has grown to a moderately-sized town and the houses have spilled along the clifftop and up the sides of the inland valley. Some ten years ago a cannery had been built, which resulted in a further population increase. The harbour was originally large enough for local purposes, but with increased shipping a long breakwater was built out from the western arm of the harbour, enclosing an even greater expanse of water. Fishing vessels can now offload directly from a wharf on the breakwater to a small steam-powered tramway which carries the fish through the narrow streets to the cannery. There is also a market for small private fishermen situated on the inner harbour.

On arriving at Pallahaxi my first interest was the investigation of the new cannery my father had mentioned. This was further out of the town, around the corner beyond the headland known as Finger Point. It seemed that the old cannery was incapable of extension; moreover, my father told me, the machinery was obsolete.

I could sense a tension between my father and me over this simple matter. Suddenly I resented the new cannery. I had known the old cannery for a long time, I knew by sight a number of people who worked there, I had watched the fishing boats unload, marvelled at the intricacy of the tramway and the machinery. The cannery was an old friend. Now my father was telling me it was obsolete and in due course would be torn down to make way for houses. It was an eyesore, he said. In order to discharge their catch at the new cannery, the boats would not even have to enter the harbour, but would offload in the estuary to the north, around Finger Point. As if all this were not bad enough, the new cannery was Government owned and my father was acting in some sort of advisory capacity there; a working holiday.

Two days after our arrival I took a walk around the cliffs and viewed the new buildings from the vantage point of a rocky pinnacle, then returned to our summer cottage on the south side of the town, unimpressed. I was beginning to feel the pricklings of boredom. The cottage was empty; father was at the new cannery and mother was down at the stores. I sat on the porch and looked across the wide expanse of Pallahaxi Bay; down below to the right I could just see the lighthouse at the end of the breakwater. Due west, not so far below the horizon, lay Asta. I think this proximity to the enemy lent a little spice to life in Pallahaxi.

The cottage was a fairly primitive wooden structure in a sloping meadow close to the clifftop; there were other cottages too, of varying shapes and sizes; lox grazed among them, scratching their backs on the timbers. On the porch of the next cottage a lorin sat in impudent mimicry of myself. I was about to shoo him off when I caught sight of a man approaching from the far end of the field. His eyes were fixed steadily on me as he walked, and it was apparent that I was his target. It was too late to retreat to the sanctuary of the cottage.

"Hello there, young fellow!" he hailed me from a distance.

I ignored him, remaining seated where I was, scuffing at the dirt with my toes and wishing he would go away. One glance, allied to his manner of speaking, had told me enough. Medium height and stocky, with hairy, jolly features and a brisk gait, he was obviously the type of person who—so my mother would say—'gets along wonderfully with children'. If you could find enough victims he would organize hikes, and slingball games and tell the kids to call him uncle. Meanwhile all the mothers, my own mother to the fore, would look on fondly and remark to one another how marvellous he was, and how the kids loved him.

And the freezing jerk would cheat at slingball, contriving to make the smallest kids and the girls win, and me lose.

"That's a sad face for a wonderful day like this." He stood before me, and I knew he was grinning before I looked up.

"Uh."

"You'll be Alika-Drove, I expect. I'm pleased to meet you, young fellow. I'm a friend of your father's; permit me to introduce myself." He held my eyes with the friendly crinkled grin, forcing me to stand up and suffer his grip on my forearm. "My name's Horlox-Mestler."

He was a long way from home, Horlox being far inland, almost at the Asta border. For a second I chased an elusive familiarity in his name, then forgot it. "What can I do for you?" I asked.

"I was hoping to see your father."

"He's not here."

"Oh. Might I ask where he is?"

His unflagging politeness was getting me down; I felt as though I was being given a lesson in good manners. "He's probably at the new cannery," I said, pulling myself together and making a real effort. "I'm sorry I can't help you any more. I expect he'll be back before too long. May I offer you a drink of cocha juice?"

"Thank you very much, young fellow, but I'm afraid I don't have time. I must get along." He eyed me with sudden shrewdness. "Bored?"

"Maybe."

"The grume will be here soon; a lad like you ought to have a boat. A boat's a lot of fun when the grume's running. Ah, well. I expect I'll see your father at the cannery, if I hurry. Goodbye." He walked off with springy steps. I watched him go, unable to make up my mind whether perhaps I liked him, after all.

I wandered into the cottage and paused to scan the map mother had pinned to the wall. Little flags indicated the position of the Erto armies as announced daily in the papers and discussed incessantly among the adults. Red arrows showed the principal areas of advancement. We seemed to be pushing forwards everywhere, but my scepticism had grown to the extent where I would not have been unduly surprised if an enemy advance party had come knocking at the door. I changed into my swimming things and went down to the beach.

A sentimental mood came over me as I stood on the familiar pebbles of the little cliff-sheltered cove. This was where I had first spoken to Browneyes, last year. I thought hard and shut my eyes, trying to project to her a mental message, the way a lorin is supposed to. *I'm here, Browneyes*, I thought. *Come to the beach and meet me.* When I opened my eyes she still wasn't there...

It was in that queer time of year between the waning of the grume and the coming of the drench that we had finally met. I had found a strange fish bopping about on the surface and Browneyes—whom I'd been watching for some time from the corner of my eye—came over to look at it. We laid the creature on the pebbles and knelt to examine it, and at last with the excuse of mutual interest had overcome our shyness enough to talk. We sat together on the beach for the rest of that day, and the following day we'd gone walking on the cliffs. The day after that my parents and I had left for Alika, and home. I had not wanted to go.

But now Browneyes was not around, and my first step into the icy water sent shivers of fear up my spine, so after a while I returned to the cottage to find mother and father had arrived back.

They greeted me in significant fashion, the way parents do when they've just been talking about you. We sat down to eat; they asked me what I'd been doing and I told them, and they exchanged glances.

My father had finished eating a ripe yellowball; he dipped and dried his fingers ceremonially and cleared his throat. "Drove... I've something to discuss with you."

"Uh?' This sounded serious.

"As you know, I have various duties in connection with my Government position which I find convenient to carry out while we are here in Pallahaxi on holiday. Normally these duties do not occupy much of my time, but unfortunately this year it will be different, so I heard today."

"I forgot to tell you, a man was looking for you. Mestler, his name was."

"Horlox-Mestler saw me. I hope you were polite to him, Drove. He is a man of some account."

"Uh."

"It seems that from now on much of my time will be taken up with the new cannery. We shall not be together, as a family, so much as I had hoped. You will be left on your own a great deal."

I was silent, trying to look suitably glum.

"And it is not fair to your mother to expect her to be continuously at your disposal. You are a boy who does not make friends readily, but I am not saying there is anything wrong in that. There are people with whom we would not wish you to make friends. However..." He paused, gazing pensively at a point some three paces behind me, trying to recall the thread of his discourse. "It is not my custom to buy you gifts," he resumed, "since I believe that a person should give value for what he receives."

"Uh."

"Nevertheless I cannot have you moping about the place, idle. The next thing, you'll be getting into some mischief or other. I propose to buy you a boat."

"That's freezing good of you, father!" I exclaimed in amazement.

He managed to smile, ignoring my slip of the tongue. "I've seen a suitable craft at Silverjack's yard. A small skimmer. You ought to be able to handle it, if you're any sort of a sailor at all."

Mother smiled at me fondly. "Isn't that good of your father, Drove?"

"Thank you, father," I said dutifully.

"You can collect the boat anytime," he said. "Just tell Pallahaxi-Silverjack who your father is."

The following morning I rose from breakfast and looked out of the window; the same twilight tinted the sky with pink, the same animals grazed around the edge of the patio; but today was different. Today I was going to Silverjack's yard to collect the boat. The dim sea stretched excitingly across to the black humps of land on the far side of the bay; today I would explore that sea. I pulled on a coat.

"Wait for me if you're thinking of going down to the town, Drove. I have some things to buy. We can go together." Mother looked up at me, smiling mindlessly over her stuva cup.

I almost told her to get frozen but thought better of it. Father was watching me, listening, waiting to cancel the boat at the first sign of unpleasantness.

My mother is short and I am tall for my age, so that it is impossible for us to keep in step as we walk. She trots along beside me, legs going like pistons, and insists that she put her arm through mine, so that the pair of us reel along the street like drunks. Added to which she talks incessantly, looking up at me all the time and smiling fondly and generally giving the impression that a very peculiar relationship obtains between us. I find myself praying that people think she is an old prostitute I have picked up, and to emphasise this effect I try to assume a shamefaced look—which is not difficult, under the circumstances.

When we reached the town it appeared that mother was not prepared to let me go yet. Together we visited store after store, where she flashed her Parl card whenever anyone showed unwillingness to serve her on the grounds of rationing. Before long I was struggling under a mountain of goods and was very relieved when mother rented a loxcart to take the stuff back.

"I'll be getting along now, then," I said when the last bag was safely loaded.

"Oh, not yet dear. I'm dying for a cup of stuva. There's such a nice little place down by the harbour but I don't like going in there alone; one meets such strange people."

On the way to the stuva bar we passed the Golden Grummet hotel and I tried not to stare in the windows too obviously, because mother knew who lived there and she was watching me covertly. I caught sight of Pallahaxi-Annlee, Browneye's mother, talking to a man so hairy that at first I thought he was a lorin, but she didn't see me. She probably would not have recognized me anyhow; I only met her briefly once, last year.

After we had been sitting in the stuva bar for a little while mother began to wave to someone on the other side of the room, uttering noises of recognition and greeting. When father is out of the way she goes berserk and is quite as adept at calling attention to herself as he. I was acutely embarrassed when a couple rose to their feet, came over and joined us; the woman was my mother's size and age, and the boy with her about my size and age, and I'll swear that every person in that stuva bar thought we were some weird sort of mirror images of each other. Mother introduced them as Dreba-Gwilda and Dreba-Wolff. She had met them yesterday.

Wolff was a smooth freezer and I knew right away that my mother thought he had nice manners and would be a suitable friend for me. In fact, I already suspected that the meeting had been fixed. No doubt Gwilda's husband was a Parl.

Wolff smiled at me toothily. "I understand you're getting a boat today, Drove."

"Uh."

"I'm a sailing enthusiast myself. At home I have a deep-hulled sloop. Can't bring it here, though. No point, not with the grume. Yours will be a flat-bottom skimmer, I expect?"

"Uh."

"You can't use it yet, of course. That would be asking for trouble. You'll have to wait until the grume runs."

"Have you ever noticed that your nose is a funny shape?"

"I'll come along with you and we'll pick it up together. I can check it over for you. You have to be careful with these Pallahaxi people. Thieves, every one of them. They've been spoiled by the tourists, of course."

At this point mother broke off her quick-fire conversation with Gwilda."That's *so* nice of you Wolff. You must be delighted to have made such a useful friend, Drove. Run along then, the two of you."

We walked down the street side by side and somehow I felt untidy and juvenile beside Wolff. "Did you know that Pallahaxi was founded by the Astans, originally?" he asked. "This is the nearest point to Asta, this side of the world. Pallahaxi was colonized by an Astan chief in the year of Renaissance 673. His name was Yubb-Gaboa. Hundreds of years later the hordes of Erto swept down from the Yellow Mountains and pushed the Astans into the sea."

"Couldn't they swim?"

"History is a fascinating subject, Drove. I find that in learning about our ancestors I learn a lot about myself and those around me. Don't you agree?"

"Uh."

"Here we are. Silverjack's yard. Now, who's in charge here? Where's your boat?"

"Listen, I don't know. I've never been in this place before."

Wolff strode off confidently into the building and I followed. It was a huge barnlike structure, redolent of wood-shavings and tar, littered with boats in varying stages of completion. Men were working everywhere, bent over benches, crawling under boats. The place was an echoing din of hammering and sawing and seagoing oaths. Everyone ignored us. Wolff tapped the nearest man on the shoulder; he jerked around and peered at us, one-eyed. A huge scar ran down one side of his face from brow to chin.

I looked away, feeling sick. Congenital deformity we hardly notice in Alika—you see it wherever you look—but the aftermath of a physical accident is another matter. I noticed a man nearby with a finger missing; he had probably lost it at work. The noise of the place pressed in on me and I felt surrounded by sickness and horror; then Wolff was nudging me.

"He says over there. Are you all right? You look a funny colour. Come on."

I found myself in a small office and the door slammed shut behind me, abruptly cutting off the din. A man was seated at a desk; on seeing us he rose to his feet and shambled towards us with an air of primitive menace; at first I thought he wore a fur jacket but then I realized he was naked to the waist—and maybe further, for all I could tell. He was the hairiest individual I have ever seen and he had a peculiar convex face; his chin sloped up to his nose and his brow sloped down to it, like a fish. As I stood goggling at him Wolff spoke calmly.

"You must be Pallahaxi-Silverjack. Is the boat for Alika-Drove ready yet?"

The brute—who appeared to be about to dismember us—stopped in his tracks. Under his hair, a wide mouth appeared.

"Why yes, lads. Of course it's ready. Never let it be said that Silverjack's late with a boat. Follow me. Follow me."

He led us through the yard, down to the water's edge. There, a few paces from the lapping waves, lay the most beautiful boat I have ever seen. It was painted blue outside and varnished within. In the early summer twilight it seemed to glow. It was flat-bottomed and tall-masted, and looked fast, expertly designed to skim the surface of the grume. It was about four paces long, small enough for me to sail single-handed but large enough to take at least three passengers, if I so desired. "Looks all right," said Wolff.

"Finest little boat in Pallahaxi," boomed Silverjack. "I'll show you how to hoist the sails."

"That's all right," said Wolff. "I've handled boats before."

"Many's the lad I've heard say that, and come to grief after," shouted Silverjack indulgently, hoisting away. I warmed to the man; I had a feeling Wolff had met his match. Pale blue sail flapped in the light breeze; it seemed a pity we had to wait for the grume.

Wolff eyed the sail. "Lateen rigged," he murmured, taking up a varnished piece of timber. "This is the centreboard."

"No, no," said Silverjack. "It's obvious you know nothing about grume skimmers, young lad. That belongs to the dinghy over there. Skimmers have no centreboard. Look at the shape of the hull, now. See those keels, shallow ones, one on either side and one in the middle? That's all you need with a skimmer. I figure you probably don't know this part of the world. When the grume runs, you see, the water gets *thick*." He made a flat gesture with his palm. "It's the evaporation which causes it."

"I'm quite familiar with Pallahaxi, thank you. I come here often."

"Tourist, eh?" Silverjack grinned at Wolff in the friendliest fashion. "There you are, you see—it's a good thing I took the trouble to explain. This boat is built for the grume. If you took it out today you'd have been in big trouble, my lad." He gripped Wolff's shoulder, roaring with laughter, and secretly I blessed him.

"There's very little swell running today," observed Wolff coldly, squinting at the flat green water of the harbour. He glanced back at the boat. "She has enough freeboard for this weather. I think we'll take her out, Drove."

I was in the grip of personalities I could not control. "Look, don't you think we ought to wait, Wolff?" I said weakly.

Silverjack was staring at us. "Whose boat is this, my lads? I was told it was for Drove, but Wolff seems to be running the show."

Wolff was gazing at me loftily. "Are you saying you're scared?"

My face felt hot as I bent down and took hold of the gunwale. Wolff lifted the other side and we slid the boat into the water. We climbed in, the light breeze filled the sail, we were moving away from the slipway. I caught sight of Silverjack's hairy back disappearing behind a large upturned boat; he did not look around.

I forgot Silverjack almost immediately in the thrill of gliding among the moored fishing boats, pleasure craft and dinghies which filled the inner harbour, seeing Pallahaxi from a new angle. Snowdivers watched us from mastheads as we passed, men paused in their work on the west shore and waved to us, sensing—in that strange way that one does—that a maiden voyage was in progress. At the east quay, the smaller fishing boats were offloading their catch directly into the open public market and hundreds of snowdivers jostled for position of the flat roof. Through a gap I caught sight of the Golden Grummet; someone was shaking a cloth out of a window. Peering around the sail I could see the opening to the outer harbour; the steam tram was puffing slowly along the breakwater. A white plume rose from the cab and seconds later the shrill sound of the whistle reached me as we passed a high stone jetty and ran smoothly into the deep blue water of the outer harbour.

Wolff spoke. "There seems to be a lot of water in this boat," he said.

FOUR

I WAS SITTING on the stern thwart, holding the tiller, while Wolff sat amidships grasping the mainsheet. We had reached the outer harbour and were running out of the shelter of the cliffs; the breeze was freshening, driving us briskly towards the lighthouse at the end of the breakwater. The water was a little choppy here and every so often a wave slopped over the low gunwales.

"Bail it out, then, Wolff," I commanded, exerting my authority as skipper

He was fidgeting about nervously. "We don't have anything to bail with."

"It's only a few drops, anyway."

"It's more than that. The boat's leaking. It's gushing in. Look!"

As I shifted position a river of icy water soaked my foot and cold fear ran up my leg. We were sinking. The water was freezing cold. I looked frantically around for help. We were many paces from the nearest boat, doomed to death from exposure preceded by the terrible onset of insanity as the coldness of the water gradually chilled our bodies and froze our brains.

Having faced the worst I was able to devote my attention to more practical matters. "We'll never reach the breakwater," I said. To our left, the cliff loomed high and black. "Maybe we could paddle in there, out of the wind. Look, there's a beach. We could get ashore. It's not far."

"What do we paddle with?" asked Wolff helplessly. All the bombast was knocked out of him and he looked suddenly shrunken, huddled on the centre thwart hugging himself and shivering as the water rose above his ankles. I could see the whites of his eyes. He stared wildly as a snowdiver swooped past us and plunged below the surface; the boat rocked sluggishly.

"We'll use the rudder. You get the sail down and I'll unship the rudder."

I twisted around and felt beneath the icy water for the nut securing the pintle. The boat rocked dangerously as Wolff, without warning, flung himself on me from behind and smashed my face against the transom. I dragged myself away, fighting clear of something clammy and encumbering, receiving a sharp blow on the back of the head and finding Wolff's crazed eyes staring directly into mine. The cold had got to him, sooner than I'd expected. I pulled my arm free and hit him in the face as hard as I could. He grunted and backed off, scrabbling for the gunwale; as his weight shifted I managed to knee him in the stomach.

He gasped and I saw the terror in his eyes as he hurled himself at me again, hitting out wildly, screeching like a sea bird. I fell back again, half across the gunwale, averted my head to avoid his blows and saw the long black shape of a scavenger sliding through the water beneath us. I'll swear its cold eye dwelt on me as it passed about half a pace below the surface. I turned back and Wolff hit me again. I seized his arm and pulled, and we rolled grappling in the bottom of the boat. Eventually I found myself astride him. His struggles weakened as I gripped his throat and forced his head back towards the water which had risen rapidly as we fought.

"Drove!" he grunted. "Let me go, you freezer! Pull yourself together. There's nothing to be afraid of!"

"Go to Rax!" I held on, but I was less sure of myself. The mad look had died from his eyes and suddenly I wondered if it had ever been there, or whether I had imagined it. "What did you attack me for, then?"

"*You* attacked *me*, remember? You h-hit me in the face!"

"Only after you flung yourself at me."

"I didn't fling myself at you. The sail came down with a rush and I overbalanced. Then you went berserk."

"What are you talking about?" I thought about it for a moment while Wolff's desperate face stared up from the bottom-boards and the water rose higher. It seemed there had been a misunderstanding. I released him, and he crawled back to his seat and we eyed each other warily. The sail lay in a crumpled mass between us; the sight of the water rising around it got me moving again. "Try to unship the freezing rudder yourself," I said irritably.

We switched positions and Wolff fumbled under the stern, uttering whimpers of fear as the cold struck into his flesh. Soon he straightened up. "I can't shift it." He was almost crying. "I can't shift the freezing thing. It's stuck." He stared around; we were under the gaunt black cliffs and I don't suppose anyone had seen us. "We don't stand a chance!" wailed Wolff.

I was diverting my mind with speculation. The boat was by now about half-full of water while, due to our weight, the water outside had almost reached the top of the gunwale and was lapping over. What would happen next? Would the sea pour in all round in a huge square cataract sending the boat and us plummeting to the bottom? Or would an equilibrium be reached resulting in the boat, though waterlogged, remain afloat?

The solution, announced by a cry of dismay from Wolff, was somewhere between these two possibilities. The skimmer filled with frightening suddenness but sank slowly and, in very short time, stopped sinking, but remained totally submerged. The only items showing above the water were Wolff and I, from the chests up, and the mast. Despite the paralyzing cold and consequent fear, I found time to hope that nobody could see me in this absurd position.

"Wolff," I said carefully, "don't move too quickly or you'll upset the whole thing. Just take the seat from under you and we'll paddle to the beach. Right?"

At the same time I groped about under the water and took hold of the stern thwart. The pair of us, shuddering violently, set about paddling an invisible boat to shore. It was an unusual situation and I wondered if there was something wrong with my theory as we worked away, but judging by the way the surface debris was receding astern, we must have been moving. Eventually the skimmer grounded us, we stepped out and pulled it up the beach.

"You're going to have to do some explaining," said Wolff. "Your father will want to know why you took the boat out."

I ignored him and took stock of our position. The cliff rose clear about fifteen paces back from the water's edge; we stood on a very small pebble beach some thirty paces long. The cliff was jagged and would have presented no difficulty to an expert, but I am scared of heights and had a suspicion that Wolff felt the same. In any case I didn't relish the idea of him scaling the cliff, leading the rescue party and being acclaimed the hero. I didn't mention the possibility of climbing; instead I pointed to a large circular hole about two paces up the cliff, from which dripped a nameless substance.

"What's that?"

Wolff regarded the cloacal thing with distaste. "That's a sewer."

"It's big for a sewer, isn't it? It's big enough to crawl into."

"Yes, well you can forget that. I don't purpose to crawl up any sewers, Alika-Drove."

I explored our territory further; I was beginning to feel claustrophobic on this narrow strip of beach flanked by sea and cliff. I walked to the extreme eastern end and climbed a large boulder jutting out into the sea, thinking there might be a way round, but merely found a further jumble of rocks, a deep pool among them and tall cliffs above. The cliffs dripped guano from countless snowdivers' nests.

I climbed down to the edge of the pool and peered into the depths. It was clear and green; seemingly empty, and I was about to turn away when I thought I saw a movement at the bottom among a nest of waving green fronds. I was looking for a stick to poke about with when a white form darted past me. A snowdiver had seen the same movement. I flinched involuntarily—the bird had passed close to my head—but I heard no splash.

When I opened my eyes the entire rock pool was opaque and sparkling; the bird's hindquarters protruded from the surface, transfixed in mid-dive. Its webbed feet were paddling ineffectively and as I watched the movement became spasmodic, then died. I shivered. The whole thing had happened so suddenly—and I might easily have put my hand into that pool. I picked up a stone and threw it; it skittered across the hard scintillating surface, bounded over the far side and splashed into the sea. Dimly I heard Wolff call me but I continued to watch the pool in unhealthy fascination. I had almost given up when abruptly the strange crystalline structure deliquesced to clear water again and the snowdiver was bobbing with the ripples, dead. As I watched, a thin strand of silver-flecked blue thread rose from the bottom of the pool and wrapped itself gently around the bird, drawing it below the surface.

I climbed back over the boulder, shaken, to rejoin Wolff. He stood with a number of kids who seemed to have materialized from living rock; they were examining the boat.

"There's an ice-devil back there," I said by way of greeting, then I was silent, staring, as they turned to me. Besides Wolff there was another, smaller boy; and two girls.

One of the girls was Pallahaxi-Browneyes.

✳ ✳ ✳

She looked at me in shy recognition then looked away again; she said nothing and there was nothing I could think to say either; except to grunt an acknowledgement of the presence of the three of them. The other girl was taller and looked as though she had a good opinion of herself—a female counterpart of Wolff, in fact. The small boy was just that; a small, dirty, scruffy boy, and beneath contempt.

He was the first to speak. "How can you expect a boat to float if you don't put the bungs in?" he asked shrilly.

Mortified, I bent down. He was right. There were two draining holes in the transom into which corks should have fitted. Due to the circumstances of our departure from the boatyard I had forgotten to check. I glanced at Wolff accusingly. He looked straight ahead, flushing a little. "You're the skipper," he said distantly. "You ought to know enough to check your own boat before putting it into the sea, Alika-Drove."

"You're *tourists*, I suppose," said the tall girl, putting a wealth of contempt into her words. "Ignorant tourists, trying to make like sailors."

"Shipwrecked sailors," added the small boy.

"Shut up, Squint. Well, it's lucky for you we're around, isn't that right, Browneyes? We know the country, you see. We live here all the year round. Right, Browneyes?"

I stole a glance at Browneyes and she looked as pretty as the pink twilit sky. I wished the others weren't there—but even if she and I had been alone, I wouldn't have had the nerve to speak. She didn't see me looking at her; she was watching a large fishing vessel disgorging its entrails into the steam tram, and I wondered if maybe she didn't like me as much as I liked her. But she had recognized me, at least.

"Right," said Squint, munching at something.

"Listen, will you hold your tongue, Squint? Now..." The tall girl regarded us triumphantly. "I suppose you're relying on us to get you out of this mess you've got yourselves into."

"They crawled out of that sewer, Drove," said Wolff wearily. "Like drivets."

"Any more of that and we'll leave you to starve, or go mad with cold. And if you went into that *storm drain* you'd never find your way out, not without our help—

it's like catacombs."

"A boy I knew got himself lost in there once," piped the irrepressible Squint through an unidentifiable mouthful. "He wandered for days and went stark staring mad and when they found him he was just a skeleton, bleached bones, and the birds had picked out his eyes."

The tall girl was silent for an instant as she digested this vivid, if inconsistent, picture; then she nodded approvingly. "I remember that. Do you remember that, Browneyes?"

Browneyes was still staring out to sea. "Leave them alone, Ribbon, can't you see they're wet and cold and if we don't get them away from here soon they'll die and if you want that to happen well I *don't*." She ran all this together as a quick gabble and her face was fiery red.

Ribbon looked hard at her, then shrugged. "Squint, stuff seaweed in those holes and take their boat back. You people, follow me." She hauled herself into the sewer and disappeared from sight.

Wolff followed her, then myself, while Browneyes brought up the rear. I looked back to see Squint hoisting the sail in expert fashion, then extended a hand and helped Browneyes into the tunnel—although she could no doubt have managed better by herself. As we moved forward I let go of her hand slowly, prepared on the slightest pretext to keep hold of it. At the same time Browneyes loosened her grip and I wondered if she was thinking the same as I, or whether I had construed more into the happenings of last summer than I should have. There had been a long winter in between, a lot of time for my imagination to work, and a lot of time for Browneyes to forget.

We could not stand upright in the tunnel but progressed slowly with a crouching gait reminiscent of a lorin. In front of us Ribbon's echoing voice uttered continual dire warnings as to the consequences of a wrong turning while around our feet I heard, or I thought I heard, scuffling noises and shrill squeaks. Despite the fact that Ribbon constantly referred to the tunnel as a storm drain, the evidence of my nostrils caused me to agree silently with Wolff; it was a sewer and a pungent one. A trickle of liquid ran down the centre; in cross-section the tunnel was roughly circular so, walking with legs apart, I was able to keep my feet out of the filth.

Apart from Ribbon nobody spoke; she had assumed the capacity of leader and presently halted at a point where daylight filtered from above. Here, the stench was particularly strong.

"We're right under the town's main fishmonger," Ribbon announced. "It's lucky for you they're not washing the place down right now, because when they do, all the fishy water comes *gushing* down here. We take this tunnel to the right, now. If you took the tunnel to the left you'd be in big trouble."

She refrained from explaining what nightmares lay down the left tunnel and we did not ask her, having by now learned the folly of such questions. We stumbled on in silence, bending lower as the rough tunnel roof sagged towards us.

"Years ago when I was just a kid, there was a cave-in," came the relentless voice from ahead. "And then all the stuff backed up; it couldn't get away. Rax, the stink."

I cannoned into Wolff who had stopped suddenly; he dug his elbow irritably into my stomach. "We've stopped," he snapped. His nerves were ragged.

"This is where I leave you," announced Ribbon with no evidence of regret. "My place is further on and I'm not supposed to go to Browneyes' place because of the *drunks*. I'd offer to take you to my place and get you cleaned up there, but my parents wouldn't like it. They're sort of *particular*, if you know what I mean."

Browneyes spoke quietly from behind. "If you'd like to come to my place and clean up, that would be fine."

"Thanks," I said. Wolff was silent.

She edged past us and climbed a series of iron spikes knocked into the wall of a vertical shaft. She fumbled about for a moment, then cracks of light from above suddenly broadened into a bright rectangle. Browneyes pulled herself through the hole and looked down on us. "Come on up," she said.

I found myself in one of the most exciting rooms I have ever seen. Low and long, the stone walls were lined with huge wooden barrels, vats and tubs, brown and aged, mysterious and forbidden like an illustration straight out of one of my mother's books. A guttering lamp provided illumination. I was surrounded by evil and it was wonderful. In a corner I saw some cans which looked familiar; I examined them and, sure enough, they contained distil. Not for use as fuel, however; this stuff was for the sodden drunks who caroused their lives away in the bar of the Golden Grummet—to paraphrase my mother. The air was rich with the heady reek of liquor, and I was enchanted.

"A beer cellar," observed Wolff calmly, missing the romance of it all. "Why the outlet into the sewer?"

"To wash out the barrels," explained Browneyes.

"Looks more like a smuggling set-up to me. I ought to tell you that my father is a Customs man, down here because of all this smuggling that's been going on since the war started. How did you get that distil? It's made in Asta."

I was not surprised to hear that Wolff's father, like

mine, was a Parl. What shocked me was that Wolff should be so interested in his father's work that he could tackle Browneyes in this aggressive fashion.

"Leave her alone," I said heatedly. "Where are your freezing manners, Wolff? We're guests here. This distil was stockpiled ages ago before the war started. Everyone was doing it. My father did it. He's a Parl, too."

For once Wolff looked abashed. "Well, it just annoys me that people can trade with the enemy, that's all," he muttered. "It's treason."

"Sorry, Wolff, but that makes no sense to me. War was declared on a particular day; are you saying that it was good business to import distil one day, and treason the next? And what about people whose boats were halfway across at the time?"

I had already found that Wolff was a sucker for the academic argument, and he fell for this one too. Browneyes gave me a look of gratitude as Wolff began to expound his theories on the ethics of war and the historical background of the present conflict.

FIVE

WOLFF AND I sat in well-padded highbacked chairs, wrapped in blankets, while Pallahaxi-Annlee fed us soup laced, I suspected, with wine. We were in the back room of the Golden Grummet waiting for our parents to collect us; every time Annlee came bustling through the door from the bar we heard the sudden roar of conversation and laughter from beyond, and for a while afterwards the whiff of liquor and smoke lingered on the air.

I was surprised by the decor of the room. Although

a fire flickered before us, this constituted the only random element in surroundings of almost unbelievable neatness and order. Ornaments stood erect like guards, aloof and untouchable; mirrors shone and reflected infinities of bright tidiness in one another. Everything seemed to be carefully positioned at exact right angles to everything else. There was even a religious motif; against the far wall was a Renaissance shelf. A statue of Phu the sun-god, in the form of the Great Lox, dragged the world from the clutches of the dead giant Rax, symbolized by a many-tentacled ice-devil. I noticed that many of the ornaments around the place bore similar religious connotations and I was unable to reconcile this with the sounds of sinful revelry from the next room.

Browneyes entered, followed by Wolff's mother and a man whom I took to be his father since he bore the look of intense suspicion befitting a Customs official. "You're a fool, Wolff," he snapped without preamble. "You always have been a fool and you always will."

"To think that I should find a son of mine in a common inn," wailed his mother softly, but not softly enough. Annlee, who had just entered, overheard. She looked as though she had been hit.

"Here are his clothes," she said quietly, handing them over. "I've washed them out. They're nice and dry."

"You haven't time to put them on now, Wolff," said his mother, accepting the bundle gingerly and holding it with her fingertips. "You'll have to wear that blanket, or whatever it is. There's a loxcart outside." She smiled with wide graciousness at Browneyes and her mother. "Thank you *so* much for looking after him."

"I can't walk through the street in a blanket!"

Ignoring his son's protests, Wolff's father seized him

by the arm and propelled him through the door. Instantly, they were gone.

Browneyes, Annlee and I regarded one another uncertainly in what seemed to be a sudden vacuum. "Did you manage to get hold of Drove's parents, dear?" asked Annlee at last.

"They'll be here later."

"Look, if my things are dry, I can put them on and go," I said hastily.

"Of course not," said Annlee firmly. "You'd miss each other on the way. You're welcome to stay here for a while; it's only early evening, after all. I have work to do, but I'm sure Browneyes will stay and talk to you. Won't you, dear."

Browneyes nodded, eyes downcast, and Annlee left, shutting the door behind her.

Browneyes sat down in the chair recently vacated by Wolff and looked squarely at me with a hint of a smile and dimples. I grinned back, but eventually had to look away in case the thing began to seem like some sort of childish staring contest. I watched her hands, which lay folded in her lap. They were nice hands, small and neat and white, and I remembered that I'd been holding one of them for a short time, earlier in the afternoon. I wished that I had the courage to hold it again, but Browneyes sat out of reach. I could hardly go plunging across the room and grab hold of her hand.

She wore a clean white dress with some sort of pink and white flowers on it, which made her look very angelic and sweet and unattainable; I almost preferred the grubby jeans and pullover she had been wearing earlier. Her knees were nice and she had pretty shoes on. We seemed to have been saying nothing for a long time, and if it went on much longer we never would say anything.

"Do you like my dress?" she asked, giving me the chance to look at her more openly.

"Yes. It's nice."

"I had to take my other things off because they were dirty."

"I suppose so. Uh... I hope you won't get into trouble for bringing me here. For bringing us here, I mean. Wolff and I." There was a huge pulse thumping in my lower chest which was making me breathless.

"Is Wolff your friend?"

"Yes," I said eagerly, glad to seize on some concrete topic. "I mean no. I only met him today. I think my mother organized it; she always wants to find suitable companions for me." I tried to smile in case there was a sting in the words; I didn't want Browneyes to think I was a freezer who held his mother in contempt.

She merely smiled back, however, and another silence followed.

"I don't really like Wolff very much," I said desperately. "It was his fault we were shipwrecked today, you know."

She smiled again, playing with something hanging from a thin chain around her neck. It flashed in the light and I recognized it. It was a crystal, possibly cultured from an ice-goblin like the one my mother had thrown away; but more likely real, hewn from a destroyed ice-devil and representing the death of evil. The sight of the thing dismayed me; there is something daunting about a religious symbol hanging around a girl's neck.

She followed my eyes downward and blushed faintly. "Mother likes me to wear it," she explained. She smoothed the front of her dress with her hand and the thin cloth molded itself over the warm curves of budding breasts. I looked away hastily, greatly embarrassed.

"Mother's very devout that way," she continued. "I mean, look at all this stuff around the room. I hope... I hope you don't think..."

"My mother's just the same," I reassured her, feeling sorry for her. "She believes everything. I sometimes think she goes about looking for things to believe—particularly recently, since the war got worse. As though she's desperate to make her peace before the Astans get her. She has a Renaissance shelf like yours, and she has a war map that she sticks pins into, and I don't know which one she believes in most. I'm not sure I believe either one." I added.

She was watching my face seriously. When she was serious she looked just a little bit sad. "But your father's a Parl," she said quietly. "And you live inland, at Alika. Here in Pallahaxi we're much closer to Asta—we used to know a lot of Astan sailors, in peacetime. We know there's a war on. We can see it all around us. We can see flashes at night, out at sea. There's no public transport any more so we have to use loxcarts or walk. And there's not much food, either, not for the general public."

"I saw plenty of fish today."

"You can get tired of fish, and even that's rationed. Most of it goes to the new cannery now, and they send it all inland somewhere."

I didn't want to talk about all this. It was a waste of time, a waste of being alone. Yet if we dropped this subject, we might find nothing to talk about again. I wondered what had gone wrong, and decided it was my own inexperience. We had started off with an intimate enough conversation, but somehow we'd been sidetracked on the way. Maybe I ought to tell her, right now, that I thought she was beautiful. The pounding was in my chest again and I knew I wasn't going to be able to say it.

"I think... uh. My father's working for the new cannery. Maybe we'll be staying here longer this year. I think Pallahaxi is a good place, don't you?"

"I thought your father worked in Alika."

"He said yesterday that he would be having to do a lot of work here." Why were we talking about my freezing father?

"So you might be staying for quite a long time. You'll like Pallahaxi when the mists come, and the warm rain. Even in winter it's much warmer than inland."

Then, just when I thought the conversation was coming under control, the door opened and the crude din of the bar filled the room. A ruddy face appeared still wearing the remains of its professional innkeeper's smile; I recognized the man as Pallahaxi-Girth, Browneyes' father.

"Hello, young Alika-Drove," he greeted me. "I hope I'm not breaking anything up." He winked extravagantly. "We're shorthanded here and I'm going to have to take Browneyes away from you. I'm very sorry, but you know how it is." He hesitated. Beyond him smoke swirled and voices brayed in animal mirth. "Maybe you'd like to get some clothes on and come into the bar; your parents won't mind, I'm sure."

"I'll get your things, Drove," said Browneyes, hurrying out. I remembered the emerald bracelet. I would have to return it, now.

Later I sat in the corner of the barroom and watched the proceedings. I found the whole thing quite different from what I'd expected. True, the smell was there and the smoke, the raucous laughter and noisy conversation, but somehow the air of evil, the air of *menace* was missing. Instead, all I saw was a roomful of people apparently enjoying themselves. It was puzzling. I sat sipping a glass of something Browneyes had given me, trying to work it out.

"Hello there, lad!" roared a voice.

I started, looking up. A large face was bent towards me, a grotesque hand was gripping my shoulder. Blackened teeth bared in a grin. I stared blankly and nervously at this apparition before sudden recognition came and I felt a little foolish. It was the trucker whom we'd left at Bexton-Post; what was his name? Grope. Behind him, his lissom-necked companion craned his long face my way, smiling vacantly over a glass of something dark.

"I thought you were at Bexton-Post," I blurted out stupidly, unable to think of anything sensible to say.

Grope lurched around the table and seated himself on the bench beside me, squeezing uncomfortably close to allow for his friend on the far side. They were both smoking long black weeds which stunk abominably. I looked around for help, but Browneyes was on the other side of the room, carrying a handful of mugs from which the foam slopped. She looked too clean and sweet to be pushing among all those uncouth bodies and suddenly I felt depressed.

Grope was shouting in my ear. "Recalled us. Had to leave the freezing truck to rot. Parls, that's what Lofty and me are now, just like your dad. The Government has taken over all the fisheries now—not just the new plant. They said it was a national emergency. No time to pick up lame trucks; leave it where it is and take another, they said. Must feed the population, stuff fish down their throats until they look like grummets, eh, Drove?" He bellowed with laughter and I suspected he was drunk.

Across the room I caught sight of Horlox-Mestler, neatly dressed yet seemingly at ease in this rough crowd. He spotted me and raised a hand in grave salute and I wondered just what the position was between him and my father. I had a notion that Mestler had in some way persuaded my father to buy me the boat. I wished he would come across and rescue me from the gross Grope. Browneyes was at the bar counter, collecting more full mugs from her father. There was no sign of her mother.

"They didn't ask," Grope was saying incomprehensibly. "Rax, no, they didn't freezing well ask—that's not their way. They just said: you're working for us, all of you truckers. That's the way of Parliament for you. They don't ask you, they freezing well tell you."

Lofty leaned around his companion to address me directly. "Slavery," he said; then, having imparted this pearl, he resumed his place, staring into his mug.

"And tell me this, my young friend. Tell me this. Where are the troops? Where are the troops to protect us when the Astan fleet comes sailing straight into Pallahaxi harbour—as it surely will, this being the nearest point by sea from their freezing country?" Grope's eyes were wide with simulated alarm as he stared at an imaginary fleet which only he saw, indicating its position with a sweep of his forked hand. It seemed to have dropped anchor somewhere between us and the bar counter.

"The grume is coming," Lofty reminded him. "The grume is coming and they'll be able to *walk* into Pallahaxi, near enough."

The roar of conversation and laughter was closing in on me and there seemed hardly enough air to breathe. Grope was pressing in from one side and a large, fidgety woman who smelled of stewed meat from the other. I swallowed, feeling sick. Suddenly Browneyes was standing before me, looking worried. "Well, hello there," murmured Grope, chuckling. "What have you brought for me, little girl?"

"Drove, we're terribly busy. Would you..." She hesitated, "would you mind very much helping?"

Overwhelmingly relieved, I stood. "I'd like to," I said sincerely. "What do you want me to do?"

"We're running out of things behind the bar. Perhaps you could bring some more bottles up from the cellar. You know where it is."

"Of course."

It was wonderfully cool outside the bar and I dawdled over lighting the lamp, savouring the fresh air. Then I made my way along the dim passage and down the steps.

As I opened the cellar door there was an inexplicable gust of cold air and the lamp went out. I stumbled forward, holding the lamp with one hand and feeling about with the other. I remembered a box in the middle of the floor which served as a table; among the various items of cellar equipment I had seen matches. Despite my care I reached the box sooner than I expected, banging my shin. For a moment I hobbled about, rubbing myself and muttering. Then I saw a square area of light beyond the box.

The hatch into the sewer was open. I distinctly remembered Browneyes closing it after Wolff and I had entered the cellar, and I couldn't think of any reason why it should have been opened since—unless Browneyes' father had been cleaning the place out. But he wouldn't have forgotten to close the trapdoor. Thieves could get in that way.

Or smugglers.

The light in the floor was flickering now, becoming

brighter, and soon a corresponding bright area appeared on the low ceiling. Someone was coming along the sewer. My imagination began to run riot. If smugglers caught me here, they would knife me. I made for the door as quietly as I could, but in my fear I lost my sense of direction and found myself fumbling at a barrel. The light grew brighter still and I watched it hypnotized, unable to move. The entire cellar sprang into brilliance as I stepped out of sight behind a huge barrel. I shuffled backwards as quietly as I could until I brought up against the wall. Then I sat down slowly—or maybe my knees gave out with fear—and peered out from under the concealing bulk of the barrel which was mounted on a stout timber frame. The hand had disappeared and the lamp sat alone on the stone floor. For the first time I noticed four cans of distil beside it.

Then two hands appeared. Large and hairy, they gripped the edge of the floor and a man hauled himself through the hole. Huge, dressed in dark ragged clothing, his face covered in fur like a lorin—I recognized him before he stood and the barrel hid all but his legs from my view.

It was Silverjack. The feet remained motionless for a while and I sensed that he was listening. Maybe his instincts were allied to his animal appearance and he had become aware of my presence in the way a lorin would. I cowered lower, trying not to breathe, trying to merge and become one with timber and stone. At last he moved, striding barefooted across the cellar to the door. Again he stopped, and uttered a low whistle.

He waited for some time then whistled again, soft and low like a newspigeon. I heard a movement beyond the door and Silverjack moved back into the cellar as another pair of legs arrived quietly, barefooted like his but not hairy; a woman's legs. There was a whispered con-versation of which I caught only a few words. The wom-an's voice was almost inaudible but I heard Silverjack say:

"Ysabel, before the grume."

Then there was a long pause during which the two pairs of feet faced each other closely, touching while Sil-verjack and the woman made little sounds and I felt my face go hot and I kept repeating to myself: don't find me here now, don't find me here *now*...

At last Silverjack turned away, lowered himself through the hole, took the lamp and was gone, letting the trapdoor down behind him. The cellar was quiet again, the woman had apparently departed and I crawled stiffly from my hiding place. I fumbled around, found the matches and lit my lamp. For a while I consid-ered the situation but there seemed no way out of it, nothing I could do except, quite simply, carry a case of bottles upstairs.

The noise hit me like a wall as I staggered through the bar door with my head down, concentrating on not dropping the case and trying to think of nothing else.

A cool hand touched my wrist and I looked up to find Browneyes smiling at me. "Bring it behind the bar, Drove," she said.

I did so. I placed the case beside a pile of empty ones and straightened up, finding myself confronted by Browneyes' father and mother. Neither spoke, and the silence was an awkward one.

"Drove brought some things up for us," said Browneyes happily. "Isn't that nice of him?" She smiled at me with her dimples, innocent and charming.

I felt dirty. I averted my eyes from her father's alarmed, searching gaze only to find I was looking at

PALLAHAXI TIDE

Annlee, whose face was pale with lips unnaturally red, whose hands were white with pressure where they clutched a brown bottle.

"It's quite all right," I muttered unhappily, edging away.

Someone shouted for beer and the spell was mercifully broken. Annlee turned away and I heard a violent rattle of glass on glass, instantly controlled, as she poured. Girth bellowed with laughter at some joke and tugged at a beer pump. Browneyes seized a number of mugs and bore them away to customers on the far side of the room. As she passed one rough character I saw him slide his arm around her waist. She twisted neatly away and passed the beer around a vociferous group as though nothing had happened. For a while I watched the man, feeling murderous and incompetent, then suddenly I wasn't sure which man it was. They all looked the same, and Browneyes was back at the bar, grinning at me. She thought nothing of all this; it was what she had always been used to. For the first time I realized how little I knew about her, and how different her life was from mine.

I don't remember much more about that evening; things seemed to settle down into a rut as several times I visited the cellar to replenish the bar stock, several times I wanted to hit men who looked at Browneyes in a way I didn't like, while all the time the drinking and shouting and laughing continued and I hardly noticed it.

Later I did notice the sudden silence when the door was flung violently open. Standing there with a face like Rax, peering this way and that through the thick smoke, was my father.

CONEY ✳

SIX

I WAS CONFINED to the cottage for an incalculably long time, seeing nobody except my mother and father and, occasionally, the various occupants of the other cottages in the field. These other folk were adult to the point of senility, however, and no company for a caged boy. During my period of incarceration the sun appeared over the horizon, the twilight brightened until eventually the days were as long as the nights. The ocean sparkled invitingly and from the patio I saw the sails of the little dinghies like white feathers drifting on the blue sea, every so often disturbed by a chuntering steamboat. Midsummer came and the tidal flow ceased; the weather remained unfailingly warm and calm as nature prepared itself for the grume.

During my imprisonment I had plenty of time to reflect on the error of my ways and still remembered clearly father's impassioned speech of outraged parenthood as we rode the motorcart from the Golden Grummet up to the cottage on the cliffs, while my mother whimpered beside him.

"I never thought the day would come when I would be forced to drag a son of mine bodily from a commom inn where I found him drinking in the company of the uncouth louts of the general public."

This was the gist of his address and it was unfair. If he hadn't come charging into the bar and laid his violent hands upon me I would have left quite willingly—in fact I had started to leave the instant I saw him standing at the door. But he hadn't given me a chance, and had subjected me to an undignified struggle right in front of Browneyes, her parents, and the entire bar full of customers. In a way it proved the validity of my previous theories concerning my father; in a crisis he will always descend to physical violence.

The following day my father had fallen strangely silent; it was as though a thick glass window had been erected between him and me. We saw each other but apparently it was impossible to converse. This would have suited me fine, had not my mother chosen to fill the conversation vacuum.

"You see, we didn't know where you were, Drove. You'd been seen taking the boat out—against all advice, so I understand—and when the boat arrived back you just weren't in it. We were terrified. I thought your father would go mad with grief. Have you no consideration for our feelings?"

"Pallahaxi-Browneyes came to tell you where I was."

"She most certainly did *not*. We heard nothing, we didn't know what to think until I contacted Dreba-Gwilda and she said they had just collected their boy Wolff from the inn, and that you were there with that slut."

"Are you referring to Browneyes, mother?" I asked coldly, but I had moved too soon. Mother was still in the ascendancy.

"I'm referring to that serving wench with whom you've seen fit to associate yourself, against all the advice of your father and me." Her face crumpled theatrically. "Oh, Drove, Drove, what are you doing to us? What have we done to deserve this? Think of your poor father, even if you have no thought for me. You've brought disgrace on his head, you've demeaned him in front of his colleagues..."

It went on like this for several days until mother at last ran out of variations on the theme and relapsed into a reproachful silence. Relieved, I was able to view the whole unfortunate affair in a saner light. I already knew the worst; now I was ready to consider the good which had come out of the incident. Firstly I had met Browneyes again and it seemed—although I hardly dared to consider this—that she liked me. I thought it just possible that she had omitted to tell my parents where I was, in order to keep me around for longer. I clung to that notion. She couldn't possibly have guessed the reaction of my parents, of course. I only hope that the unseemly brawl with my father in the bar had not soured my image.

Next there was the fascinating question of Silverjack. There was no doubt in my mind—the man was smuggling liquor across from Asta and supplying the Golden Grummet, and possibly all the inns in Pallahaxi. This was a delightful piece of knowledge and my only regret was that I had nobody to share it with. Father had mentioned Silverjack in conversation with mother several times—apparently the hairy fellow was on the verge of taking up some sort of piloting job for the Government —yet here he was trading with the enemy under the very noses of the Parls. In my eyes he had assumed the stature of a romantic hero.

So I had some pleasant thoughts to keep me company during the slow passage of days. At last father asked me to pass the salt one breakfast time and mother, taking her cue, laid me out some fresh clothes. After father had departed for work she glanced at me speculatively a few times and eventually spoke.

"You have a friend coming to see you this morning, Drove."

"Uh?"

"I saw Dreba-Gwilda yesterday and we arranged a big surprise for you. Her nice boy Wolff is coming to see you, and you're going out together. Isn't that nice?"

"Rax. It was Wolff who got me into this freezing mess. Wolff's a fool, mother."

"Nonsense, Drove; he has such *nice* manners. And please don't swear like that. I hope you don't swear in front of Wolff. I must go now. Enjoy yourself, dear." Smiling at me widely and fondly, she gathered up her things and departed for the stores.

Wolff arrived about mid-morning, casually dressed yet still contriving to look dapper in a way I could never achieve—and never wanted to. "Hello there, young Ali-ka-Drove," he greeted me breezily.

"Look, what did you tell your parents that day?"

He looked pained. "That's all in the past now, Drove. Today marks the beginning of a new era in your entertainment and education. It has been arranged that we go on a fishing trip with our mutual friend Silver-jack, in order to see how the general public obtain their livelihood."

His pseudo-adult manner appeared to have developed further since last I had seen him, but the idea of a boat trip appealed. Anything which resulted in my getting away from the cottage would have appealed. "Are you taking fishing things?" I asked. "I must find my gear."

"Fishing tackle will be supplied," he said. "I tell you, Drove, it's all organized. Our people have some connection with this character Silverjack, added to which they seem to want to bring you and me together—can't think why. Maybe they think we're suitable companions for each other." There was a twisted sarcastic smile on his face which I didn't like.

We set off down the hill in the direction of the harbour. When we reached the point where the steep road overhangs the outer harbour, Wolff stopped and leaned against the wall, gazing at the boats at anchor. "I ought to tell you that some strange things have been happening while you've been out of circulation, Drove." Snowdivers soared below and beside us, riding the updraft, occasionally tilting and dropping vertically with folded wings to disappear momentarily beneath the rippled surface. "Now take a look down there," he said, pointing directly below.

I leaned against the wall. The cliff dropped away sheer, ledged with birds nests, to the little beach on which we'd been shipwrecked. I could even see the rock pool where the ice-devil lurked; but at present the water was calm and beguiling but ready to crystallize the moment the creature judged prey to be within range. "What about it?" I asked.

"I made a few enquiries about the storm drain."

"The sewer, you mean?"

"I wish you wouldn't keep calling it a sewer. That storm drain branches out all over the place and runs under most of the town. Now here's my theory. At night when it's dark the boats come close around the far headland, then straight across the bay towards the coast under your cottage." He pointed. "Then they keep close in under the cliffs to this beach, where they unload. Then the stuff is delivered through the tunnels."

"You're still not talking about this smuggling nonsense, are you?" I asked uneasily.

"I hardly think they deliver milk through the tunnels."

"What makes you so freezing sure they deliver anything?"

He stared shrewdly into my face. I'd never realized how close together his eyes were. "Because I've seen them," he said.

"Seen them?" I muttered. Recently I'd decided the smuggling incident had better be left unmentioned. It wasn't Silverjack I was scared for; I was sure the hairy man could look after himself. It was Girth and Annlee's position which worried me—and through them, Browneyes. I was sure Browneyes knew nothing of the smuggling, or she would never have sent me down to the cellar that night when a delivery was due; but nevertheless her parents were involved and she would be affected by any revelations of criminal activities.

"I've been investigating the affair ever since my suspicions were aroused in the cellar of the Grummet. Usually every third night a boat unloads down there. I'll know it again; it has a yellow deckhouse. Here's where I'm going to need your help. On the night of the next delivery we're going to conceal ourselves by that rock pool, and observe the proceedings from close range. We'll use your boat to get to the beach."

"You freezing well won't!"

He turned away and we continued walking down the hill. "Think about it, Drove," he said casually. "It's an interesting exercise, if nothing more. Much better than turning the whole thing over to my father for an official investigation, don't you think? I mean, I may be mistaken. Ah, well, let's talk about something else, shall we? Have you seen anything of that little girl from ther Grummet recently, what was her name?"

"Look, you know freezing well what her name is, and you know freezing well that I haven't seen anyone for days and days!"

"Jumpy, aren't we?" he said distantly as we crossed

the fishmarket and entered Silverjack's yard. He enquired for the owner in peremptory fashion; Silverjack himself appeared almost immediately and escorted us to the water's edge. A small steam launch, already fired up and showing a white plume at the safety valve, rode quietly at the quayside next to the slipway. I glanced around for my own boat and saw it, apparently in good shape, under cover.

"A steam launch," I observed. I rate steam launches as little better than floating motorcarts.

Silverjack sensed my feelings. "A fine craft," he said quickly, strangely deferential. "We'll come to no harm in this. All aboard, then."

"Wait a moment," said Wolff. "There are more of us to come, yet." He looked back towards the town, expectantly.

"You didn't say anything about anyone else," I complained. "I thought it was just going to be the three of us, fishing. There's no room on that boat for any more."

"Here they are," said Wolff.

A smartly-dressed young girl was walking towards us, stepping directly over the debris which littered the slipway, holding the hand of a younger boy, equally well turned out. At first I failed to recognize them but as they came nearer I was able to penetrate the disguises of Pallahaxi-Ribbon and her younger brother, Squint.

"Wolff!" I whispered urgently. "What the Rax is she doing here? I can't stand the sight of her. Have you gone mad?"

"Hello, my dear." said Wolff smoothly, ignoring me, taking Ribbon's hand and assisting her on board. Squint followed, scowling ferociously, and Silverjack cast off. The engine panted and we began to glide among the moored boats; there were noticeably fewer compared with the last time I had seen the harbour. Numbers of the deeper-hulled vessels were being laid up preparatory to the grume.

Silverjack was in fine fettle during the earlier stages of the voyage as he sat at the helm smoking an ancient pipe and telling tales of the sea. In essence the tales were similar to those by Grope the trucker except that the events ocurred on water instead of land and involved storms and whirlpools rather than earthquakes and floods. Meanwhile, his audience had divided itself into two factions. Wolff and Ribbon on one side of the cockpit paying scant attention to the raconteur as they trailed fishing lines and murmured inaudibly to each other, while Squint and I sat in uneasy alliance opposite. Squint listened to Silverjack with open-mouthed gullibility and I quietly brooded over the perfidy of Wolff. Not that I'd ever had a high opinion of him; but I'd never expected him to sink to this.

"And look at the sky now, young lad." Silverjack was addressing Squint as the only attentive member of his audience, "To see the sun Phu shining there, you'd never believe what it's like in the south, right now. I've been there, I can tell you. Great rolling clouds and mist and sea so thick a man could near walk on it. Evaporation, you see. And if you go near shallow water an ice-devil will seize your ship and he won't let go for half a year, not until the rains come. Years ago, when I was younger, I used to work the grume. We'd wait out in the southern ocean while the sun shone so close it charred the masthead and the sea disappeared all around us in steam and there was only one place in the whole ocean where a man could see through the clouds—that was at the Pole itself. So we'd wait there, near dying from the heat and humidity while the clouds closed above in a great spiral, with the sun gone away north. And when we couldn't see any more, then the water would begin to pull us, and we'd follow like a loxcart, the current taking us on the journey north. So we'd follow the grume..."

Squint munched winternuts, eyes wide.

"What about smuggling?" Wolff broke in abruptly. "Have you come across much smuggling in your time, Silverjack?"

A wiggle appeared in our otherwise straight wake astern and I wondered if Wolff noticed it. He couldn't know of Silverjack's involvement with the Golden Grummet, surely.

"Smuggling?" I could see alarm in the small eyes under the hairy brows. "Smuggling? Yes, I've heard tell of smuggling."

"Well, tell me *who* hasn't," trilled Ribbon. I regarded her sourly. It was difficult to imagine her as I'd last seen her; dirty and ragged, crawling through a sewer. She sat beside Wolff but rarely looked at him; in fact she rarely looked at anyone, seeming content to regard the sea and smile secretly from time to time at her personal, mature deliberations. I preferred her as she had been: objectionably domineering but at least genuine.

We had rounded Finger Point and the stark black cliffs were falling away to the flatter land of the estuary, where the new cannery was. The waves were higher and the launch bounced noticeably as it puffed along. We were trailing two lines but had not caught any fish.

"Well?" said Wolff into the hiatus.

Silverjack launched into a long and complex yarn the moral of which was that smuggling didn't pay— particularly in times of war. As he approached the conclusion, great hairy paw waving before him indicating the wrongdoers swinging from the scaffold, his voice shook with emotion and the whole performance took on the atmosphere of repentance, of a confessional. He finished, his fictional wife sobbing into her handkerchief while the lorin carted his autobiographical hero off to the burial grounds. He kept glancing at me as if for reassurance that he was putting on a good show. I felt hot and uncomfortable, wondering how much he knew I knew—and if he knew I wouldn't tell anyone. Then he rose to his feet and excused himself, asking that I take the helm; he needed a rest. He eased himself down the steps into the tiny cabin and shut the hatch behind him, leaving the rest of us looking uneasily at one another. It seemed we had upset the captain.

Then we ran into a shoal of fish and for a while there was intense activity as the other three wound the lines in, detached the fish in a flapping spray of blood and scales, threw lines out and instantly had to repeat the performance. I noticed that Ribbon, in the excitement of the moment, dropped her poised act and worked away eagerly with Wolff and Squint, hands crimson and dripping. I struggled to concentrate on my steering, a little annoyed that they seemed to be having all the fun. A small steam dinghy lay in our path; I could see no sign of its crew and at first thought it was drifting aimlessly, but as we approached I saw a fishing rod projecting over the gunwale.

We were quite close to the estuary and the new cannery. Although the cliffs were not so lofty and precipitous as those back at Finger Point, there was still a fair jumble of rocks and boulders at the water's edge where the waves churned into white foam. It again seemed to me that the steam dinghy was drifting in that direction and I surmised that its occupant had fallen asleep. I blew a few short blasts on the hooter.

Ribbon paused from wrestling a fish off the hook. "Do you *have* to play around like a kid?"

I indicated the dinghy, now about twenty paces away. Fishing forgotten, they stood and regarded the drifting craft. We slowed down as I throttled back. We could see a man lying on his back on the bottomboards, head pillowed on his hands.

"He's had a heart attack," guessed Squint. "He was fishing and he hooked himself a big one and the excitement was too much for him, and he dropped down dead."

"Shut up, Squint," commanded Ribbon. "Make yourself useful. Go and fetch Silverjack."

"Pull alongside," said Wolff, just as I was pulling alongside.

Squint climbed from the cabin, looking pink and a little scared. "I can't wake Silverjack," he said. "He smells funny."

It was quite unreal, the manner in which responsibility had been thrust upon us. A moment ago we had been fishing happily; now, without warning, we had two bodies on our hands. I remember wondering wildly if it was putrefaction that Squint could smell in the cabin. The pressure gauge on the boiler had fallen and I was not sure what to do about it. The other boat was bumping against us and Wolff and Ribbon were looking to me for orders, having conveniently chosen this moment to disclaim command. The water was choppy and the cliffs looked close. The wind was freshening, swinging us around.

"I feel sick," said Squint.

"Ribbon," I said decisively, " you go and try to wake Silverjack. Squint, get over to the leeward side. Wolff, get the boathook and poke that man with it." As they leaped to obey, I realized the advantages of responsibility. Once he has given his orders, the man in charge is free to relax. I sat down and allowed events to take their course.

Squint vomited over the side. Ribbon glanced at him briefly, then stared belligerently at me. "Wake Silverjack yourself. That cabin's no place for a woman."

Meanwhile Wolff had seized the boathook and, overbalancing slightly as the launch rolled with the swell, drove the pointed end into the stranger's ribs.

Any doubts we had as to the health of the man were resolved as he screamed in agony, scrambled to his feet clutching at his side, then cut loose with a tirade of abuse which stopped as abruptly as it began. Suddenly everyone was silent, everyone stared wide-eyed as the boats bumped together.

We watched as the stranger took up his fishing rod and reeled it swiftly in with strange, spatulate fingers. Moving economically he checked his gauges, seated himself at the helm and thrust the throttle forward. He didn't look in our direction again. The engine puffed rapidly and water boiled around the stern. Gathering way smoothly, the steam dinghy accelerated on a wide curve and headed towards the mouth of the estuary.

We looked at each other and I know that we were all frightened. For a while nobody spoke, then at last Wolff voiced our thoughts as he said almost meditatively:

"Odd that he should have spoken in the Astan dialect."

Squint was more forthright. "He was a spy," he said decisively. "A dirty Astan spy."

SEVEN

"*AFTER HIM!*" URGED young Squint as I fingered the throttle irresolutely.

"What are you waiting for?" asked Wolff.

The dinghy was receding rapidly and was clearly a speedier vessel than Silverjack's fishing launch. There was undeniably a temptation to set off at once in pursuit, but it seemed to me that such a policy would be shortsighted. You don't pursue anyone unless you intend to catch him—and I didn't relish the idea of catching an Astan spy, desperate and maybe armed. "Let him go," I said. "We'll report him later."

"Let him go?" said Wolff incredulously. "What sort of patriot are you, Alika-Drove? The least we can do is investigate. Catch the man up and confront him, then if he's on the level there's no harm done."

"I didn't see you doing much confronting a moment ago!"

"It was an awkward situation, Alika-Drove. You can't confront a man you've just stabbed in the ribs. Besides, we were all taken by surprise. You don't expect to meet an Astan spy face to face in these waters."

"Hurry, hurry!" yelled Squint, capering about and rocking the boat dangerously. "The freezer's escaping!"

"Go and see what Silverjack says, Wolff," I suggested desperately.

He disappeared into the cabin and Squint continued to leap and shout. Ribbon was watching me speculatively. I knew she was going to tell me I was scared, so I busied myself loading dried bark and small logs into the tiny furnace. The fire had burned low, which explained the drop in boiler pressure.

Wolff was standing over me. "Silverjack's drunk," he said. He seemed quite matter-of-fact about it. "He's in no shape to make any decisions."

I straightened up, surveying the ocean. The only vessel in sight belonged to the receding spy. Midsummer is always a quiet time at sea; the deep-hulled vessels are being laid up and the water is not yet suitable for the skimmers. "We must take the boat back to Pallahaxi, then," I said.

"Since when did you become captain, Alika-Drove?"

"If you remember, Silverjack handed me the helm before he went below."

"You're wasting time! You're wasting time!" Squint was beside himself.

"Right, all of you." Wolff addressed Ribbon and Squint. "Who's in favour of following the spy?"

"Me! Me!" shouted Squint. Ribbon nodded poisedly.

"I have a majority," observed Wolff with satisfaction. "Move over, Alika-Drove. I'm relieving you of your command."

"That's mutiny!"

He seized my arm, dragging my hand away from the throttle—symbol of my authority. I put up a token struggle but was very conscious of the fact that they were all against me. Shrugging, I left the cockpit, edged around the cabin and made my way to the foredeck to sulk. I sat down and watched the shore, thankful that the cabin roof concealed me from my conquerors. I hated them quietly and intensely; Wolff with his supercilious manner, Ribbon with her domineering personality. Rax, I thought, they deserve each other.

The boat trembled beneath me as Wolff urged the engine to full speed. I looked ahead to see the steam dinghy passing between the low headlands of the estuary; it seemed to have reduced speed. I heard Squint's excited voice. The spy was heading inland and I wondered just where he was making for. Whatever his reasons for being in Erton waters, he must have a base to operate from; that tiny dinghy would never survive in the open sea. There must be traitors in the area.

Soon our quarry disappeared from sight among the fishing boats moored in the estuary. I wondered how the cannery would receive its supplies when the grume came; with the fall in water level the estuary would be navigable only to the smallest skimmers. On the headlands stood square buildings; at the time I thought they were merely lookout posts guarding against a surprise attack on the cannery.

Suddenly thick columns of smoke rose rapidly from each lookout post and after a moment the pounding of powerful engines was borne across the water, audible even above our own puttering unit. We were almost between the headlands; men stood looking down at us and gesticulating. They wanted us to stop. I jumped to my feet and made my way aft; I had no confidence in the boat's new commander.

On stepping down into the cockpit I found a situation of total anarchy. Squint, his small face set in determined lines, was clinging to the throttle which he had thrust full ahead, while Wolff struggled to detach his hand and steer at the same time. Ribbon was shouting at her brother but this only served to reinforce the youngster's determination to push on at all costs.

It was none of my business. If they wanted to wreck the boat that was their concern, not mine. I was about to sit down when I saw Squint's eyes widen in sudden fear. His mouth dropped open as he jerked the throttle back frantically. As the engine slowed I looked forward.

Something was rising from the water ahead of us, something huge and black, dripping and weed-festooned. In the first terror-stricken moment I thought only of Silverjack's eerie yarns of unknown waters and the strange creatures that dwelt there. Before us reared Ragina, queen of the ice-devils and legendary lover of the dead planet Rax. It did not occur to me to wonder why so regal a monster should trouble herself with four youngsters in a boat. The thing before us became a swaying tentacle, barring our course.

The boat heeled violently as Wolff put the helm down. As we stumbled about the cockpit, off balance, the spell was broken. We were running parallel to a thick, rusty cable from which vertical chains dangled into the water, all slung between the two buildings on the headlands and obviously designed to protect the estuary and consequently the cannery from alien invaders. Yet they had let the other boat in... The columns of smoke were emitted by steam winches, which, on the approach of a strange boat, hoisted the apparatus from the bottom of the sea.

"Somebody's coming," said Squint nervously.

A fast launch swept out from a wharf below one of the headlands. As Wolff swung the boat around and headed back for the open sea I saw men grouped on the foredeck, working at a large and complex piece of machinery. Suddenly they were enveloped in a white cloud and I heard a curious noise; a hissing thud. Water suddenly fountained up a few paces off our bows.

"That's a steam gun!" grunted Wolff in alarm. "Rax. We'll have to stop." He throttled back and we pitched gently on the waves while the gunboat drew rapidly nearer. His face was flushed and his fear changed quickly to temper. "What right do they have to fire on us, that's what I'd like to know! This is Erto! Have they taken leave of their senses? I shall speak to my father about this!"

"You do that, Wolff," I said sarcastically. "Meanwhile, talk us out of this. You know as well as I do that the cannery is a restricted area. That gunboat thinks we're Astans!"

He gave me a venomous look which turned to an ingratiating smile as the gunboat drew along side. I noticed that Squint, Ribbon and I had automatically crowded to the forward end of the cockpit leaving Wolff alone in the stern, holding the incriminating helm.

"It's only a bunch of kids," I heard someone shout, then the boat rocked as a man jumped aboard. He wore the dark-blue uniform of the Erton navy and he stood in the centre of the cockpit, dominating us. "All right," he said. "Whose boat is this?"

"It belongs to Pallahaxi-Silverjack," said Wolff eagerly. "He's drunk in the cabin and we had to take over. We were coming to you for help."

There was a brief struggle around the cabin door as the naval man, who didn't believe in wasting words, thrust us aside and climbed down into the cabin to check Wolff's story out. Squint was staring at Wolff accusingly.

"What about the spy?" he whispered loudly. "You didn't tell him about the spy!"

"Shut up!" Wolff hissed back. "We can't change our story now, and it's better this way. They'd never believe a spy, but at least we can prove that Silverjack's drunk."

The man emerged from the cabin, wiping his hands fastidiously on a piece of cloth. "Yes," he said. "Are you

aware that the estuary is a restricted area for the dura-
tion of the war? We have more important things to do
than play nursemaid to a bunch of stupid kids. You realize you might have been killed, going under our guns
like that? And suppose you'd run into the boom?"

"Yes, but we thought it would be all right," babbled
Wolff, demoralized by the naval officer's manner.

Personally, I was not demoralized. I was infuriated;
the man was just the type of supercilious freezer I
seemed to be meeting too often, the type who—like
Wolff himself—assumes that all but he are fools. He had
boarded the boat without permission and now he saw fit
to lecture us. Through a red curtain of rage I found I was
speaking.

"We wouldn't have been killed because your captain
would have the sense to make sure of his facts before
sinking us—even if you wouldn't. The same goes for any
guns on the headlands. And I'm quite sure the winches
are started up at the first sight of approach, so any fool
has time to avoid the boom. And if you don't agree with
me, then there's proof right here under your freezing
nose. We're still alive. We were never in danger."

The officer was watching me coldly, tall and indom-
itable, and suddenly I knew that was a pose, too, that the
man was beaten—that all he had left was his age and his
uniform. Underneath he was merely an intelligent life
form; like myself, but inferior.

Wolff grabbed himself a ride on my rising morale.
"And I think you ought to know that my friend's father
holds a very important position at the cannery. His
name is Alika-Burt."

Freeze you, Wolff, freeze you, I thought. Can't you
understand that I don't *need* my father? I don't *want* my
father?

"Is that so?" The man was still looking at me.

I believe that there is a point in our lives when our characters crystallize like an ice-devil; when, after all the uncertainties, the external influences, the subjection and irresponsibility of childhood, a person will decide: that is the way I am going. I have seen it all, I have listened to the views of my parents and teachers, and although I concede there are facts I do not yet know, nevertheless my character is now so formed that I will not be thrown by new facts. They will increase my knowledge of the world but they will not change my attitude to that world or my conception of my own role in that world. At last I know enough of other people to know when I am *right*.

Thus I did not deny that my father had influence in the cannery, because to do so would be to display a childish obstinacy, a lack of appreciation that a man must use the weapons he has. In front of me stood a tall man in uniform, symbolic of adulthood, symbolic of authority—and he had to be *beaten*. And when I had beaten him, then I would have rid myself of the smothering burden which had hampered the development of my personality since the cradle.

"That's right. My father is Alika-Burt. My name is Alika-Drove. And now if you'll get your ass out of here, we'll resume our voyage. I'm quite capable of handling this boat myself."

He shrugged and there was a curious expression behind his eyes as he murmured, "I'm sure you are. Have a pleasant voyage." He swung himself on board the gunboat, which sheered off and sped away. The confrontation was over so quickly that it was almost as though it had never happened—but not quite...

I made my way to the stern and Wolff stepped aside, relinquishing the helm. He eyed me with respect. I knew it wouldn't last, but just for the moment he eyed me with respect. "That was an impressive display, Alika-Drove," he said.

We discussed the spy on the way back to the harbour. Squint was in favour of an expedition at the dead of night, during which we would scour the country around the cannery for the mysterious foreigner. Ribbon pointed out the fault in his reasoning: at the dead of night the spy was likely to be in bed asleep and therefore difficult to locate. Wolff had a better suggestion.

"Why not ask your father if any of the men at the cannery have Astan accents, Drove?"

This solution appealed to me—partly because it would give me the chance to try out my new-found maturity. I would, quite simply, demand an explanation, man to man. I might even reprimand my father for sending me out with a drunken skipper.

After I had piloted us expertly through Pallahaxi harbour and tied the boat up at the quay, we agreed to meet the following morning. It was late afternoon and the light was fading rapidly as Wolff, Squint and Ribbon departed and I entered the boatyard. I wanted to make sure my skimmer was all right; I hadn't had a chance to look at it for days.

While I was examining the hull and worrying about a few scratches in the varnish, Silverjack came shambling up, rubbing huge hairy fists into his red-rimmed eyes. "You should have woken me, lad," he said. "When did we arrive back?"

"Not long ago."

"I was asleep."

"You were drunk."

"Come now, lad." He was regarding me in alarm. "That's not a pleasant thing to go spreading around, is it now?"

"Oh, forget it." I made to walk away, but he caught me by the arm.

"You won't tell your father, eh, lad?"

"I don't see why I shouldn't. I reckon I'll tell him I saw you smuggling distil into the Golden Grummet, as well." Immediately I wished I hadn't said that.

"Come into my office, will you Drove," he said quietly, letting go of my arm and allowing me to take my own decision. I followed him. "Sit down," he said, sliding behind his desk and lighting up a vile weed. "You and I have some talking to do."

"There's nothing to discuss."

He looked at me steadily; he seemed to have pulled himself together. "All right," he said. "Then I have some talking to do. Now, first of all, I want you to take a look around this place. Nice little business, would you say?"

"I imagine you do all right."

"Well, I don't. This place has been losing money for years. Then last year the Government brought in the new fishing regulations to cut down on the numbers of small boats, and to cut down on the smuggling, I reckon. I'm just not equipped to build the big trawlers so I have to make a living building a few pleasure craft, like your skimmer, and doing repair jobs. You follow me?"

"So far."

"Right, so I make a little money on the side with a few, uh, deliveries, just to keep my head above water. Times are hard, with the war—and I knew a lot of Astan sailors, good fellows, during the peace; so I have plenty of contacts. We ship in a few necessities, we ship out a few things *they* need, and everybody's happy. And in any case I'm getting out of that business soon because your father's offered me a job with good pay. If you go spreading stories around he's going to change his mind."

"I'm not sure father ought to hire a traitor."

Suddenly he stood. He didn't look threatening, merely sick and exasperated. "Your father's a Parl and I suppose that's the way you think, too. Now just listen to this, lad. Here in Pallahaxi we wouldn't know there was a war, if it wasn't for the Government and their rationing and their freezing restrictions and their nasty little secrets. We still trade with Asta—although we have to do it on the quiet; we still produce as much fish and grain as we ever did—but Parliament tells us we can't use it, and takes it away from us. The inland towns are starving, they say. Then how did they manage before the war, that's what I'd like to know? It seems to me this is Parliament's war, not ours. Why they can't leave us alone, and fight the Astans by themselves, I don't know!"

His voice had risen to a shout and I stared at him. "It's a good thing everybody doesn't think like you." I said, using a favourite phrase of my father's.

He gripped my shoulder tightly. "But everybody does, Drove lad," he whispered. "Everybody does. You'll find Parliament has no friends here in Pallahxi."

I did some serious thinking as I walked slowly back to the cottage. There was a feeling of elation within me and it took some time to pin it down; but as I paused on the steps to the clifftop and looked across the harbour at the boats riding at anchor, the houses on the opposite hillside with the old cannery among them, the people working and playing and sitting around the quay just watching, I knew what it was.

I loved the town of Pallahaxi in an all-embracing way; the boats, the life, the atmosphere. And if Pallahaxi was against Parliament and the discipline and regulations it represented, then so was I. In my growing awareness of myself as an individual I think I had been needing a cause to identify with; I had probably realised that nobody can go it completely alone—and here was my cause. Pallahaxi. As I resumed my climb I passed an old woman. She looked hard and worn and tired, yet undefeated; and suddenly she seemed to symbolize the town under the yoke of the Government and I wanted to seize her arm and say: Mother, I'm on your side.

Realizing that although symbolic she was human and probably dominated by an unmarried daughter while constantly complaining about her arthritis and wetting the bed, I kept my hands to myself.

My parents wanted to know every detail of the trip but I gave them an edited report, omitting to mention Silverjack's shortcomings. Then I asked the question. "Father, we came across a man fishing and he had an Astan accent. He went up the estuary and we were following to find out who he was, but they wouldn't let us in. What would an Astan be doing near the new cannery?"

He smiled with disappointing ease; he seemed in great humour. "He'd be working there, Drove. We had several refugees; people born in Erto who were living in Asta when war was declared, who managed to get out before they were interned. Some of them had been living in Asta since their childhood but they still had to get out or be locked away."

"They lost everything they had," put in my mother. "That's the sort of fiends the Astans are."

EIGHT

AFTER BREAKFAST ON the following morning I made

my way down to the quay. Over the past few days the brilliant sunshine had given way to the slight haze which presages the onset of the grume, but it was nevertheless a fine day and I found myself hoping it would be uneventful. A few early newspigeons fluttered about the tall tower of the message post and, at the waterside, snowdivers lined the roof of the fishmarket. There were fewer seabirds than ususal; large numbers had already flown northwards, sensing the approach of the grume. Business at the fishmarket was slow but I paused for a few moments to watch the auctioneer selling off a varied catch; as usual I was unable to comprehend his rapid-fire patter and after a while drifted on. In a short while, when the grume began to run, the days would not be long enough for the auctioneer to dispose of the vast catches and the auction would run long into the nights. Lamps would be lit and portable heaters installed, and whey-faced buyers from far inland would nod their bids and arrange shipments to Alika and Horlox and Ibana.

Always provided that Parliament, with its insatiable desire for control, did not take the whole thing over, arrange quotas, and allow half the catch to go putrid in some forgotten warehouse.

Beyond the fishmarket stands a monument to some long-forgotten event. I have never understood Parliament's compulsion to erect monuments to this, that and every minor event or person—but the obelisk at Pallahaxi does serve as an excellent meeting place. Everyone knows where it is, even if they don't know its purpose. Leaning against the railing overlooking the water, their backs to me, stood Wolff, Ribbon, Squint—and Browneyes. Suddenly I had that breathless feeling again and I knew I was going to make a fool of myself. I tried to remember that since yesterday I had come to terms with myself and ought to be able to take such encounters in my stride.

"Hello," I said, coming up behind them. Wolff and Ribbon ignored me, of course, carrying on some absorbing private conversation, but Squint turned around and so did Browneyes.

Browneyes smiled faintly and Squint said, "Right, then. Are we all ready?"

"Ready for what?"

"We're going to catch that stinking spy, aren't we? Lay him by the heels."

"There isn't a spy," I said. I told him what my father said, but he didn't want to be convinced.

"Well anyway," he said, "we've decided to go for a walk up around Finger Point, so we can sort of poke about at the same time."

"There's no point in going there," I said irritably.

Wolff turned around casually, acknowledging my presence for the first time. "Suit yourself," he said. "We're going anyway. Come on, Ribbon." He took her arm and they began to stroll away.

Squint said, "Come on, Drove," and since I didn't know what Browneyes' attitude was, and certainly didn't wish to be left out of anything, I followed.

The road to Finger Point follows the harbour before climbing steeply into the heavily-wooded area above. We paused for a while at the small beach at the leeward end of the breakwater and watched the fishermen laying up the deepboats in preparation for the grume. It was an unusual procedure. About twenty men would split into two teams and take hold of either side of a floating boat. At a given signal they would heave, legs pumping and feet constantly slipping on the round pebbles that rolled away from under them, and haul the boat on to a series of short logs laid parallel to the water's edge. A few lorin helped, wet fur matted against their stocky legs. The theory was, of course, that the boat would then roll up the logs to its resting place well up the beach—but things never worked out that way. Due to the size of the pebbles the logs would not revolve but remained obstinately stationary, sinking into the beach under the weight of the boat. I always felt they would be better off without the logs, but the whole thing had become traditional, and the men wore special clothes and sang chants as they pulled, while spectators lined the harbour wall.

One day, someone would think to have a preacher pray to the sun-god Phu for a successful grume, and the whole performance would be rounded off.

I preferred to watch them beach the larger boats. This was accomplished in a crude but practical manner which appealed to me. Temporary track was laid from the old cannery tramway down the beach, the steam engine was hitched to the bows of the boat and, with a staccato bark of exhaust and scream of spinning wheels, it dragged it relentlessly to the required position.

We climbed up into the shade of the trees where the road degenerated into a track. A few lorin watched us from among the branches and, in the manner of their kind, warned us with a chattering whenever we approached too close to the sentient mantrapper; the dangerous anemone tree common in this region. Some say that the mantrapper was originally a water creature, but due to being left behind on the low tides of countless grumes it adapted itself to life on land, and now infests most coastal areas. It is much larger than the inland variety; apparently it is distantly related to the ice-devil.

Wolff stopped with an exclamation, staring down at the harbour which was still visible through the trees.

"Look! Down there, that boat with the yellow wheel-house!" He pointed, "That's the boat I was telling you about. That's the one they use for smuggling!"

We left the track and advanced through the trees to the edge of the cliff, which hereabouts crumbled away in a cataract of mighty boulders to the blue water far below. The boat in question was riding at anchor in the outer harbour, about halfway along the breakwater. As we watched, a figure emerged from the deckhouse, made his way forward and hauled steadily on the anchor chain. Events seemed a long way off, and remote. Eventually the tiny figure laid the anchor on the deck, and re-entered the wheelhouse. Puffs of smoke rose from the short funnel and the boat nosed its way among the moored craft, making for the beach where the laying-up teams worked.

"That was Silverjack," breathed Squint in awe. "Silverjack's a smuggler."

Wolff turned away with the air of one who has seen enough. "Remember what I said, Drove?"

"He can't do any smuggling if he's laying the boat up," I objected.

He regarded me pityingly. "You don't think a little detail like the grume would stop a man like that, do you? He'll be getting his skimmer ready, mark my words. And when he does, we'll be waiting for him. We'll catch him red-handed as he unloads the stuff." He glanced suddenly at Browneyes. "What do you think of that?"

She blushed, but I'm sure she knew nothing of her parents' involvement with Silverjack. I'd noticed before that she always blushed when addressed unexpectedly. "Do you really think he's a smuggler?" she asked quietly.

"I'm sure of it, girl, I'm sure of it." He took Ribbon's

arm again and they led the way back to the track.

Browneyes and I walked silently behind, while Squint capered around the four of us, unable to suppress his delight. "Silverjack's a smuggler," he chanted, over and over until Ribbon told him brutally to shut up. Momentarily chastened, he fell behind, scuffing his feet in the dirt and whistling.

I watched Ribbon and Wolff as they walked ahead, arm in arm, heads bent together as they conversed in low tones. Ribbon was wearing a short dress which showed off her undeniably good legs and I found I was watching the backs of her knees as she walked.

"Ribbon looks very pretty, doesn't she?" said Browneyes.

I fouled it up. I had the ideal opportunity to praise Browneyes appearance at Ribbon's expense, but I didn't have the nerve. "She looks all right, I suppose," I muttered.

"Do you like tall girls? I wish I was tall like Ribbon."

I turned to look at her. She was smiling up at me with her eyes warm and beautiful and her sweet dimples showing. I hesitated. I think I was about to say that I liked girls who looked like Browneyes, but Wolff had stopped talking and might have been listening.

"They're building a wharf down there," he said. "Look."

We had rounded the point of the headland and the path had veered to the very edge of the cliff. Far below, men were working, shovelling, leading lox which hauled cartloads of boulders, wielding picks, hacking at the cliff face. A rough road ran from the wharf along the foot of the cliff, winding out of sight beyond an overhang.

"The water's deep, there," observed Ribbon. "It must

have taken an awful lot of rock to build that road. What's it all for?"

Wolff was silent. He didn't know.

"When the grume comes, they won't be able to take the big fishing boats up the estuary to the new cannery," I explained. "They're building this so they'll have somewhere to unload; then they'll take the fish to the cannery by loxcart. They might even build a tramway. Offshore there," I pointed, "is the Pallahaxi Trench, which goes right out to the middle of the ocean. That'll never get shallow, not even during the grume, so the boats can always approach from that direction and come right up to this wharf."

"I know all about the Trench," said Wolff.

"Look out there," said Browneyes.

The clear blue of the sea was interrupted in several places by the brown and foaming white of protruding rocks which had not been there yesterday. The sea level was falling fast; soon the grume would be here.

We began to descend the escarpment from Finger Point and the trees thinned out; the countryside lay stretched below us. Far in the distance we could just make out the Yellow Mountains where the desert began, then the hills rolled towards us, green and fertile. Close below, the estuary narrowed to a river, sinuous and gleaming in the hazy sun, then disappeared among the inland hills. The new cannery lay directly below, an untidy jumble of buildings and heaps of excavated soil; a new road ran like a scar around to our right, back to Pallahaxi. Nearby, I noticed a warren of large lorin holes in a grass-fringed bank. Such holes are common in the soft soil around Pallahaxi; they are reputed to form networks as deep as fifty paces down. A few fishing boats moved about the estuary and we could see the tiny figures of men, walking between the buildings and around the riverside. Trails of dust rose from vehicles.

"It's like a picture," said Browneyes, entranced. I wondered how often she was able to get away from her parents and all the work at the Grummet; how often she had the chance to really *see* the place she lived in.

As she said, it was like a picture and therefore just a little unreal. I found myself wondering if those tiny figures were really men—if they really thought and urinated and battled with their wives and children—or if they were merely a moving tapestry provided for my pleasure. I felt powerful, watching them from on high while they toiled unknowing; I felt as though with a stroke of my mind I could wipe them all out...

Later we walked through the river valley and stopped at a small wayside store to buy food. The place belonged to an old woman who looked as though she'd been there as long as the river itself; gnarled she was, and all covered with hair the way old people get. She looked like Silverjack's mother and Wolff and Ribbon treated her with contempt, calling her grandma and joking with each other about her appearance and the look of the store; I must admit, the place could have been cleaner.

But that was no reason to make fun of the old woman and I felt hot with shame for the two of them as they baited her endlessly—until I thought: if I'd been alone with a girl of Ribbon's type who I was trying to impress, I might have acted the same. So then I merely felt bitter for the three of us. Browneyes I absolved from blame because she was too innocent; Squint because he was too young.

"Look," I said at last. "Will you two cut out the freezing funny stuff and let's get some food?" Browneyes looked gratefully at me but that didn't do any good; I was as guilty as the other two—or would have been, given the circumstances.

We ate dried fish and yellowballs and washed it down with some beverage of the old woman's making which Browneyes, our expert in such matters, assured us was non-alcoholic and therefore not likely to knock us out for the afternoon. "You can tell by the way it feels in your throat," she said wisely.

Afterwards Wolff and Ribbon became serious and began to discuss the purpose of the expedition, as if it mattered.

"Are we going to reconnoitre the area around the cannery, or do you intend to play around all afternoon?" Wolff asked us sternly.

"Reconnoitre!" shouted Squint enthusiastically, spraying particles of winternut.

"I'll go along with that," said Browneyes.

"Right." Wolff stood on a stump, gazing about the countryside. "The cannery is over there; I can see the chimneys. The river's between us and the cannery. And before we reach the river, it looks as though there's some sort of swamp."

"I've heard stories about that swamp," remarked Ribbon.

"We'll make for the river," decided Wolff. "Then we'll be able to observe the cannery from this bank without actually entering the restricted area and having to use Drove's freezing father. Then we can make our way inland along the river bank, reconnoitring as we go, until we hit the Pallahaxi road. Then we go home. Right?"

There was a murmur of agreement and we left the road, striking across the rough grassland towards the river. There were few trees here; the vegetation consisted mainly of low scrub of a harmless variety and, further on, tall reed. Soon the ground became soggy underfoot and before long we found ourselves jumping from tussock to tussock, flailing our arms to keep balance while water gleamed in the grass.

"Hold it," said Wolff as we reached a drier patch than most. "We're getting off course. We need to head that way." He pointed over to the left.

"We'll get our feet wet over there," I objected. "The ground's dry this side."

Wolff looked at me in simulated astonishment. "Are you scared of getting your feet wet, Alika-Drove?"

It had taken me a long time to learn my lesson, but I'd gotten things straight now. "Yes, I'm scared of getting my feet wet," I said firmly. "Does that bother you?"

"Oh, well, in that case we'll go this way and you can go that way."

"I'll come with you, Drove," said Browneyes, grinning.

Squint regarded the two factions anxiously. "Just what am I supposed to do?"

"You have a choice, Squint," replied Wolff.

"Well, thanks." He frowned unhappily, sensing that Wolff didn't want him in his party, yet still inclined to stay with his sister. "Get frozen the lot of you," he said suddenly, stumping off in another direction. "I'll go it alone."

Browneyes and I set off on the dry ground and the voices of the others faded into the distance; soon they were hidden from sight by reeds. A small stream lay in front of us and I jumped across, then held my hand out to Browneyes. She took it and jumped too—and this time I made sure I didn't let go. Hand in hand we walked among the coarse grass and bushes, heading roughly east. I wondered what to do next. Conversation had ceased in the way it always did when she and I were alone.

"I'm glad you came today, Drove," she said at last, just when I felt like screaming at my mind for its lack of ideas. "I was worried about you. I haven't seen you for so long and I thought maybe you'd got into a lot of trouble, you know, *that* night."

"My father doesn't believe in alcohol. Except for the motorcart."

"My mother blamed herself. She didn't know, you see, that your father was like that."

It was incredible. We were holding hands, yet we were talking about our parents. Animals never had this problem; they couldn't talk.

"I blame my father."

"What for?"

I had forgotten. I'd lost the thread of the discussion. I let her words hang there, and turned my head so that I could see her face as we walked. She was looking at the ground, her expression serious. Her legs—I moved a little away so that I could see them better—were, yes, much prettier than Ribbon's. Sturdier and more healthy looking.

Watching her, I tripped on a protruding stump and stumbled, and her hand tightened in mine. We had stopped walking now, and were standing looking at each other. Her eyes held mine and her face tilted up just a fraction as she looked and looked, and my insides turned to shivering slush. I wanted to say something but I knew that if I tried, it would just come out a groan, and she would laugh.

"I... I'm glad we're here," she said. "It's nice, isn't it? Being together like this, I mean."

"I like it too," I managed to say.

"I was scared the others would be around us all the time, weren't you?"

"It was lucky they don't mind getting their swamps wet," I said idiotically. "I mean their feet."

"Drove..." she said, and gulped suddenly; and at last I realized she was just as nervous as I. "I... like you, Drove. I mean, I really *like* you."

I stared at her and wondered how she had managed to say that—and hoped she knew I felt the same way. I opened my mouth a couple of times and closed it again, then tugged at her hand and we started walking again. There was a scrub bush nearby and as we walked the branches formed three crosses in line with a tall tree in the distance. I'll never forget that place.

Soon my elation with what she'd said turned once again to impatience with myself for failing to follow the matter up. I wasn't quite sure what I should have done, but anything would have been better than standing there like an idiot and letting a girl do all the talking.

But we were still holding hands, and as we walked I squeezed hers and she squeezed back, so I was very happy again. We came to a large shallow lake which meandered off among the reeds and bushes, and we stood still for a while, watching it and not saying anything. This time, however, it was an easy silence because we both had plenty to think about.

Then, suddenly, everything changed.

I think Browneyes saw it first. Her grip on my hand tightened and she gave a little gasp—and just about that time I saw the surface of the lake tremble.

It came around the corner, from where an arm of the lake disappeared from view; it came as an icy gleam across the surface, extending a scintillating arm of crystal, then another, an immediate filling-in of the gap with diamond-shaped wedges of jewelled glitter, reaching forward, reaching out, while all the time the lake groaned and creaked and was suddenly silent, inert, crystalline solid.

We heard a distant scream, terror-filled and shrill; then an urgent male shout.

"There's an ice-devil in the lake!" cried Browneyes. "It's got somebody!"

NINE

THE ENTIRE SURFACE of the lake now glittered like polished silver in the afternoon sun; the cracks of the crystalline progression had disappeared and the lake was one single homogeneous mass. Except that somewhere, under all that glitter, the ice-devil lurked... As I shifted my feet I heard a crackling. The ground, which a moment ago had been soggy and resilient was now firm, glowing through the grass with the same cold lustre. Again we heard Wolff shouting.

"Come on," I said, drawing Browneyes along. We trod carefully from clump to clump on the tough, coarse grass, dreading to step on the glossy hardness all around in case the ice-devil sensed our presence. I found myself in a blind alley, teetering on an isolated tussock, knowing that the distance to the next was too far to jump. I looked around to see Browneyes, too, swaying precariously. "What shall we do?" I asked her. "Can you go back?"

"I can..." She turned and looked back the way we'd come. There was a distant scream from Ribbon. "But I don't think it'll help, Drove. The ice-devil has frozen all the water around here. We'll never get out unless we walk on the surface."

"Is that safe?"

"They say it is. They say so long as you keep going, and so long as the ice-devil has something else to think of... If it wanted to capture us, it would have to let go of who it's already caught."

"All right. I'll go first."

I stepped on to the crystal lake. Underfoot it was rock-hard; I bent down and touched the surface nervously; it was cold, but not too frightening. It was not slippery, either, not like real ice. I nodded to Browneyes and she stepped down from her tussock, holding tightly on to my hand. I remember thinking with the ridiculous sentimentality of my age: if we go, we'll go together.

"Whereabouts are they?" asked Browneyes. "I thought Wolff was shouting from somewhere over there." She indicated a point where the arm of the lake disappeared from sight among the reeds. It looked a long way off. "That was where it first started going solid. Around that corner."

We began to walk, treading lightly in order not to disturb the monster underneath, talking in whispers. After a while we reached the far shore and followed a winding, glittering path among the spinethickets and reed. Wolff yelled again and suddenly I caught sight of him and Ribbon beyond a bush, about thirty paces away.

Ribbon's face was white with pain and Wolff was bending over her ankle. He looked up as we approached. "The ice-devil's got her foot," he said.

They were siting on the surface of the lake itself, several paces from the nearest patch of grass. "What were you doing out here?" I asked. "You knew there were ice-devils about. I told you we ought to keep to dry land."

"Yes, well we didn't, did we? It's too late for all that, now. We ought to be thinking about what we're going to do, instead of holding a post-mortem."

He was right, of course. I knelt beside him. Ribbon's right foot was locked solidly into the lake. The leg was cut off short just above the ankle, and through the translucent crystal I could faintly see her foot and, rather pathetically, the red shoe still in position. The pressure must have been considerable and I was surprised that she wasn't making more noise.

"What shall we do?" asked Wolff.

They were all looking at me and I couldn't see why I should be expected to dream up a solution when nobody else could. "Browneyes," I said, "would you look after Ribbon for a moment? I must have a talk with Wolff." That way, I thought, we could discuss the hopeless situation freely, without further alarming the trapped girl.

Wolff and I withdrew amongst the scrub. "I saw this happen to a bird the other day," I said. I described the death of the snowdiver. "So long as Ribbon keeps moving, the ice-devil will know she's alive, and it won't attack. I don't think its tentacles are very strong—not even for a big ice-devil like this one. They're just thin tendrils for wrapping around a body and pulling it down."

"Ugh," grunted Wolff, shuddering. His face was pale and sweaty. "Shouldn't we send to the cannery for help? We could get men with picks. They could chip her free."

"That wouldn't work. As soon as the ice-devil felt it was losing its grip it would liquefy and re-crystallize instantly. That way it would get a better grip on her, and maybe some of the men too."

"So what do we do?"

I thought hard. There was a possible way out, but I wasn't sure if Ribbon was capable of taking it. It was worth a try, anyway. I explained to Wolff and he looked as doubtful as I felt.

We returned to the girls. Browneyes looked up hopefully, but on seeing our expressions she averted her eyes. Wolff seated himself beside Ribbon, taking her hand.

"Ribbon," I said, "I want you to try something. I want you to be as still as you possibly can. Just don't move, not at all, for as long as you can. That way, the ice-devil will think you're dead. Right?"

She nodded. Her cheeks were shiny with tears.

"Then as soon as he relaxes and the lake turns to water again, jump backwards." I pointed. "There's a clump of grass right there and you could just make it before the ice-devil catches on, and crystallizes the lake again. We'll stand back there and grab you when you come."

She looked at Wolff. "He means I wait here until the ice-devil starts reaching for me, Wolff?'

Wolff glanced at me. "That's right. Ready, then?"

We withdrew to safety and left her sitting there. She looked at us and actually tried to smile as she hugged herself and forced her body to keep still. As I watched, I knew she wasn't going to be able to do it. The cold was striking into her from the hard lake and no matter how hard she tried—and she did try—she could not control the involuntary shuddering that comes with the fear that cold brings. As much as Ribbon told herself she was not frightened, her body insisted that she was, and trembled to prove it... We watched her and we sorrowed for her, we murmured encouragement and we told jokes, but it was useless. She remained trapped in the pitiless crystal.

"It's no use," she muttered at last. She flapped her chilled arms and shifted about.

I couldn't think of any other solution. The ice-devil wouldn't free her until she was still, and she wouldn't be still until she was dead. Even if we could bring ourselves to knock her unconscious, the creature in the lake would still be able to sense her breathing, her heartbeat. It was expert in such matters. That was how it lived.

We stood over her and from time to time Wolff would make an impractical suggestion and then berate the rest of us because we would not accept it. "After all," he said belligerently after we had turned down his scheme for pounding the lake with steamgun fire, "we've got to try everything. Do you want to just leave her here to die? Have you any better ideas? Surely it's better to try everything, rather than just give up!"

Ribbon said, surprisingly, "Wolff, will you please shut up and let us think?"

About that time I had an idea. I couldn't tell the others the details because it might have been a stupid idea —and whether it would work or not, I wasn't sure that they would agree to it. Wolff, for one, would condemn it as defeatism, as clutching at a straw, as the fantasy of a diseased mind.

"I think I can get her out of this," I said carefully. "But if this is going to work, you and Browneyes will have to go away and leave us here for a while, Wolff." I looked away from the hurt in my girl's eyes.

Wolf was puzzled, but relieved. He was being absolved from responsibility. He made a token gesture, of course. "I hope you know what you're talking about, Alika-Drove," he said. "If you fail and Ribbon dies, you'll be held personally responsible."

With this threat he took Browneyes' arm and they departed.

Ribbon was silent as I sat beside her, then after a

while she looked up from contemplation of her invisible foot and said: "Well?"

"Do you think you can stay calm for maybe a long time, and just trust me?"

"I... I don't know. Look, what's all this about, Drove?"

"It won't work if I tell you, because then you'll start hoping for it and I think maybe it's too much to expect. It's a thing that happens sometimes when you're in trouble, that's all. Provided that you don't get so scared that you demand it."

"Oh." She tried to smile again. "Then maybe you'd better not tell me. Uh... Drove...?"

"Yes?"

"Please sit closer and put your arm round me. That's better... Don't look so worried; Browneyes can't see. Oh..." she winced, clutching her ankle. "It hurts, Drove. It hurts so much." She tensed in my arms, then relaxed shudderingly. "It's so cold here."

"Talk about something, Ribbon. Try not to think too much about the pain. Tell me about yourself. You might have time to tell me the story of your life." I tried to grin into the wan face next to mine. "Make a start, anyway."

"You don't like me very much, do you? I know it's mostly my fault, but you can be freezing irritating yourself, Drove. You know that?"

"I know, but let's not talk about hate. Instead think of yourself as an animal in trouble. Animals don't hate. They don't blame people because their foot hurts. They don't even blame the man who set the trap."

She cried a little, then said, "I'm sorry, Drove. You're right. It's not your fault I'm stuck here. It's mine and that fool Wolff's. Rax. If I ever get out of this I'll tell that freezer just what I think of him and that stupid nose of his!"

"Ribbon!" I reproved her. "It won't work unless there's no hate." But she was right; Wolff did have a long nose. "Have you ever noticed how close together his eyes are?" I asked interestedly.

"Frequently." She actually giggled, but then her eyes clouded over again as the involuntary movement brought more pain.

"Ribbon," I said quickly, "I think you're very nice. You're right that I didn't like you much when I first met you, but now I know you better I think you're very pretty and... nice," I finished lamely, wondering how I'd had the nerve to say that, then realizing it was because I didn't mind too much what *she* thought of *me*.

"You're all right yourself, Alika-Drove, under that chip of yours." Her eyes were blue. She thought for a long time, then said, "If I ever get away from here, you know, I'm... I'm going to try to be better. Maybe... maybe if more people knew what I was really like, then they'd like me more. I know I give a bad impression, just like you do. Afterwards... will you promise me something, Drove?"

"Uh," I said noncommittally.

"If I get out of this and you think I'm going bad again, you know, being bossy and horrid, will you tell me?"

"Right."

I was sure she was sincere, and we talked some more, huddled close together and shivering from time to time. She tried to laugh sometimes; she cried a lot more —but softly from the pain, because she couldn't help it. I thought she was very brave about the whole thing. She was much too good for Wolff.

Then, at last, the lorin came.

I didn't see them arrive, but gradually became aware

of them watching us from the other side of the lake. There seemed to be eight of them standing motionless in the shade of a low tree but it's never easy to tell with lorin; their bodies are so shaggy that they blend into one another, at a distance.

I was worried about Ribbon's possible attitude. "Ribbon." I said quietly, "over there are some lorin, and I think they're going to help us. That's what I've been waiting for. Now you won't start yelling or struggling if they come over here and touch you, will you?"

She swallowed, watching the shadowy forms uncertainly. "How many are there? There seem to be a lot of them. Are they safe? What are they going to do?"

"Take it easy. They'll touch you, that's all. Just relax and let them come."

I held her close to stifle her shuddering and she buried her head in my clothes. The lorin watched for some time then, moving together, they advanced towards us over the crystalline surface of the lake. Closer they came and I think Ribbon sensed their nearness, because her shivering became less violent and she slipped her arm around me and squeezed me—and I was calm enough to enjoy it.

She whispered, "Drove, are they near? I'm not so frightened now. I'm sorry for being such a kid."

"They're here," I said.

They stood around us, looking down at us with no expression detectable under the thick hair of their faces. I sensed the calm in their presence, the feeling of hope they engendered. I stood back and they went to Ribbon.

She watched them as they squatted around her and there was no disgust in her eyes, no loathing. When they laid their hands on her she didn't flinch. She looked at me in mute enquiry as they drew closer about her, cradling her in their arms.

"Just let them take over," I said. "Relax and don't worry. Go to sleep."

After a while her eyes closed and her body slackened, supported by the arms of the lorin. I backed away to the grassy patch and stood in safety, watching and feeling the balm of the lorin's minds, so that I began to feel drowsy too. The lorin were motionless now, heads sagging on their furry chests as they grouped about Ribbon, a silent tableau on the glittering lake. I was sitting down...

The next thing I knew, the lake was lapping liquid near my feet and the lorin were splashing towards me, carrying the inert form of Ribbon while behind them a slender tentacle waved in frustration. They laid her beside me then the largest one looked into my eyes for a long moment. Then they were gone.

I turned to Ribbon. She was utterly still, her face pallid yet calm. Glancing around guiltily I laid my hand on her soft breast but could feel no heartbeat, no respiration. There was not even warmth...

Maybe I left my hand there longer than I should; anyway, after a while there was a faint thump within her chest and a flutter, and her colour returned rapidly as the beat steadied and she began to breathe again. I snatched my hand away as warmth returned and she opened her eyes.

"Oh..." She looked at me with a faint smile and touched herself briefly as though remembering something, and I felt my face go hot. "What happened, Drove? How did I get here?"

"The lorin pulled you out of the lake," I said briefly, and stood. Our period of intimacy was over; we had shared something and we knew each other better as a result, and I think we were both glad of that—but now circumstances were back to normal. "Let's go and find the others," I said.

She jumped up, completely recovered with no sign of shock, unharmed except for a faint blue bruise around her ankle; such is the way of the lorin. "How long was I asleep?"

"You woke up almost immediately after they put you down."

"Oh. Uh... thanks, Drove." She took my hand. "Friends?" She was very serious.

"Uh." I grinned sheepishly.

We walked through the swamp, keeping to the dry ground. "I hope you can express yourself better with Browneyes," she laughed, glancing at me mischievously. "Otherwise she's going to be very disappointed."

I could feel my face flaming. "What makes you think I...? Uh... what makes...?"

Suddenly we saw Browneyes and Wolff standing near the riverbank, and I let go of Ribbon's hand as though it were red hot.

"That's what makes me think you, uh," she mimicked, laughing.

After the explanations and a few searching glances from Browneyes—who apparently resented the intimacy into which Ribbon and I had been forced—we resumed our walk along the riverbank. It was late afternoon and the sun was getting low, so we cut down on the reconnoitring with a view to reaching Pallahaxi before dark.

A trail of smoke arose from the cannery opposite while a few fishing boats unloaded their catch at the wharf. Several of the deep-hulls were already pulled up on the bank, while others stood in the shallow water with legs attached to prevent them toppling when the estuary dried out. A steam truck puffed its way out of the yard and raised a cloud of dust as it rolled on to the Pallahaxi road.

After a short interval of suspicion Browneyes was holding my hand again and, as we dropped behind the other two and I made it clear that I preferred her company to Ribbon's, she began to squeeze it and chatter happily. I watched the pair ahead with some amusement; Wolff had taken Ribbon's arm and was bending towards her as they walked, and I saw that his nose was indeed long—pointed, too. He looked like a large angular bird. I told Browneyes so and she laughed, then said after a short pause:

"But don't you think Ribbon's very pretty?"

I seemed to have heard this before, but this time I was going to give the correct answer. I wondered where all the confidence had come from.

"She's pretty, in a sort of doll way," I said judicially. "But I think you're much prettier, Browneyes."

As she looked at me her eyes widened until the sungod Phu seemed to shine out of them, then she smiled a broad, dimpled smile of satisfaction. "Do you really think so?" she murmured. She squeezed my hand until I felt a cracking in the joints.

At this happy moment Wolff interrupted us, as he had a habit of doing. "Look over there, you two," he said. "What do you make of those?"

There were several of them; they were large, whatever they were, and covered by tarpaulins. They were placed at regular intervals along the riverbank; turning, I saw that the line continued almost as far as the headland. I couldn't imagine what they might be but felt there was something sinister about them; something relentless about the way they marched along into the distance.

"I'll ask father," I said doubtfully. I could just visualize the blank expression on his face, as he pretended he didn't know what I was talking about. If we were meant to know, the objects wouldn't be covered up like that.

We discussed the mystery all the way back to Pallahaxi, when it was driven from our minds by the news that Squint had not arrived home yet.

TEN

RIBBON'S HOUSE LAY on the north side of the town, well back from the harbour. As we made our way from the outskirts she invited us in for a drink; we were all hot and thirsty and her house was the nearest. I think Wolff was a little annoyed at Browneyes and I being included in the invitation. The house was very small and I guess it was a blow to his pride to have it so spelled out that he was associating with the daughter of an impecunious fisherman. However, we soon forgot all that.

Ribbon's father confronted us in the tiny living room. "Just tell me how you came to lose him. He's only a child. You were responsible for him!" His name was Pallahaxi-Strongarm and the name was well-chosen; he was a menacing figure as he seemed to fill the little room with his rage.

"You know how adventurous he is," put in the mother, Pallahaxi-Una. "You know how you have to watch him all the time."

"Mother, he just went off," said Ribbon helplessly.

"So you said. What I don't understand is, why didn't you look for him? Why did you come back without him?"

Ribbon's face was pale; she was trembling and on the verge of tears. "We thought he was ahead of us, you see. We thought..."

"You thought? You thought? The trouble with you is that you don't think!" roared Strongarm in uncanny repetition of one of my father's favourite sayings. "I tell you this, my girl, I'm going to take a strap to you. You've been asking for this for a long time and now you're going to get it, by Phu!"

Ribbon was crying now and Wolff stood silently by, face stiff with embarrassment. Somebody had to do something.

"Ribbon got caught by an ice-devil!" I blurted frantically. "It took us ages to get her free and we really thought Squint had gone on ahead of us!"

"She what?" An extraordinary change came over the huge man's face as he regarded his daughter. "Where did it get you, girl? Are you all right? How did it happen?"

"It... It took my foot," she sobbed. "It's all right now, really it's all right."

Strongarm was kneeling now, tenderly caressing the bruised area on Ribbon's foot with his coarse hands. "My poor little girl," he murmured. "Does it hurt much now, darling? I'm sorry... I'm sorry I shouted at you." He eased her shoe off. "Sit down, darling," he said. He looked up and I saw his eyes were moist. "Una, fetch some warm water, will you?"

They bathed Ribbon's foot and rubbed ointment into it, consoled her and generally made a sickening fuss of her—and I began to get an even clearer picture of why Ribbon was the way she was. When you live with parents who keep telling you you're beautiful and clever, then I imagine you can get to believe it, after a while.

Afterwards Strongarm, a changed man, thanked me repeatedly for my part in the rescue and promised me the world, should I ever want it. Even though I was, as he put it, the son of a freezing Government bum. At last we returned to the problem of Squint—who still had not arrived—in a quieter manner than before.

"The little freezer's probably down at the yard fooling with that waster Silverjack," guessed Strongarm. "I've always said he spends too much time there. I'll go and see. You, Browneyes, try the Grummet. Drove and you, what's your freezing name? Wolff, go along to your houses and check. We'll all meet back here. Right?"

It was dark as I walked through the town and climbed the hill beside the harbour. I was becoming alarmed. I could think of no reason why Squint should call on my parents—and I was quite sure that Silverjack had fallen in the kid's estimation since the episode of the steam launch, so it was unlikely that he would be at the yard. I couldn't think where he was. I was beginning to wonder if maybe he'd never reached Pallahaxi at all, but was lying down by the river somewhere with a broken leg—or worse, in the grip of an ice-devil or an anemone tree.

As I expected, he was not at my house when I arrived. Both my parents were in, however, sitting in the living room. I've often wondered what my parents *do* when they're alone together. They must be pretty dull company for each other. I imagine they discuss the war, and father helps mother find the right places to stick the pins in her map.

"We wondered what had happened to you," said mother. "We worry about you, you know, Drove."

"I only called in for a moment to see if Pallahaxi-Squint was here," I explained. "He's lost. I'm going back to help search."

"You most certainly are not." Father's voice had taken on the adamant tone I knew so well. "I'm not having any son of mine tramping the countryside at night looking for a fisherman's brat. You'll stay right here, my boy, and go to bed."

"What's wrong with a fisherman?" I asked hotly. "You wouldn't get far with your freezing cannery if it weren't for fishermen!"

Mother uttered a little gasp of alarm as belatedly she sensed a full-scale row brewing up. "Your father considers fishermen a very estimable breed of men, Drove," she twittered. "And so do I. But that doesn't mean that we consider their offspring to be suitable playmates for you, dear."

"Playmates! Rax, mother, do you think I'm still a freezing kid?"

"I will not tolerate your swearing at your mother like that, Drove!"

"Well, that's too bad, father, because I'll say what I freezing well like!"

"Oh, Phu... oh, Phu..." lamented mother.

"All right," said father grimly. "All right. This time you've gone too far. You never know when to stop, do you? I can only assume that you learned this sort of behaviour from your friends, because you certainly never learned it from your mother or me. Now go to your room and stay there. I'll see you later."

I knew there was no point in arguing further because physically he was stronger than I. Mother, to my disgust, was crying noisily. I went to my room with the feeling that I could be there for a very long time. Opening the window I looked out. I was tempted to climb to the ground and make a run for it, but was deterred by the fact that it would solve nothing. I saw lights at the entrance to the field and watched as a motorcart came chuffing quietly across the grass.

At first I thought it was Ribbon's father, come to fetch me, but then I realized that he would never have access to a motorcart. It must be one of father's freezing associates from the cannery, I decided. The vehicle halted just short of the cottage and gave a quick, short blast on the whistle. I withdrew behind the drapes as I heard the front door open. Father strode across to the motorcart and a man climbed out to greet him quietly. I recognized Horlox-Mestler.

There was something furtive about them; I wondered why they didn't go into the house, and concluded that it was because they didn't want mother or me to hear what they said.

"You know about the search for the boy Squint, of course," Mestler was saying.

"My son told me," said father, equally quietly. "He wanted to join in, but I stopped him."

"Why?"

"Well..." My father was confused by this. "I mean, it would have looked strange... the son of a Parliamentarian..."

"Burt, you're a fool and you don't understand kids," snapped Mestler to my delight. "It'll look strange if he *doesn't* join in the search. Relations are bad enough between the town and us already; at least have the sense to let your son show that we're not totally divorced from the life and needs of the general public."

"It's not going to be easy..." father muttered. "He was intolerably rude."

"That's your problem. Anyway, that's not what I came to see you about. There's bad news, I'm afraid. The Ysabel's been delayed."

"Again? Rax, at this rate she'll barely beat the grume!"

"That's what I'm afraid of. As it is, she'll probably have to offload at the new wharf—which is something we didn't want. Anyway, I want you to organize that side of things first thing tomorrow. We must have everything ready. Make sure the cliff road is completed as soon as possible."

"Of course. Of course."

Mestler suddenly chuckled. "Don't look so alarmed, Burt. It'll all work out, you'll see." He climbed back into the motorcart and puffed away.

A short while later, father entered my room. I looked at him blandly.

"I have been giving the matter of your abominable rudeness some consideration," he said woodenly, "and I have concluded that there may have been extenuating circumstances. In your anxiety over your friend, you forgot yourself. You are young, and the young lack control, lack discipline. As you grow older, I trust you will begin to realize—"

"Look, are you trying to say that you'll let me join in the search for a small boy who may be lying in the cold and dark with a broken leg?"

He swallowed hard. He opened his mouth and shut it. At last he managed to speak. "Get out of here," he jerked out.

Outside Ribbon's house I found a large crowd of people assembled, holding torches which flickered crimson in their faces as they listened to Pallahaxi-Strongarm. I joined Browneyes and held her hand in the darkness while Ribbon's father addressed us from the upper window of the house.

"I'd say we have about fifty people here," he shouted, "and I'd like to thank you all for turning out like this. We've sent a message to the new cannery asking them to let us have the use of their vehicles."

"About time they did something for us!" a man shouted, and there was a murmur of agreement.

At that moment a team of lox shambled around the corner, led by a lorin and dragging a large cart. Several more followed until the narrow street became crowded. The beasts stood patiently in the flickering light, heads hanging.

"Meanwhile we'll use these, which have been kindly lent us by the old cannery," Strongarm continued. "We don't want to waste time, so let's all climb aboard and get going!" He disappeared from sight; seconds later he emerged from the front door and pushed his way urgently through the crowd, his face expressionless. His wife and Ribbon followed him and they mounted the lead cart, followed by a number of bystanders.

"Come on, Drove," said Browneyes, pulling me forward. We climbed into a nearby cart which smelled strongly of fish and sat on boxes lining the inside of the vehicle. Others joined us and soon we were all jammed together, about fifteen of us, grateful for the mutual warmth. The air was fresh with the night chill and I noticed numbers of people left the nearby public heater with some reluctance. The dead planet Rax glinted stonily in the blackness above. I was very conscious of Browneyes sitting close beside me and after a moment I put my arm around her. I saw white teeth flash in a grin from the opposite side of the cart and the flicker of the torch revealed Browneyes' father Girth watching us indulgently.

Then the lox lunged forward and the cart lurched into motion, throwing us against one another. We rumbled through the narrow streets and soon reached the main road out of town; the lorin had transmitted the urgency of the occasion to the lox who moved with unaccustomed speed, their shaggy heads thrust forward. There were two lighted torches in our cart and a further bundle on the floor for use when the search began; for the time being, however, we had all the illumination we needed. The crimson glow reflected back from the windows around us like a multitude of eyes and suddenly I was conscious of the cold, and shivered. Browneyes glanced at me enquiringly then huddled back into her thick loxhair cloak. I tightened my arm around her and she smiled to herself. Then I think we both remembered just how serious the situation was, and I know that I felt ashamed of my errant thoughts while Squint was lost in the cold somewhere.

Then I told myself that my feelings towards Browneyes made no difference to Squint's predicament, and I felt better.

The lox's claws scrabbled at the loose road surface as we climbed the long hill out of Pallahaxi and the lorin moved closer, its thick arm around the neck of the lead beast while it presumably emitted thoughts of encouragement. I saw Silverjack sitting in the next cart ahead and caught the glint as he raised a bottle to his lips. I looked from him to the lorin and was struck by the resemblance, remembering a somewhat unlikely story I'd heard recently, that Silverjack's mother had lain with a lorin out near Finger Point, years ago.

At last we reached the top of the hill and the lights of the cannery lay below us, looking a long way off. The four carts drew alongside one another and Strongarm stood, holding a blazing torch.

"We'll start from here," he shouted. "We spread out

and beat downhill towards the river, keeping in a straight line as far as possible." Although his voice was steady enough, the strain showed in his gaunt face. "Be careful when you reach the swamp. There are ice-devils in there. Now, I want a small team in either cart to form advance parties with a roving commission. Listen out for cries or anything which might strike you as strange. In a short while the vehicles from the new cannery will be here, then we'll really be able to get moving."

The messenger had returned, having ridden on lox-back up the hill from the new cannery. He said something to Strongarm.

"What!" the man roared. "What?" He turned to the rest of us, his face haggard in the glow. "They say we can't have the vehicles," he rasped. "The guards say they don't have the authority! What sort of freezing country is this, anyway?"

"Let's ride down there and smash the place up!" yelled the cyclopean man, and there was a chorus of agreement.

"No!" shouted Strongarm. "For pity's sake don't forget what we're here for. First we find my son. Then..." His voice dropped and he spoke so quietly that I barely heard the words. "Then we deal with the cannery..."

I remember it occurred to me at the time that Squint was lucky in his father; there couldn't have been a better man to organize a search. It was not merely because he was personally involved; he seemed naturally to have a way of getting things done, of bending people to his will by sheer force of personality and maybe a little physical intimidation. Later Browneyes told me that although Strongarm held no office in the town he was nevertheless highly respected and looked on as a leader in local affairs.

Browneyes, Ribbon, Wolff and I were placed in the middle of the straggling line and told to make for the place where we had last seen Squint. As I looked left I could see torches in the distance almost as far as Finger Point; to the right, the line stretched far inland. While the searchers were getting themselves organized, further volunteers had ridden up from the town and by now we must have been well over a hundred strong. Down in the river valley below, more lights moved as loxcarts and their crews conducted a random search.

We made our way slowly downhill, torches held above our heads until our arms ached. From time to time Browneyes and I would see a huddled form in the bush, but when we got closer it always turned out to be a sleeping lorin, or a lox, or even a spinethicket. I found myself wondering about the lorin. If anyone could find Squint they could, with their uncanny ability to detect the emotions of people in trouble.

Later progress slowed as the line began to pick its way through the swampy area towards the riverbank. We passed the place where Browneyes and I had first confessed our feelings, then moved on to the point where Ribbon had been trapped, all the while treading with the utmost caution as the dancing lights of the torches glittered over dark water. We saw nothing and heard nothing more than the occasional shouted query and reply further along the line. At last we reached the river; I joined Browneyes and together we gazed across the slow-moving ripples of the dark estuary to the lights of the cannery opposite. Further along the bank I could see Wolff and Ribbon standing together.

Suddenly I heard an exclamation from Wolff. He was bending down, showing something to Ribbon.

"What is it?" I called.

He turned. "It's a yellowball skin. It's..." He turned back to Ribbon and they muttered together, pointing. "Come over here!" he shouted.

We joined them and Wolff indicated the mud before us. The gradual falling of the tide had revealed a wide margin of black ooze between the bank and the water and at this point I could make out marks, imprints in the mud. I moved closer, stepping down from the bank and sinking into the slime, holding the torch high. I saw a long single furrow running out into the dark water and, parallel to the furrow, a line of small deep imprints. Quite obviously someone had pushed a boat into the estuary at this point, climbed in and rowed... where? The destination could only be the cannery.

"They could be Squint's footprints," said Ribbon. "They're small enough. And it would be just like him to go prowling around the cannery because he knows he wasn't supposed to."

"What have you found?" The shout came from along the bank. A column of jiggling lights marched in our direction. The searchers were reassembling for a further briefing. Soon there was a large crowd gathered around us. Strongarm arrived, thrusting his way through and staring belligerently at the marks as though willing them to yield up their secret.

"He must be in the cannery," he said at last. "He found a boat here, got inquisitive, and rowed across. Right." He stamped away upstream. "Make for the freezing cannery, men!" he shouted, and the column of burning torches trailed him along the riverbank.

The bridge which carries the Pallahaxi road over the river was some distance away but Strongarm set a furious pace and before long we had crossed to the other bank and were marching in a body towards the new cannery. There was hope in the air now, and I think we all believed that in due course we would find Squint asleep on a heap of sacks in the boilerhouse.

At last the high wire fence and glaring noticeboards delineating the restricted area glittered in the light of our torches. We halted and Strongarm beat on the tall gates with a cudgel. "In there! In there!"

A guard stepped out of the tiny hutch beyond the wire. He stared at us, eyes screwed up tight against the light. "What do you want?"

"Don't act so surprised, man!" shouted Strongarm. "You must have heard us coming. Now open up and let us in, will you? My boy's in there."

"There's no boy in here," replied the guard flatly.

"You're not a Pallahaxi man, are you? I don't know you—but if you knew me, you'd know I have a habit of getting what I want. Now open up the gate and I'll say no more about the vehicles you wouldn't let us have."

"This is a restricted area. I have orders to admit nobody."

"Now look here, you!" yelled Strongarm. "Open up that gate and let us in before I smash the freezing thing down! Do you hear me?"

There was a pause and I found Wolff plucking at my elbow. "I don't like this," he muttered. "My father works for the Government. I don't want to get involved. You ought to have more sense yourself. I'll see you tomorrow, maybe..." He crept away and I looked after him in disgust. Ribbon hardly noticed him go; she was watching her father apprehensively.

"Are you deaf?" shouted Strongarm, then receiving no reply: "Right. You asked for this, my lad. Where are the lox? We'll tie them to this gate and pull the freezing thing down." There was a movement at the back of the crowd; it parted to allow men through, leading the animals.

"What's happened to the lorin?" I asked Browneyes, conscious of the foreboding. If Squint were in there, I would have expected the lorin to sense it. Yet they were nowhere in sight. The lox were uneasy, peering this way and that with questing eyes as they stood at the gate.

"All right, that's enough!" shouted the guard. A row of uniformed men had appeared inside the compound. They held springrifles, cocked and levelled at the crowd.

"The next man to make any move towards the gate gets it," said the guard coldly. "You've had your fun; now go home, all of you."

I thought Strongarm was going to rush the gate and attempt to tear it down with his bare hands as I saw the veins bulge on his neck and his fists clench. His wife caught his arm; and Ribbon ran to them, pushing herself between him and the gate.

He stood motionless for long seconds, staring over their heads at the guard. Then he relaxed, shrugged, and turned away. I saw his face in the torchlight as he walked past me; his mouth hung open and there was a dreadful emptiness in his eyes.

ELEVEN

IN THE DAYS that followed I was conscious of a growing feeling of unity among the people of Pallahaxi. It is possible that this had always existed and only now that I had become acquainted with a few townspeople had I noticed it. In previous summers my parents had always been with me and we had driven about in the motorcart, visiting beaches, going with organized boat trips, hardly ever speaking to anyone other than the occupants of the other cottages in the field—all of them, like ourselves, were on vacation.

Nevertheless I was quite certain that people were drawing together in some way that was almost instinctive; as though they had been hurt, and they knew they were going to be hurt some more, and they needed the company of one another. Attendances at the Phu temple increased greatly—not because people had suddenly got religion; but because they wanted to be together. The local newspaper, instead of merely printing the incoming news from the message post, began to report local gatherings and publish letters and opinions of Parliament's conduct of local affairs. People gripped one another's arms when they met, they stopped berating the storekeepers for the rationing and sympathized with them instead. In the evenings they sat outside their houses and chatted to neighbours, burying the feuds of decades.

I'd heard that in times of adversity people came together like this, so to a certain extent it was understandable. The only thing which perturbed me was: whom were we uniting against? The logical answer would have been the enemy, Asta—yet I scarcely heard the war mentioned. Asta was not blamed for the rationing; the Government was. The shortage of distil fuel, the proliferation of restricted areas, the occasional loss of a vessel at sea; any disaster, any hardship, was laid at the door of the Government.

During the state of armed neutrality which existed between my parents and me, I mentioned this to my father.

He looked thoughtful. "I'm aware of the sentiments of your friends in the town, Drove," he said at last with remarkable restraint. "Of course it worries us. The cannery is an important project and, right now, there are many inland towns which would not survive if it weren't for the supplies which we ship out of here. There are Astan saboteurs in the area whose prime target is the cannery, so we have to take stringent security measures. But as far as the general public are concerned, they have had to suffer hardships so naturally they look for a scapegoat. Asta is a long way over the horizon, but the Government is close at hand, so the Government is blamed. It's regrettable, but it's the way people think."

I'd been watching him in some surprise; for the first time ever, he'd spoken to me as though I was an adult. It felt good. "Maybe if the cannery had been more helpful over Squint, then people might be more friendly," I said mildly.

"A very unfortunate incident. The guards involved were most sternly reprimanded. We carried out a thorough search and the young lad was nowhere to be found on the cannery premises." He seemed almost to be apologizing. "It illustrates my point, however, Drove. With all the region to choose from, with the ocean to the west and the Yellow Mountains inland, why should the general public choose to assume that the boy had disappeared into the maw of the cannery?"

This made a certain amount of sense, but left me with horrifying images of Squint, overbalancing as he investigated some giant machine, falling into the whirling blades and eventually emerging in the guise of a stack of cans...

Since the confrontation at the cannery gates Wolff had been lying low. From time to time I saw him with his mother, walking about the town and buying supplies in such quantity that I had no desire to admit our acquaintance in public. I couldn't understand why the Government didn't make it clear to its employees that flashing cards around and ignoring rationing made for bad public relations.

Meanwhile the trucks continued to thunder through the town and away up the inland road, carting produce to towns less fortunate than ourselves. I spent much of my time with Browneyes and frequently we visited Ribbon's house—at first to express sympathy and find out the latest news on Squint; then, as the days went by and hope dwindled, to console and try to divert them from their sorrow. They were a close family and had taken it very badly. Ribbon blamed herself and hardly spoke, and Strongarm blamed *himself* for his remarks to us on the evening of Squint's disappearance which had contributed to Ribbon's decline.

In the evenings when we sat in Ribbon's room trying to cheer her up while she sat on the bed and looked unseeingly through us, the house received a number of visitors. The bedroom was at the front of the house and I could watch people arriving. Some of them carried parcels which would contain food or liquor as a gift for the bereaved family—but others, and these were usually men, came empty-handed. They approached with purposeful tread, sometimes in twos and threes, and Strongarm would receive them into the living room and shut the door firmly—reopening it only to call to his wife for more drink. Often he would have twelve or more people in that room and one night I counted more than twenty. Browneyes' parents were there that night and later she asked them what it was all about, but she couldn't get a satisfactory reply. We asked Ribbon, but she didn't know and didn't care.

It seemed that an action group had been formed, but we couldn't guess the nature of the action to be taken.

Meanwhile the grume arrived.

We took Ribbon down to the quay one day; we had difficulty in getting her out of the house but once we reached the harbour the activity all around us seemed to brighten her up. All the deep-hulled boats were laid up by now, and the basin was filled with brightly-painted little skimmers. The water level was very low; the surface had a heavy, undulating appearance like molten lead.

I untied the rope of my skimmer from a bollard and pulled; the rope dripped slow viscous drops like treacle as the little craft slid towards us. We climbed in and I hoisted the sail. Tired ripples spread around us with the movement of the boat, but died almost immediately. The wind caught us and we glided gently towards the harbour mouth. All the snowdivers were gone, now; with their buoyant lightness they were not suited to the dense water of the grume. They would not have been able to descend beneath the surface—besides, the grume brought new enemies.

The grummets had arrived, winging in from the south, following the grume. A large number of the great white birds perched on the roof of the fishmarket, eyeing the offloaded catches avidly. As we sailed through the gap into the outer harbour a grummet came in low, skimming the surface with downslung feet, wingtips raising little ripples. It landed heavily on the slow water, settled, shrugging great wings across the broad back and watched us coldly as we passed. I gazed at it fascinated. These birds symbolized Pallahaxi to me, and the whole meaning of our annual vacation.

As though reading my thoughts, Browneyes asked, "When are you going back home, Drove?" Her eyes were sad.

CONEY ❋

"Rax. Don't talk about that now. It's a long time yet
—besides, father's all tied up with the new cannery."

I didn't dare say it, but at the back of my mind was
the feeling that we might never go home, that we were
in Pallahaxi for always. The thought was almost too
wonderful to contemplate. Certainly my parents never
spoke of Alika; and usually about this time my mother
would start talking about how nice it would be to get
home again. I found myself hoping that my father ran
into all manner of difficulties with the cannery, which
necessitated him staying here on a permanent basis.

Ribbon was looking at me gravely. She said, "Perhaps you'll stay here, Drove." I wished she hadn't said it.
It was tempting fate. But it was good to hear her speak
and I made some noncommital reply while Browneyes
smiled hopefully.

The sullen water was suddenly flecked with sparkling silver as a shoal of tiny fish, unable to maintain
depth, broke surface and skittered among the boats, pursued by snapping, twisting glubb. A flight of grummets
swooped, a huge bird picked off a stranded glubb as it
lay writhing on the surface, unable to regain safety underwater.

"Hello, kids!" The shout came as a skimmer moved
nearby, half-full of fish, the unmistakable figure of Silverjack at the tiller. The two active members of his crew
were busy with vast nets slung like nets from either side
of the boat, barely touching the surface and scooping
stranded fish as the boat slid onwards. The bay of Pallahaxi is particularly good for grume-fishing. Fish tend to
become trapped within its confines as the grume moves
northwards, chasing the mass of marine life before it.

We glanced at each other and I began to think of
spies, and smuggling, and inevitably Squint, all topics

we wanted to avoid on this therapeutic trip for Ribbon. I looked at her; she smiled faintly and her eyes slid past me. She was regarding the shipwreck beach where the storm drain emerged. Silverjack was passed and so, I hoped, was the dark moment.

Eventually we reached the end of the breakwater with its small lighthouse, and passed into the open sea. The bay was alive with fish dancing like windborne tinsel on the surface, the grummets swooping in a continuous white cloud and filling the air with their screams of greed. Among them plied the skimmers, sails straining as they ran before the wind with nets outspread, reaping the rich harvest of the grume.

It was early days yet, but it looked like being a record grume. In days to come the larger fish would be forced to the surface; the giant wingets and flatties, the man-eating snint. Around that time the mammalian grume-riders would arrive from the south, bounding over the surface with flailing flippers. There would be bloody battles on the turgid water. Lastly the bellets would come; the slender sharp-toothed scavengers whose way it was to eat anything left behind by the grume; anything. It was unwise to go swimming when the grume was on the wane...

Ribbon was looking distinctly more cheerful, watching the activity with interest and exclaiming over the strange creatures which littered the ocean around us. Suddenly she pointed. "What's that?"

Far away in the ocean but making for the bay was a large vessel, trailing smoke. "That's a deep-hull," I said, as momentarily the blizzard of whirling grummets parted and I got a better view. "She's left it late. They'll have to beach her."

"Where?" Browneyes stared interestedly out to sea.

"She'll never get near the estuary. It's too shallow, now. And the estuary shelf drops off sheer into the Trench. So they'll have to bring her into the inner harbour among all the private fishing boats and things, and then there'll hardly be room for anyone else. There could be a lot of trouble, if they did that."

It was interesting, the way we had tacitly assumed the ship belonged to 'them', and that its arrival would inevitably be to the detriment of Pallahaxi.

"Much better if the Astans sank it before it reached here," I said.

When we arrived back at Ribbon's place she turned to us and said, "Thanks."

"What for?" asked Browneyes. "You're welcome to come with us any time, isn't she, Drove?"

"Uh," I said.

"Look, I don't like to be in the way," said Ribbon, her eyes on my face.

I had reached another crisis and it had crept up on me without me seeing it coming. I'd overcome my adult domination to a certain extent, I'd gained confidence in my own worth and was beginning to find that I really was the equal of anybody—previously I'd only told myself I was. Now—how far did I want to go? Did I want to stamp on people?

Did I want to be the cause of Ribbon being lonely and miserable, because I would selfishly rather be with Browneyes all the time?

Impulsively I grabbed Ribbon's hand. "Please come along with us any time," I said. "We like to have you around."

Her whole face glowed, and for the first time since the disappearance of Squint she looked really happy.

Later that evening Strongarm asked us, "Well, are

you coming to the temple?" He and Una were putting on their coats.

I looked at him in astonishment. "I never go to temples," I said.

He laughed. "Oh, you won't hear anything about the sun-god Phu or the Great Lox or anything like that, lad. This is a meeting of the townsfolk. A representative of the Government will be there."

"Not my father, I hope."

"No. I don't know if you've met the man. He's been around a lot lately, and he seems a reasonable sort of fellow. His name's Horlox-Mestler."

When we reached the temple there was a good crowd and I saw many familiar faces. Significantly, those on the platform were mostly the people I had seen coming and going at Strongarm's place. Ribbon, Browneyes and I sat with the body of the audience but Strongarm mounted the improvised stage and, presently, hammered on the table for order.

"People of Pallahaxi," he shouted. "We've met tonight because there are a whole lot of things we don't like about the way Parliament's running things. Now Horlox-Mestler here is a Parl and he's been good enough to come and be shot at. I'm not much for talking myself, so I'll let Mestler get on with it."

He sat down to ragged cheering and Horlox-Mestler stood regarding the audience thoughtfully. "I must begin by telling you that this meeting has no official status—"

Strongarm leaped to his feet, instantly purple with rage. "Now cut that out, Mestler!" he roared. "We're not interested in freezing status and we're not interested in your freezing evasions. We brought you here to straighten things out. So get on with it!" He sat, and this time the audience thundered their applause.

Mestler was smiling faintly. "I'm very sorry; the fault is mine, Strongarm is right. The meeting exists here and now. Status has nothing to do with it." He paused, and then began to summarize the progress of the war so far. I'd heard it all before from my father and my attention wandered. I diverted myself by allowing my hands to dangle by the sides of the chair and presently found myself holding Browneyes' hand on one side and Ribbon's on the other, which was what I'd hoped for.

"And so the latest news is that we're holding the Astan advances on most fronts," Mestler was saying after a while, "although they have broken through in the south. Certain key towns have fallen to their forces and we cannot overlook the possibility of an invasion by sea, in which case Pallahaxi might well be a target."

"So where are the guns?" shouted somebody.

"Adequate protection for the town is being organized, you can be sure of that," replied Mestler. "Although you will of course appreciate that we are unable to divert supplies from the front. Right now, the guns are needed by those brave men who are fighting to save this land of ours!"

He paused, but if he expected applause he was disappointed. There was, indeed, a sceptical muttering. A man behind me summarized the feeling of the meeting on that point. "Rax to this land of ours!" he shouted. "What about Pallahaxi?"

"Even in Pallahaxi the war situation is critical and is being kept under close observation," continued Mestler. "There have been reports of enemy agents in the vicinity of the cannery—and, since the cannery is so vital to our war effort, it may in due course be necessary to redefine the restricted area. But we hope not. We hope not."

He went on to denounce those who took matters

into their own hands with no thought for the common good, who prowled the countryside at night in mobs, thus providing cover for Astan spies, who organized illegal and unrecognized gatherings, thus wasting the time of Parliament—time which would be better spent in pursuing the war effort. In short, he took the offensive, talking all the while in his quiet persuasive tones and allowing his jolly-uncle smile to take the sting out of his words.

I wouldn't say he carried the audience along with him, but at least they didn't storm the platform. Strongarm was scowling and his henchmen were whispering among themselves, but they made no move to interrupt.

"And so after a long and painful consideration, Parliament regrets that it has no alternative but to take this unpopular measure." Mestler was saying, and I must have missed something again, because I didn't know what he was talking about. The audience was muttering angrily.

"What authority do you have?" called Browneyes' father from the platform table. "A direction like this could ruin my business. Is that place a cannery, or is it some sort of freezing Government department?"

"This is a war situation and we have the power to take emergency local measures," Mestler infromed him. There was a growing uproar from the audience.

"What measures?" I whispered to Browneyes.

"A curfew."

"What! What are they frightened of?"

"Ribbon's father and his followers, I think... Drove, this means we won't be able to go out in the evenings." Her expression was forlorn.

Around us the audience was leaping about and shouting and I saw the templekeeper looking nervous;

his trinkets would be endangered if there were a riot. A symbolic crystal would be a handy missile for throwing at Mestler.

Then there was silence, amazed silence, as a group of uniformed men appeared from the rear of the platform and took up position behind Mestler. The Parl spoke into the quiet.

"No, we are not imposing martial law. A number of troops will be stationed in the town to assist the local police and for obvious defence purposes. Rest assured that the measures to protect this town in the event of Astan attack are in hand. Thank you all."

"Wait a moment!" Baffled, Strongarm was on his feet. Somehow the initiative had been lost, the meeting turned into defeat. "We're quite capable of defending ourselves! We don't need these thugs!"

Mestler looked at him sadly. "Pallahaxi-Strongarm—what do you want? You claimed the Government wasn't looking after you—now we give you the protection you asked for, and still you're not satisfied. Really, I'm beginning to think you're just a troublemaker..."

TWELVE

THE FOLLOWING MORNING I called for Browneyes and we planned to walk up to Finger Point to watch the arrival of the large ship. From the high vantage point we would be able to gauge whether it was making for the harbour or, as Browneyes had suggested, the new wharf.

"They were saying in the Grummet that it dropped anchor off the Point last night," she said. "It might be bringing some sort of war supplies. Somebody said it was attacked by Astan men-of-war out in the ocean and the engines were damaged. That's why it's late. It should have been here before the grume."

Once again I wondered at the way in which the Golden Grummet acted as a clearing house for news and intelligence. The news Browneyes told me was usually more up-to-date and accurate than the newspapers my father so avidly read.

We called for Ribbon, feeling sorry for her after the way her father had been treated at the meeting. She seemed cheerful enough and was obviously grateful for the diversion, as Strongarm was still furious and talking wildly of organizing a militia. Leaving Una to shoulder the burden alone, we made our way through the main street to the harbour. For a while we discussed the meeting then out of consideration for Ribbon, we dropped the topic. It appeared that the curfew was to be imposed tonight, which did not please Browneyes. The loss of trade suffered by her father would be considerable.

Wolff was standing near the monument, for once without his mother and looking at a loose end. Unfortunately he caught sight of us and came hurrying up, smiling easily with no hint of embarrassment; he had, after all, been avoiding us for many days and I'd been thinking that we'd seen the last of him.

"Just the people I wanted to see," he greeted us breezily, actually taking Ribbon's arm as he fell in step. She glanced at him without expression and suddenly he recalled himself. "Uh... Any news of young Squint?"

"Nothing," said Ribbon very quietly.

"Too bad. It's a very terrible thing. You know, I was thinking about that, and I had a thought. Do you suppose—"

"Look, shut up about all that, Wolff," I snapped as I

saw Ribbon biting her lip unhappily. "Let's talk about something else." It had been well over twenty days since Squint had disappeared and there was no point in re-opening the topic.

He looked down his long nose at me, in aristocratic surprise. "Well, now, Alika-Drove. When a child's life is at stake I should have thought *any* suggestion would have been worth consideration. After all, I was there when Squint was allowed to go off on his own and I feel very much to blame—and so ought you. It seems to me that mere selfish..."

His voice trailed away as Ribbon jerked her arm from him and buried her face in my shoulder, sobbing noisily. "For Phu's sake make him be quiet, Drove," she wailed desperately. "I can't stand it!"

I was not equipped to deal with the situation. I stood there on the crowded quay of Pallahaxi harbour, holding a sobbing girl while bystanders eyed me curiously—none more so than Browneyes, whose sympathy for Ribbon seemed to have evaporated rapidly. I couldn't think of anything to do, or to say; the best I could achieve was a facial expression which I hoped combined gravity and concern in the correct proportions. My one hand still lay inertly in Browneyes' cold grip, while the other arm was draped unenthusiastically around Ribbon's shoulders.

My one consolation was that Wolff was even more discomfited than I. His mouth had dropped open and his face had changed colour. "Uh..." he stammered. "Uh, I'm terribly sorry, Ribbon, I didn't realize, I mean..."

At this I was able to forget the spectators and achieve some measure of righteous indignation; after all, I was Ribbon's hero and protector, defending her against this lout. Morally I had the upper hand. In fact, had I been in Wolff's shoes I would have made a run for it.

"Just shut up, Wolff," I snapped. "The trouble with you is—"

Then I saw my mother approaching, laden with shopping.

I wheeled Ribbon around and let her go. "Let's get out of here," I said urgently, tightening my grip on Browneyes' hand and propelling Ribbon along with an unceremonious palm on the butt. Wolff loped alongside, puzzled. I think I was the only one who had seen my mother. We rounded the corner of the quay and joined the Finger Point road.

"Listen, I'm frightfully sorry," Wolff panted. He thought we were running away from him.

Safe among the beached boats, I drew to a halt. They stopped too, regarding me in bewilderment. "All right," I said. "That was my mother back there. I'm not frightened of my mother so you can save your comments, Wolff—it's just that I don't want her seeing me involved in some sordid public scene. I couldn't face the inquest afterwards. Now, are you all right, Ribbon?"

She smiled at me wetly. "I'm fine now, Drove, thanks."

"If you want to come along with us you can cut out the funny stuff, right, Wolff?"

"Uh." He looked abashed.

"We're going up to Finger Point to watch the big ship. Is it all right if he comes, Ribbon?"

"I don't mind," she said quietly.

In this way Wolff rejoined our little group, willingly accepting a drop in rank.

We stood on the Point and looked across the bright, slow sea. The surface was speckled with dancing fish and the grummets swooped endlessly, snatching a mouthful of live food, gaining height as they swallowed until they were riding the upcurrent of air level with the clifftop. Then—and some of them hovered so close we could see them gulping—they would wheel and spiral downwards, levelling out just above the oily waves, gliding so close that their feet occasionally trailed a thin wake while they scooped more fish into their downhung pouched beaks.

The ship had raised anchor and was moving towrds us although still almost a thousand paces offshore. She was being towed in unusual fashion; four steam launches had lines aboard her, two on each side; but the tugs were so positioned that they were pulling sideways against each other as much as forwards.

Ribbon explained. "She's a deep-hull boat caught in the grume, you see. The thick water's raised her and made her top-heavy; that's why she called for the tugs. Now they're stretching tight lines from either side to keep her on an even keel. You see that man in the crow's nest?" She pointed to a vaguely familiar figure perched on a platform half-way up one mast. "He has a list indicator and he controls the tugs. When she starts to heel over, he signals to the pair of tugs on that side to slacken off, while the pair on the other side pull harder—so they bring her back upright. All the time, they're edging her nearer the wharf. When she's close enough they'll attach cables from land, in place of two of the tugs, and they'll winch her in sideways."

"You must have seen all this before, Ribbon," said Wolff kindly.

"A few times. Often they use my father as the pilot in the crow's nest, but he's not there today. It's a Parl ship and he won't work for *them*." There was a world of contempt in the way she said this but Wolff took it in his stride, asking more questions and generally behaving with revolting consideration and politeness.

After a while I said to Browneyes, "Let's go for a walk."

We left the others sitting on the clifftop and strolled among the trees. Browneyes had been quiet for some time, but once we were out of earshot she said acidly, "Funny how she turned to *you*."

There was a sinking feeling in my stomach. "What do you mean?"

"I mean it's funny how Ribbon started c-cuddling up to *you* down there on the quay when she was crying. And she always comes everywhere with us. You and she always seem to be talking together, always." She sniffled, and I realized with despair that she was going to cry. It was not my day. "And don't think I didn't see you holding her hand at the meeting last night."

I sat on the grass and pulled her down after me. It was warm mid-morning, and only the trees were near. She sat upright with head bowed, her hand resting passively in mine. "I wouldn't have asked you to come for a walk if I'd wanted to stay around her," I said reasonably.

She sniffed again, her shoulders shook once, then suddenly she tossed her hair back from her eyes and looked straight at me. "I think I might be losing out, Drove," she said in a voice of surprising calmness. "It's not your fault so I think it must be mine. I can't really blame Ribbon. But I think I'm going to lose you and I don't know what to do about it."

You're not losing me," I muttered unhappily.

"Listen. There's something about you and Ribbon, I know there is. Somehow you're always the one who gets her out of trouble, or are around when she's unhappy... you seem to share a lot of things. It's... it's as though you were meant to be together. Nothing's ever happened to you and me. We just sort of walk around holding hands, and nothing ever happens to bring us closer."

"How do you mean? We can't make things happen."

She didn't answer. She looked at me steadily and there came over her face an expression so thoughtful, almost calculating, that it wasn't like my Browneyes at all. She took her hand away from me, smoothed her dress down and lay back on the grass; her expression had changed further so that she looked almost sleepy. I was uneasy about the way she looked at me, and when she lifted her arms and tucked them behind her head, arching her back a fraction, I had to avert my eyes. I think I blushed.

"Look at me, freeze you, Drove," she whispered.

I regarded her apprehensively, and it was as though she were a deep lake and I didn't know what lurked down there and was frightened of it, yet fascinated. Her eyes still gazed into mine, still with that drowsy look. Her lips were plump and parted, and I saw the flicker of her tongue.

She wore a blue dress and there was no chain around her neck. My eyes passed hastily over the hypnotic beauty of her new breasts down to her waist and, greatly daring, I reached and touched the outside of her hip, where the little belt encircled her waist and the dress suddenly filled out with the roundness of her. I stroked the material gently while I let my gaze move on, to where her brown thighs emerged from the blue. I wondered idly if it was wrong for me to feel the way I was beginning to feel; then I decided it must be all right because instinctively I knew Browneyes wanted it that way. I looked at her dimpled knees and plump calves, then from her little white shoes back to her face; and now there was a lazy smile on her lips.

"Is it nice to have a girl as pretty as me, Drove?" she asked softly.

"Browneyes..." I mumbled. "I..."

"Then kiss me please, Drove," she whispered.

I leaned over and pressed my lips inexpertly against hers. Her arms went around the back of my neck and something happened inside my chest; suddenly our lips were much softer and much more together, and I felt her tongue touching against mine as she uttered a long wordless sound of delight.

When at last I thought it was time to sit up again, she was looking at me uncertainly. She wanted to say something, but it took her a little while to get started.

"Drove," she said at last. "Promise you won't laugh?"

"Uh."

"I want to tell you something but it's the sort of thing people much older say," she said hurriedly. "So it might sound funny. Drove...?"

"Yes?"

"I will love you for all of my life, Drove."

When we joined the others they were sitting apart, staring down at the water, conversation having flagged. Ribbon looked up in obvious relief on hearing our approach.

"Whatever have you two been doing all this... oh..." Her expression changed as she looked at us searchingly, then a faint smile crossed her face. Wolff continued to stare silently at the ship beneath us. It had edged considerably nearer the wharf and now I recognized the man in the crow's nest.

It was Silverjack.

"I suppose he was the best they could get," said Ribbon after I had pointed this out. "After all, he does know the waters well. If only he wasn't so unreliable."

We watched as the ship moved closer. It was the largest vessel I had ever seen; two-masted—but all sails were now furled. A shattered spar and some unidentifiable wreckage aft bore testimony to the Astans' guns. Amidships stood a tall funnel flanked, on either side of the hull, by giant paddle wheels. These, too, were damaged; jagged timbers dangled as they revolved slowly. On the deck stood a number of objects covered by white canvas and, presumably, the holds were full of cargo. Despite this, she rode the water far too high, perched top-heavy on the grume like a floating snow-diver.

"They're having trouble," said Ribbon suddenly, an edge to her voice.

Figures were gesticulating on the deck, waving at Silverjack. A dangerous list had developed and the tugs, manoeuvring carefully to avoid the rocks protruding from the surface, were slow to correct it. The steamer heeled slowly until one huge paddle was half underwater and Silverjack hung over the sea from the slanting mast. A fusillade of harsh puffs ascended from the two starboard tugs as they strove to haul the steamship upright. We heard faint cries from the wharf below.

For an age the ship hung there, teetering on a thick balance as the thick water churned slowly about the sterns of the tugs.

"It's all that deck cargo," Ribbon murmured. "Pull, freeze you!" she urged the tugs. "*Pull!*"

She was the daughter of a fisherman and had a feeling for ships and the men in them; a sense of responsibility in such matters which I couldn't be expected to possess. So I didn't blame myself too much when I found I was hoping the ship would capsize. The whole thing was so exciting that it would be a crippling anticlimax if the steamship were safely berthed.

Slowly, reluctantly, she righted herself, water spilling in thick dribbles from among the damaged paddle mechanism. The cables tightened on the opposite side, holding her, and Ribbon breathed a groan of relief...

The disaster occurred with slow inevitability. One of the port tugs seemed to fidget in the water, propeller churning, simultaneously uttering a blast of alarm on its whistle. The long cable attached to a post in its bows had broken—or maybe the post itself had fractured with the tremendous strain. The cable rose in the air, curling towards the steamship like a striking snake but more slowly, high and heavy. There was a fierce grinding crash as the tug ran backwards into a rock and the screw bit into granite and shattered. Then came the splintering, rending scream as the flying cable sliced through stays and shrouds, looping all over the deck of the steamship as men flung themselves in all directions, finally wrapping around the mast and felling it in a tangle of ropes, wires and canvas. As the mast toppled towards the water the figure of Silverjack broke free in a clumsy dive. He surfaced almost instantly, swimming strongly towards the wharf.

Meanwhile the steamship was heeling over again and this time nothing could save it. Ribbon looked away and there were tears in her eyes; to her the ship represented all ships, and anyone of the men might easily have been her father. I put my arm around her and held her as we watched. I knew Browneyes wouldn't mind, now.

The deck cargo on the port side broke free, item by lumbering item of machinery, and rolled across the deck to crash into the starboard cargo, dislodging some of that, too. The steamer heeled further and men jumped into the sea as the cargo dropped over the side, raising low, slow splashes. I saw that the underside of the hull was painted green and flecked with weed and shellfish as it lifted slowly from the water.

The tragedy of the thing had got through to me now, maybe communicated from Ribbon's trembling body to mine. Browneyes was gripping my hand as she stared miserably down, and Wolff wore an odd expression of fastidious disgust as though the whole drama was too strong for his gentle sensibilities. So we watched the steamship capsize, and soon only the long, curved green bottom was visible, with the tugs standing by helplessly, defeated.

The majority of the crew were swimming towards the wharf; swiftly and easily, buoyed up by the grume. There was no danger there; the only tragedy lay in the loss of the living ship. Some of the men climbed on to the tugs where they immediately began to gesticulate in furious altercation. Meanwhile the grummets swooped around and I remember thinking it was fortunate the grume was no further advanced; at the time of maximum density the deadly grume-riders would have been bounding across the surface to the scene. And later, the scavengers...

We heard a deep rumbling roar, seemingly from within the ocean itself. The spine of the upturned ship erupted in a geyser of steam and debris as water reached the furnaces and the boilers burst. Timber, machinery, other shapes terrifyingly manlike were flung into the air; I watched a large piston rod suspended for a long second at the summit of its arc almost level with the cliff-top, before it fell away and hit the water with a soft plop, hardly a splash.

Giant slow bubbles arose like dying gasps as the long cigar of the ship disappeared beneath the surface and sank irretrievably to the bottom of the Pallahaxi Trench.

THIRTEEN

I WAS OF an age when the concerns of the adult world around me rarely entered my consideration. Although I was technically at the mercy of the world, I paid scant heed to its climate, rarely bothering to enquire the reason whenever I saw my parents creeping about the house in sepulchral silence, glum of face. Whatever the crisis was, I had confidence that it would soon go away. An offshoot of this attitude was the scepticism with which I regarded my mother's war map. Although she could be practically in tears when moving back an Erto flag—thus conceding our native soil to the Astans—to me it was just a flag, nothing more. I could not appreciate the symbolism behind the strip of coloured paper.

In the rapid events which followed that day on Finger Point, however, I was forced to acknowledge the existence of this other world, and the fact that it applied to me, here and now.

We received an early visitor on the morning after the sinking of the steamship and this in itself should have alerted me; but it was pleasant in bed, and through the window I could see right across the bay. Whatever discussion was proceeding around the breakfast table was of no interest to me. I heard a motorcart arrive, I heard voices from the front door and later downstairs, but I paid no heed. I lay there dreaming of Browneyes and the things we'd said to each other yesterday.

At last I put some clothes on and went downstairs.

My mother and father sat at the table, looking grave; and with them was Horlox-Mestler. He smiled at me cheerfully. As the conversation resumed I had the distinct impression—and this is nothing unusual—that the topic had been adroitly switched with my arrival. Things had been under discussion which were not suitable for young ears.

At present they were discussing the time and place of some unspecified event. A favourite gambit of my father's is to carry on an intriguing conversation with another adult without actually mentioning the crux of the matter, thus driving me insane with the suspense.

"The fish-market will be quieter by mid-morning," he was saying. "The early catch will have been sold off."

"The evening would have been best," Mestler said thoughtfully. "But we can hardly contravene our own curfew. No, it will have to be mid-morning."

"The temple?"

"I think so. There's something so... undignified, about an open-air meeting."

"A meeting about *what*?" I asked.

Father barely glanced in my direction. "I quite agree" He wiped his lips methodically and rose. "I'll see to the announcement and organize the temple staff."

"I'll be down later," said Mestler, remaining seated. "I'm in no hurry. I always like time to collect my thoughts before these occasions. Then I don't become flustered by hecklers."

"Hecklers?" Father's expression was grim. "By Phu, there had better not be any hecklers!"

"Oh, go along with you, Burt," chuckled Mestler. "There are always hecklers. It's part of the game."

Grunting, my father left and shortly afterwards I heard the puffing of the motorcart. Mestler turned to me.

"Perhaps I can give you a ride down to the town later on, Drove. My cart is outside."

"Oh, that is kind of you, Horlox-Mestler," said my mother before I could reply. "Thank Horlox-Mestler, Drove."

"Uh," I said.

"I noticed you in the temple the other day with young Pallahaxi-Browneyes and Ribbon," said Mestler with twinkles in his eyes.

"He spends *so* much time with them," lamented mother. "I've spoken to him again and again but it's no use; he just won't listen. The daughter of an innkeeper and the daughter of a political agitator."

"Don't forget Wolff, mother," I put in. "The son of a Parl."

Mestler laughed outright. "Don't worry about the boy, Fayette. Let him choose his own friends. Besides, there's no harm in your son being acquainted with the general public. It might even come in useful."

I didn't like the sound of that last remark, so I preserved a careful silence while mother chatted on about shortages and rationing—subjects about which she knew nothing. Ignorance, however, has never inhibited her conversation.

Later Mestler and I climbed into his motorcart—it was an even more imposing vehicle than my father's—and drove to the town. The crier was standing at the foot of the monument, portable steam-whistle fired up beside him. As we passed, he pulled the handle of the machine and the basin of the harbour echoed to the shrill squeal, then he began to announce the meeting in his stentorian voice. I noticed sullen faces around; the people had divined that any meeting called by the Government was likely to have unpleasant consequences.

Instead of heading for the cannery Mestler took the Finger Point road and soon we were bumping along the track among the trees, the water gleaming far below. I was annoyed. I'd intended to get off in the town and call on Browneyes, but he hadn't given me a chance. He stopped close by the place where Browneyes and I had sat yesterday, then motioned me out and together we walked to the edge of the cliff and stood looking down at the water. The grummets were even more numerous than before and I saw several small skimmers below, their inquisitive crews peering into the depths for signs of the wreck. There was very little activity on the new quay; the crane stood idle and two or three men sat around a lox and cart.

"So you know Strongarm pretty well," said Mestler unexpectedly.

"Uh."

"I understand he's the best seaman hereabouts... I'll put it to you frankly, Drove, we're in trouble. The sinking of the *Ysabel* yesterday makes matters very awkward for the Government. You'll hear all about that at the meeting."

Ysabel. The name was familiar.

"We want to raise her," he continued. "To do this, we need a man with a complete knowledge of local waters and the grume. We need an expert sailor—but more than that; a man who can round up crews, persuade bubble-divers to go down, estimate the tide and the density and the currents. We need Strongarm."

A curious thought had occurred to me; I don't know why. Mestler was unaware that I had witnessed the sinking of the *Ysabel* from close range—he probably thought the only witnesses, apart from those actually involved, were the few fishermen who may have been passing at the time, too far away to see much.

"After the way Strongarm was treated at the last meeting, I don't think he'd help the Parls," I said firmly.

Mestler's eyes widened, he looked almost comically bewildered. "What's going on?" he asked. "What's going on? If he helps Parliament, he helps himself and all of Pallahaxi. How did this hostile attitude come about? Do these people in Pallahaxi realize who the enemy is? Has everyone gone insane?"

"Well, if you don't know, I'm sure I don't," I muttered. I wanted to get back to town. I wanted to get away from Mestler because I thought he was going to try to persuade me to use my influence with Strongarm.

"The grume..." Mestler was murmuring, recovered from his outburst. "That's what's at the bottom of it all. That's why the people around here think they're different from anyone else. The grume knits them together; their whole lifestyle is molded around one phenomenon..." He was staring at the ocean as he spoke almost to himself. "Inland, it's either desert or farming or industries. Until the war broke out there was an expanding motorcart industry in Horlox, do you know that? The biggest in Erto. But we've never been able to raise the sugarplant successfully here, so we had to import nearly all our distil from Asta. And when the war came... there were a lot of people thrown out of work in my town, did you know?"

"I wouldn't know anything about what happens up there," I said shortly. Adults infuriate me, the way they always ramble on about hard times.

He was looking at me closely. "You wouldn't, would you? In a way you're much closer to Pallahaxi than even your own town. I wonder why that is. The grume seems to get into the very blood of you people." He smiled, and despite myself I felt flattered at the way he included me with Pallahaxi. "I'll swear that if a Pallahaxi man cuts himself at this time of year, the blood runs thick. And yet they're ignorant. They accept the grume for what it is, and they never pause to consider the reason, the implications."

"Why should they?" I was annoyed. "The grume is a fact. It happens. Isn't that all that matters?"

Below us a large skimmer was ghosting quietly across the water with net-booms stretched like welcoming arms. It weaved its way carefully through the protruding rocks then tacked, sail swinging lazily and headed out to sea, along the line of the Trench. The man at the tiller was Strongarm and I wondered what he was doing there, well off his usual fishing grounds.

"You disappoint me, Drove. You speak like the people here, as though the grume has always been with us. Remember, everything has to have a beginning. Once there was no grume. The water remained the same consistency, and at almost the same level, all the year round."

This was hard to conceive, and I said so. "Our world revolves around the sun Phu on an elliptical orbit," I quoted from my learnings. "In summer we come close to Phu, and the ocean evaporates, causing the grume. In the drench comes the rain as the water condenses from the atmosphere. Winter is cold, because the sun is a long way off. It's quite simple."

"Then why does the grume *flow*, from south to north? Why is the sky clear now, when it ought to be cloudy with evaporation?"

"How should I know?"

"You ought to, Drove, because at some time in the past you should have been inquisitive enough to find out. Now..." He pulled a piece of paper and a charcoal stick from his pocket. "Our world rotates on its axis at right angles to the direction of its orbit around the sun Phu. Look."

He then drew a circle in the bottom half of the paper, representing Phu, and a series of smaller circles in an elliptical path around it, representing our world during the seasons. "Of course ," he said, "the scale isn't right, and our orbit extends much further away in winter than I've shown here. Still, it suits the purposes."

Strongarm's boat was receding into the distance now and I was becoming interested in the astronomy lesson against my better judgement. Maybe Mestler was a good teacher or—more likely—he was explaining something I'd always wanted to know, but had been too lazy to find out.

He lettered the positions of the world from A to H. "Position A is midwinter," he explained. "That's when the world is furthest away from the sun and the days and nights are of equal length. Now, I said that the axis is at right angles to the orbit." He drew diameters, north to south, on the circles. "But there's another important point. With respect to the sun, our world revolves slowly, counter to the direction of its orbit. This means that at the start of the summer—Position C—the sun will shine on our south pole, whereas about 80 days later it will be shining on the north pole. You see?"

I regarded the paper with the charcoal marks, and tried to visualize it. It would have been easier if I'd had a couple of slingballs handy; but I wasn't going to give up now. "I see," I said.

"So this is what happens. At the start of the summer the sun shines continuously on the south pole causing the massive evaporation and the tidal flow through the

narrow isthmus of the Central Ocean north to south, to
replace the waters of the Southern Ocean which continue to evaporate. Then by midsummer—Position E—the
days in Pallahaxi are as long as the nights again, the heat
is off the south pole to a certain extent, and a position of
total equilibrium is reached. The enormous cloud forma-
tions of the south pole are retained within those polar regions by the normal circling actions of the winds.

"Then gradually the world swings and presents the
north to the sun."

Now I was getting the picture. "So the Northern
Ocean evaporates instead," I said. "But when the water
flows through the Central Ocean and past Pallahaxi to
replace it, it's not normal water. It's already been subjected to evaporation. So it's thick. That's the grume."

Mestler grinned enthusiastically. "It's a fascinating
subject. Even now, there are many things we don't understand." He indicated his drawing again. "Anyway,
the grume is at its height in Position G. After that, the
world is moving away from the sun, cooling rapidly,
and the clouds spreading inwards. By Position H the
drench begins and continues until the dry winter comes.
Then it all starts over again."

I looked at the sea. Despite the low tide, there was
still a great depth of water where the Pallahaxi Trench
ran out into the middle of the Central Ocean. "I just can't
imagine evaporation making a difference to this quantity
of water," I said. "There's so *much*."

Mestler nodded. "Yes, but this is the Central Ocean.
It's deep and narrow, and it's said that it was caused by
a giant earthquake in the days when our continent circled the globe. The split appeared, separating Erto from
Asta and joining the Northern and Southern Oceans—
the coastline of Asta is very similar to the coast around

here, did you know? You could almost fit them together. But the polar oceans have always been there, and they're shallow like huge pans. The constant sunshine almost dries them out. All that's left is the grume."

A dense flight of grummets was approaching from the south on heavy wings. Near the cliff they swooped low, skimming the surface and feeding voraciously. I thought for a while. Then I said, "But it hasn't made any difference, has it? You can't prove what you've told me, and I'm no better off through knowing. We haven't proved it's wrong to be ignorant. The grume still goes on."

He grinned his jolly grin. "Such is life. So you feel I'd be wasting my time in trying to get help from Strongarm?" He stood with an air of finality.

I gathered up the piece of paper and slipped it into my pocket, hoping he hadn't noticed. "You could try," I said. "But you wouldn't get anywhere."

I called for Browneyes at the Golden Grummet—by now I was in the habit of walking boldly into the bar—and found a handful of customers discussing the meeting. Browneyes was busy for the moment, so I hung around, listening. Her father was doing the talking.

"Why they call it a meeting I can't think," he was saying hotly. "It'll be just like last time. Horlox-freezing-Mestler will get on his hind legs and talk crap and we'll have to take it, and right at the end he'll spring some new regulation on us and then run out, protected by his bodyguards. There'll be no discussion, no chance for any of us to ask questions. I've half a mind not to go. We ought to boycott the freezing thing."

"Which reminds me," murmured an elderly man, "I haven't seen much of the military police today."

Girth instantly recovered his temper and boomed

with laughter. "And you're not likely to. They're lying low, scared to show their faces. A few of the boys roughed them up last night, and they haven't been seen since."

Grope the trucker looked alarmed. "Maybe that's what the meeting's about. What about our own police, though? Didn't they stop it?"

"They weren't around at the time. I tell you, it's unwise for a Parl to show his face in town these days." Girth glanced at me. "I don't include you in that, Drove. You're like one of us." His wife Annlee smiled at me in reassurance.

"But I'm a Parl. I hadn't realized," muttered Grope. "I work for them, now."

"Then you'd better go armed. Well..." Girth emerged from behind the counter with an air of finality as Browneyes entered the room. "We might as well close down for the rest of the morning. Horlox-freezing-Mestler's stolen all our customers again..."

The scene in the temple was much the same as before, except that this time I did not hold Ribbon's hand, although she sat next to me. We were in the front row, and I caught my father's disapproving eye as he looked down from the eminence of the platform to see Browneyes sitting very close to me and holding both my hands. I could almost hear him thinking that this was neither the time nor the place for that sort of thing.

Mestler did not keep us waiting. He stepped forward to the pulpit with his hands clasped behind his back, his expression unusually serious. "I don't have any good news for you this morning," he said.

If he thought Pallahaxi would appreciate his honesty he was sadly mistaken. "Then shut up and go home," someone yelled. "We've enough problems without you,

Mestler!" There was a general fidgeting and muttering and a few shouts.

"So I'll tell you the worst, right away!" Mestler roared back, for once losing his temper. "There's nothing you or I can do about it, so sit down and listen!" He stared around belligerently.

After a while there was comparative quiet, and he resumed. "As you all know, the steamship *Ysabel* was lost yesterday off Finger Point, fortunately with little loss of life. Now as I've said before, your Parliament has always had the best interests of the general public at heart and has appreciated the wonderful efforts of all you people in these difficult times. In return for such loyalty it is, of course, the duty of your Parliament to protect Pallahaxi against the Astan hordes. And such was our intention." He regarded us sadly. "And such was our intention."

Ribbon leaned close to me and whispered: "but unfortunately..." and I chuckled aloud, which earned me a sharp glance from father.

"But unfortunately our hopes were dashed," continued Mestler. "Sunk to the bottom of the Trench with the steamship *Ysabel*. Yes, my friends. On board *Ysabel* were the guns, the ammunition, the war supplies with which we had hoped to defend this town of ours." He paused, looking at his audience tiredly, allowing the extent of the disaster to penetrate its thick Pallahaxian skull.

Strongarm asked, "Are you telling us that we're not getting anything to protect ourselves with?"

"No. Fortunately replacements will be available, and will be sent by road. But that will be many days yet. Many days."

"How many?" asked someone loudly.

"Oh... about thirty." Mestler hurried on, drowning

out a few scattered shouts of despondency. "Our industrial workers are labouring magnificently, but as I said before most of their production must necessarily go to the front. And here again I'm afraid the news is bad. The enemy has broken through at many points and is presently at the very gates of Alika!"

Suddenly the war came home to me and I saw the house in which I'd been born, occupied by hostile forces. "Does that mean that Parliament might be captured?" asked Girth hopefully. "I mean, I understand that Alika is our capital. It says so in the teachings. So I suppose the Members of Parliament have been issued with guns and are right now heroically defending this land of ours?"

The outburst of hilarity which greeted this witticism left no doubt as to the audience's sentiments and Horlox-Mestler flushed a deep red.

"Right, you freezers!" he yelled. "Have your fun. Enjoy it while you can. You won't be laughing when the Astans come pouring across the Yellow Mountains!"

Strongarm walked across the platform, standing very close to Mestler so that the Parliamentarian edged away nervously.

"We won't be running, either," he said quietly.

FOURTEEN

THE DAYS WENT by and the grume intensified until the old men were saying, as they sipped their beer in the Golden Grummet and nodded wisely, that it was the densest grume in memory. Phenomenal catches were offloaded at the fishmarket and the breakwater wharf, so nobody begrudged—except on principle—the large quantities of fish that were diverted to the new cannery. Most of these latter hauls were delivered to the new wharf beyond Finger Point, out of sight of the townsfolk, although some were taken by road from the harbour. The estuary had dried up long since.

The military police were hardly seen in Pallahaxi despite everyone's fears. Occasionally they would show the flag literally and in force, marching down the main street in a body, dressed in scarlet uniform quite unlike the sombre blue of the cannery guards, carrying to the fore a tall staff from which fluttered the Silver Lox of Erto. Although our national emblem is said to represent strength, persistence and fortitude with further religious connotations, it is not popular with the people of Pallahaxi and its display on these unfortunate occasions was considered no less than an insult. Attempts were made to organize a counter-march, but these eventually fell through when it became apparent that Strongarm was against it.

"All this wearing finery and marching in step like they only have one mind between them," he muttered. "That's the way of Parls and such people. All that prancing about and ceremony you hear about in Alika. Do we want to be like them?"

When someone timidly suggested that at least Pallahaxi must have its own flag which would be hoisted in opposition whenever the Erto flag was displayed, he said, "We have no need of a flag or any other fake symbols. The name of our town is enough—that tells who we are and what we are. We live here and work here and sometimes we like one another and help one another—but that's enough. We're still individuals and we'll keep it that way." He grinned suddenly. "It makes a difficult target for the Parls."

Although I liked Strongarm, there were times when I tended to agree with Horlox-Mestler's view that he was overly insular and that his view was rapidly obscuring the real issues. I had not even bothered to mention Mestler's proposal for raising the *Ysabel*, because I knew what its reception would be.

However, in the course of time two events occurred which brought home to Pallahaxi the fact that it was part of a nation at war, and that occupation by the Astan forces was a poor alternative to the present comparatively benign government of the Parls.

"Alika has fallen," said my father at breakfast one morning as he read a single, ominous news-sheet which had been brought direct from the message post.

My mother burst into noisy sobs, rose from the table and hurried from the room.

For a moment I sat there wondering if she had gone to stick an Astan flag into Alika, or whether the war map would now be quietly disposed of, in favour of increased praying. Then my previous vision of Astans sleeping in my room returned, and I knew the news was not funny. Much as I loved Pallahaxi, Alika was where I was born and lived most of my life. It would never be the same. Even if we counter-attacked and threw the Astans out, they would leave their mark about the place. There had already been furious fighting and it was possible that our home was destroyed.

I wondered how my mother was reconciling this news with her announcement to me, not so many days ago, that the sun-god Phu was on our side. I toyed with the idea of suggesting to her that Phu's favours were conditional on the flow of the tide, remembering Mestler's astronomy lesson some days ago, but an unexpected onset of pity prevailed.

Instead I rounded on father. "What's Parliament doing about this?" I asked. "Where is the Regent?" I had visions of his august presence in a loxcart, trundling through the desert towards Bexton Post followed by the Members of Parliament in their robes, in lesser carts.

"Parliament has withdrawn," he said. "You may as well know this; everyone will know it soon. Pallahaxi has been chosen for the temporary seat of Government. We are indeed honoured, Drove. A certain Member of Parliament will be lodged in our own home, and other arrangements will be made with various suitable households in the town. A suite has been prepared for the Regent at the new cannery."

There seemed to be a funny side to that somewhere, but I was more concerned at the prospect of a stranger in the house. We had no room; this was only a summer cottage. I didn't want another person around, to whom I had to be polite. "Rax," I muttered. "He can have my room. I'll stay at the Grummet."

To my amazement there was no fit of temper. Instead father regarded me thoughtfully. "Possibly that might be the best arrangement," he said at last. Of course, the last thing he wanted was a disruptive influence in the house while a Member was here. "I will arrange for the requisitioning of a suite there. You must be suitably housed."

"I'll see to that, if you don't mind, father." I said hastily.

"If you like." His expression had become abstracted and he was already working out ways he could impress the member, now that I would be out of the way.

Pallahaxi had been chosen as the new seat of Government because it was the furthest point from Asta by land and therefore the last place which the enemy hordes would reach. I wondered what our own hordes were doing these days; we seemed to have precious little good news recently. I have always found that verbal information can create a distorted mental image, and I was suffering from one of those images as I walked down to the town that morning. I was visualizing the Astan hordes sweeping us into the sea, thus reversing the defeat which they had suffered at the same spot around the year of Renaissance 1000. They would be yelling on the beach, waving springrifles while we waded out into deeper water and the bolts raised little splashes as they fell around us.

Yet when the second crisis occurred, on that same day, it came from the direction which Parliament had not, apparently, considered...

I went straight to the Golden Grummet and told Browneyes the news that I was to stay at the inn—if her parents agreed, of course. We stood in the geometrical room at the rear of the bar and she threw her arms around my neck and gave me a long, long kiss of delight and possessiveness. Round about that time Annlee and Girth entered, having heard her squeals of joy. Browneyes lost no time in breaking the news.

"Well, I don't know about that," said Girth doubtfully, looking at me.

"Are you *sure* your father said that, Drove?" asked Annlee. Apart from seeing him on the platform at the temple, her most vivid recollection of my father centred around the unsavoury tussle in the bar some time ago. On that occasion he made it abundantly clear what he thought of Girth, Annlee, Browneyes, the customers and even the very structure of the building.

"Look, there's a member coming to stay and father needs my room," I said. "I'd just stay here like an ordinary guest, really."

Girth smiled broadly. "In that case you're very welcome, and you'll be no ordinary guest. See that he gets the very best room, Browneyes."

She led me up the stairs which, although well-carpeted, creaked excitingly, along a twisted passage of variable pitch to a thick door with a bright brass knob. This she threw open then stepped aside, watching me expectantly as I entered.

The first thing I saw was a bed, which would have slept a team of lox. Broad and decorated with brasswork it seemed to occupy most of the room with its opulence. To the right stood a heavy, dark chest of drawers and against the other wall was a panelled dresser. I walked to the window and looked out; I could see right across the fishmarket to the boats in the inner harbour. The opposite hill rose in trees and grey-roofed houses to the skyline slashed by the diagonal of the road to Finger Point. I saw a man leading a lox and cart up the long slope; a lorin sat astride the lox.

I turned back to Browneyes. "It's a wonderful room," I said. "I'll make sure your parents get well paid."

"I don't think they're so worried about that," she said. "They're glad you're staying here."

We sat on the bed and bounced a few times, then kissed. Somehow we fell backwards while kissing and, since it seemed more comfortable, we stayed that way. Then Browneyes said, "My legs are getting stiff, hung over the edge like this," so I released her for a moment and she crawled right onto the bed; I followed and we lay together. I could feel the whole length of her body against me as we kissed again.

"I love you, Browneyes," I said for the first time.

She was looking at me as I lay half across her and her face was indescribably lovely. She smiled and said,

"That's just as well, Drove, because we seem to be in bed together."

I smiled back but I think I may have coloured a little as the implication hit me. I kissed her again to cover what I was thinking, but then I found that my own body had betrayed me and she must know what was in my mind. She held me hard for a moment, wriggling against me just a little, then we moved apart mutually and she was looking worried. "Look here, Drove," she said quietly. "Maybe we'd better stand up, huh? We... we shouldn't be like this. We're not old enough."

Hastily we scrambled from the bed and stood staring at each other. I could hear footsteps on the squeaky stairs.

I said, "Anyway, we weren't in the bed. We were on it." And we laughed, and the awkward moment was over.

Annlee came into the room. "Well, you two certainly look happy," she said alarmingly. "Do you like your room, Drove?"

"It's the best room I've ever seen. Are you sure I can have it?"

"If it's good enough for the Regent it's good enough for you," she laughed.

Browneyes was grinning at me. "I didn't tell you, in case it put you off. The Regent slept here when he was in Pallahaxi once."

"Oh..." I regarded the bed in some awe. I wondered what the Regent thought about, while he was lying in it, and what he dreamed about when he slept. I wondered if there had been guards posted outside the door. I wondered if he hadn't thought Browneyes was the prettiest girl in all Erto—and I thought: if he had, then I would assassinate the dirty freezer...

"Of course, I don't remember much about it," said Browneyes. "I was only three at the time." And I laughed.

Later, after Annlee and Browneyes had had some sort of mother-to-daughter private talk, Browneyes and I walked through the fishmarket towards the monument. The stones were slippery underfoot with fish scales and fishy water, so we held hands in case one of us fell.

"The fish are getting bigger," she observed. "You can tell the state of the grume by the size of the fish." Men moved about with villainous spikes, spearing fish and tossing them into baskets. We walked along the quayside.

"What did your mother say to you?" I asked.

She stopped, rested her arms on the rail and gazed at the water heaving stickily below. The usual assortment of strange objects floated there; odd lengths of rope, net-corks, dead fish, soggy paper. Even in the detritus of Pallahaxi harbour there is romance. Browneyes had changed into a yellow pullover and blue jeans, and I'll swear that she looked prettier than ever. I wondered if it was love that did it.

"Mother said it wasn't right for me to be in the bedroom with you," she said. "So I said a bedroom was just another room, wasn't it? And she said: well, not *exactly*, my dear..." Here Browneyes gave a remarkable imitation of her mother's worried voice. "Anyway, the outcome was that I promised not to go into your room between the hours of sunset and sunrise, which are the dangerous times, it seems."

"Uh." I was disappointed.

"But mother's a simple soul and she forgot to make me promise not to have *you* in *my* room."

"Fine." I wanted to change the subject, now. I had a

feeling that events in that direction were moving beyond my control. "What shall we do this morning?"

"Call for Ribbon?"

"Look, why not let's go without Ribbon for a change? I think Wolff's seeing her this morning, so she'll be all right. Let's take my skimmer out."

Browneyes agreed enthusiastically and we entered Silverjack's yard. The man himself was nowhere in sight so we made our way through the wood shavings and upturned boats to the slipway. Soon we had rigged the skimmer and were slipping through the harbour. Browneyes lay in the bows and I sat at the tiller. We seemed to be looking at each other all the time, and every so often I would have to make a violent course correction to avoid running somebody down.

People waved to us from the quay and called us by name from the other boats, and for the first time I realized how conspicuous we were, how people *noticed* the son of a Parl and the daughter of an innkeeper constantly in each other's company. At one time this would have caused me infinite embarrassment, but now I found I was enjoying it, feeling proud to be seen with my beautiful girl.

We passed into the outer harbour and ran parallel to the breakwater. It was occurring to me that there was something different about Browneyes' clothes, something to do with the yellow pullover.

"Uh, Browneyes," I said tentatively. "You look sort of... sexy, in that."

She gave a sudden broad grin and looked down at herself. I felt the pulse beating strongly in my throat, and my heart was thumping. "Do you really think so?" she asked happily. "I thought perhaps you might; that's why I put it on. It's too small for me, really. Next year I won't be able to... Uh, Drove, do you think there will be a next year for us? I love you so much, I get scared."

"I'm going to stay here all winter," I said confidently. "I'll be here always, now that..." The thoughts came back...

"I'm sorry to hear about Alika," she said softly.

"That's all right. This is my home, now..." Yet in my mind there was an inevitability about leaving. Every year we had come to Pallahaxi for the summer, and every year we had gone away afterwards, before the drench started. This was the way things were. I could imagine my father ignoring my protests and dragging me off to some outpost in the wilds by main force, the way he always did when our verbal deliberations reached an impasse.

We tacked at the point of the breakwater and headed towards Finger Point. The fishing boats were out in strength and there were three large skimmers of unusual outline further out to sea. Frequently we had to duck as grummets swooped past us, intent on the fish and ignoring anything else. We kept close in under the cliffs, watching the rocks slip by.

"Drove..." said Browneyes after a long and comfortable silence, "I think there's some sort of organization building up in Pallahaxi. I thought I ought to tell you. This morning in the Grummet people were talking about how Members of Parliament were going to be staying here, and a lot of people were saying it wouldn't work out. They said if Members were going to be around the place, with privileges and ignoring rationing and the curfew and living in our houses, then the Members might pretty soon find themselves dead. I know it's a horrible thing to say."

"It's getting that bad, is it?" The townsfolk didn't talk

so freely in my presence, wrongly imagining that everything got back to my father.

"It's serious, I think. I mean, I couldn't care less about the Members myself, but you were saying that one of them is staying with your parents. I wouldn't like to think of anything happening to your mother and father, for your sake."

There were plenty of cynical replies I could have made to that, but I refrained. Browneyes was too sweet to understand.

"Look over there!" I pointed. "By the rocks." There was something big at the water's edge, moving gently with the waves.

"Oh..." Browneyes looked away.

I moved in closer. Hereabouts the rocks were jagged and although the water held little motion, I had visions of ripping the boat open on some spike. The thing floated head down, buoyant on the dense water. "It's a lorin," I said.

"What a shame... what shall we do, Drove?"

I was trying to make up my mind when there was a curious whistling noise and a section of rock above us crumbled with a loud report and came cascading down, falling into the water with a subdued splashing which subsided instantly. I wheeled around to see the three steam skimmers we had noticed earlier, now close by, skirting the outside of the breakwater. Puffs of white arose from steam guns on their decks.

They were Astan men-of-war. They were shelling Pallahaxi.

Like the *Ysabel* they were paddlers, but here the resemblance ended. The Astan ships were skimmers. In the interests of manoeuvrability they bore no sails, but had two oversize paddlewheels on either side. Suddenly they all turned in unison almost in their own lengths, and darted out to sea again. With paddlewheels whirling they appeared almost to run over the surface of the grume like motorcarts. Their funnels beat a harsh quick chaff-chaff-chaff and columns of pale smoke fountained vertically as they accelerated, veered south, and came dashing back towards the harbour with guns thudding.

Astan or not, they were magnificent machines. Each craft bore two tall funnels and a large superstructure amidships; the engines must have been huge. Being skimmers they had scant freeboard but, at full speed, it seemed that the hulls barely touched the water. There was a short mast forward at the head of which fluttered the sinister Astan flag; the gold stylized sugarplant on a red background. The decks bristled with steam guns.

Men could be seen working rapidly at these great weapons as the Astans made another pass. I wondered why the enemy didn't slow down and bombard the town at his leisure, but then realized that the Astans would be expecting answering fire at any moment. I actually caught a glimpse of a large ball travelling overhead; it smacked into the cliff near the floating body, but this time there was no landslide.

Browneyes flinched. There was no fear in her eyes, only a sorrow and a deep concern as she saw the missiles arching over the outer harbour and disappearing into the town. "There's nothing anyone can do," she said helplessly. "Why won't they give us guns, Drove?"

"They said they will," I muttered. I felt in some way responsible, being the son of a Parl. "These things take time, Browneyes."

The attack was over. The skimmers were racing out to sea, overrunning several small fishing boats as they went. Soon they were lost in the haze of distance, a violent memory on the placid water. The grummets dived, the fish glittered and thrashed. The enemy was gone.

The damage was slight. There was an impromptu meeting at the monument later in the afternoon, and it was reported that the only damage sustained had been two smashed loxcarts at the old cannery, three fishing boats sunk at sea and two more in the inner harbour, a ball through the roof of Olab's bakery—and a lot of Pallahaxi pride. It was a stormy meeting and there was wild talk of a march on the new cannery, but Strongarm came sailing into the harbour and managed to calm them down. "The time will come," he said ominously.

Ribbon met us shortly before the curfew sent everyone hurrying for their houses. "Look, have either of you seen Silverjack?" she asked. "Father's been trying to find him all day, ever since I told him he'd been piloting the *Ysabel*."

"Uh... we saw him," I replied unhappily.

"I don't remember that, Drove. Where?" Browneyes was puzzled.

"He... uh, you remember that body under the cliff? That wasn't a lorin, Browneyes. I'm sure of it. The water rolled it and I saw the side of the face. I'll swear it was Silverjack."

The girls regarded me in horror. "What shall we do about it, Drove?" asked Ribbon.

"I'm going to tackle Mestler," I said. I had a sudden, terrible suspicion—and I remembered Mestler didn't know we'd witnessed the sinking of the *Ysabel*...

FIFTEEN

WITH THE GRUME at its maximum the Government were faced with a practical difficulty in enforcing the curfew which, apparently, had not previously occurred to them. They were men from the interior, away to the south-east, from Alika and Horlox. Even Mestler, for all his astronomical knowledge, failed to remember that the time was approaching when the sun would shine continuously and there would be no darkness, no excuse for the curfew—and no secret hours for the mysterious comings and goings of Parls and supplies. Now, the trucks to and from the cannery thundered through the town in full view of everyone, and the military police were no longer able to carry out their clandestine missions under cover of darkness.

Understandably, for a few days after the Astan attack Mestler and his men lay low. There were ominous mutterings in the town and hardly a standard day went by without an impromptu meeting at the monument. There were those who called on Strongarm to lead a deputation to the new cannery—which was now recognized as the focus of Parl activity—but the fisherman remained adamant. There was nothing to be gained; any such gathering at the gates would, he knew, be turned away at gunpoint.

I called on my parents on a couple of occasions to find their mood increasingly grave. On the second occasion there was a stranger in the house; father introduced him to me as Zeldon-Thrawn and I thought I vaguely

167

recognized him from my infrequent visits to the Parliament buildings in Alika.

"Are the other Members all here?" I asked. "I haven't seen any strangers around town."

Father's face hardened. "And you're not likely to. I regret that there is so much hostility among your friends in Pallahaxi that it's not wise for decent men to enter the town. Zeldon-Thrawn is safe up here with us—but can you imagine a Member walking through the streets, with that animal Strongarm at large? Most certainly not. The Members are having to be accommodated at the cannery—in conditions of the utmost privation, I might add."

"Oh, come on, Burt," said Thrawn smiling. "It's not that bad."

"I am ashamed to be associated with this town. The inhabitants are no more than ignorant louts with no respect whatever for their rulers!" Father was staring into my face, all set for a bout of temper and entirely forgetting the presence of Thrawn. "Horlox-Mestler is speaking to them today but I've told him it's a waste of time and dangerous, too. But then..." He forced a smile, recalling himself. "Mestler's like that. The man's fearless, when it comes to the performance of his duties."

We talked some more and I formed the impression that Thrawn was a pleasant enough, sensible type of man who would recognize my father's ridiculous tubthumping for what it was. Later I spoke briefly to my mother in the kitchen and asked after the war map, but she was not disposed to discuss the subject and after a while I left, in some relief.

I heard the blasting of the crier's steam-whistle as I walked down to the town and by the time I reached the fishmarket Mestler was standing on an upturned crate, addressing a small crowd in informal fashion. He had forsaken the splendour of the temple for the grass-roots approach—at the same time cutting out the advance publicity and relying on the smaller audience to convey his points to the rest of the town by word of mouth. In this manner he eliminated the possibility of organized opposition and consequent unpleasantness.

The acoustics under the fishmarket roof were not good and grummets were constantly swooping in through the open sides, causing people to duck nervously, and disputing possession of morsels of fish with harsh cries. Nevertheless we were all able to gather the gist of Mestler's oration.

It seemed there had been an unavoidable delay in the supply of munitions for the protection of Pallahaxi due to the Astans having overrun key industrial cities inland. This was most unfortunate in view of the recent attack by Astan men-of-war—but people were to consider themselves assured that the Government was doing everything in its power to rectify the situation. The Government was very grateful for the war efforts of our great town and in recognition of this were relaxing certain security measures which it fully realized were unpopular, but which had been very necessary at the time. The curfew was being countermanded. The military police were being withdrawn.

"I thought you said the police were for our protection!" someone shouted, but it was too late; Mestler, smiling and nodding, had stepped down from his box and was climbing into the waiting motorcart.

I ran across, pushed my way through the crowd around the cart and called, "Can I have a word with you, Horlox-Mestler?"

Already seated, he glanced up and saw me. He

smiled, said something to his driver, then motioned me
to climb in beside him. Soon we were moving through
the streets of Pallahaxi while people jeered, hissed and
threw stones. I found I was shivering, appalled by the
concentrated hostility with which I was surrounded. I
decided that maybe it wasn't such a great thing to be a
Parl, after all. For a while the stones rattled off the wood-
work, then we were clear and climbing out of town.

Mestler told the driver to stop, then turned to me. "I
don't suppose you want to come to the cannery," he
said, smiling. "Now, what can I do for you, my lad?" His
eyes were sparkling with charm and delight as he radiated his wonderful-with-kids personality at me. The an-
tagonism from the town had hardly touched him; he had
forgotten it already. My mother would have said: how
kind of Horlox-Mestler to take the trouble to talk to you,
dear.

"Look here," I said brutally. "Have you seen Silverjack?"

There was a pause and I heard the exhaust of a truck
harshen as it passed through the level main street and
begin to climb the hill behind us. There were few houses
around here, although I saw an old woman watching us
from the window of a tumbledown cottage opposite.

"Silverjack was a friend of yours, wasn't he?" asked
Mestler, the twinkle gone.

"Not exactly a friend. I knew him. Wait a moment."
The significance of our use of past tense occurred to me
and I wondered if I'd been led into a trap. "What do you
mean, *was*? Are you saying he's dead?" I thought I inject-
ed the right note of alarm into my voice.

The truck was blasting on its whistle as it pounded
up the hill towards us, but there was plenty of room for
it to pass. Mestler frowned slightly.

"Didn't you see the list? It was posted at the temple. Silverjack was one of the poor souls lost when the *Ysabel* sank. He never stood a chance. It was a terrible affair."

My heart was thumping now, and my palms were moist. As the din of the truck hammered nearer I turned to him, staring into his face and getting ready to jump from the motorcart. This was it; this was when I made the final break with the Parls, with my mother and father, with the whole freezing murdering lot of them. He saw it in my face and there was no friendship in his eyes now, no avuncular condescension. I opened my mouth to denounce him when his eyes slid past mine, widening as he stared back down the hill.

"What's happening? Get away from the cart, boy! Quickly!"

We scrambled from the motorcart as the driver of the truck leaped from his seat and rolled in the dirt at our feet. Some distance away, surging up the hill, came a large mob, silent and purposeful. The driverless truck hammered past us; I turned and saw it puffing on but slowing now, swerving to one side of the road with a grinding of metal wheels, lurching to a halt in a ditch.

The driver had jumped to his feet and was clutching at Mestler's sleeve with a deformed hand. "Let's get out of here!" he yelled. It was Grope.

"What's going on?"

"The truck!" he cried. "She's going to blow! I did my best, Mestler; by Phu I did my best. I got her out of the town."

With one backward glance at the ominously smouldering steam truck we ran down towards the town, halting behind the reassuring bulk of a public heater. We were immediately joined by the townsfolk storming up the hill from the opposite direction. Strongarm was in the lead; he seized Grope by the arm. "Do you realize you've injured at least three people back there, driving like a maniac?"

"The safety valve jammed, coming down the cliff road," explained Grope, almost in tears. "I was already going into the town and the pressure was rising fast. I had to keep going. I had to get through the town before she blew! I risked my own life, can't you understand?"

Strongarm's expression was grim. "If anyone dies, then your life wasn't worth risking," he said quietly. He stared up the hill; some two hundred paces away steam drifted from the abandoned truck with deceptive quietness. She was a woodburner; there was nothing anyone could do except wait while the furnace blazed and the pressure built. If she had been fired by distil like the motorcart, the burners could have been shut down and the truck might have been saved. We watched in silence.

"At least she was on the return trip to the cannery," someone said. "She'll be empty. The only loss will be the truck."

"Let's hope that's all," said Strongarm ominously.

Grope was trembling violently, completely transformed from the self-possessed and opinionated oaf whom I'd known before. Sweat was trickling down his thick neck, leaving pink channels in the grime. His fatty breasts quivered. "Let's get out of here!" he wailed suddenly. "We're too close!"

Mestler was looking old and defeated. He had been silent for some time, watching Strongarm. At last he spoke. "I think it would be better if you sent these people back to their homes, Strongarm," he said quietly. "We don't want anyone else injured when she explodes. I'd be extremely grateful if you dispersed the crowd."

At first Strongarm looked surprised; then his eyes

narrowed. "That's all right, Mestler," he said. "We'll take the chance. I'm sure the townsfolk will think it's worth the risk, to see a Parl truck blow."

Ribbon arrived but her father was too busy scrutinizing the truck to notice. I told her what was happening and her eyes widened with excitement. "Browneyes will be sorry she missed this," she said.

"Where is she?"

"At the Grummet, waiting for you."

"Rax. I can't go now. The truck might blow at any moment."

Ribbon grinned at me. "Are you saying that a mere steam truck is more exciting than your Browneyes?"

Wolff hurried up at that moment. "Ah, there you are." He looked around at the large gathering with aristocratic distaste. "Rax, what a mob. Let's get out of here, Ribbon. It's a good day for a walk along the quay, I think."

Ribbon stared at him haughtily. "If you think I'd leave all this just to walk along the quay with *you*, you must be simple-minded. In any case, you haven't taken the *trouble* to ask what's happening; I suppose you think we're all just standing here *mindless*, like *lox*."

It was a perfect example of Ribbon as I'd first known her—and first hated her—and I was delighted that Wolff was on the receiving end.

Mestler moved close to us, gripping our arms. "Both you lads, get back home, there's good lads, eh?"

"Get frozen, Mestler," I said.

Wolff's mouth dropped open as he stared incredulously from me to Mestler to Ribbon. Ribbon chuckled and took my hand. Wolff saw this, swallowed, then said, "Certainly, Horlox-Mestler." He turned and loped off down the hill.

Mestler was still regarding me; the aged look was there and something else. "Drove and Ribbon, do this for my sake," he said. "Just for me, not for the Parls or the Regent, right? Ask Strongarm to break this up and send everyone home, please."

"Well *really*, Mestler," trilled Ribbon. "I have no influence with my father *whatsoever*. And I'm *quite* sure—"

I took her around the waist and whirled her about, whispering in her ear, "Ribbon, dear, please listen."

"Oh yes?"

"I honestly think it might be important to get people away. There's something else behind all this, something we don't know anything about. Mestler's serious, you know. I know he's a crook but I don't think he's the worst of them."

"Say you think I'm pretty."

"Phu, you know I do. Just don't tell Browneyes I said so, that's all."

"Oh dear, isn't life so *complicated*," Ribbon twinkled, turning back to Mestler. "All right, I'll do what I can. Because Drove asked me, you understand?"

She walked over to her father and drew him aside. I saw him glance my way as she spoke quietly to him.

There was something shrunken and pathetic about Mestler as he watched them. I touched him on the arm and he started violently.

"All right," I said. "Now tell me why you people killed Silverjack."

His eyes dropped and he said nothing. After a while Ribbon joined us, looking serious.

"I'm sorry, Drove," she said. "I really tried. But father thinks there's something funny going on. Something to do with the truck cargo. He says everyone ought to be here just to see what's in there."

"But there's nothing in there," I muttered, trying not to think about it...

Mestler said, "Thank you anyway, Drove. And you, Ribbon. Your father's a good man, my dear. He's the kind of man it's good to have on your side, when you don't know who your enemies are... I'll leave you now. Look after each other, and that nice little Browneyes..."

He began to walk away, moving almost casually through the crowd and there was an air of finality about our parting. I ran after him, caught his arm. "Mestler! What happened to Squint?"

He looked round but I couldn't tell whether he'd heard or not; I think I forgot my own question when I saw the desolation in his eyes. He detached himself or I let go, and he walked away from the crowd, up the hill.

"Mestler!" roared Strongarm. "Come back! I want you here!"

He thought Mestler was escaping from us, maybe hurrying for the sanctuary of the cannery. I knew instinctively that it was a different sanctuary that Mestler sought...

Mestler climbed into the cab of the steam truck and sat there, looking quiet and thoughtful and ordinary. The crowd was quiet too as we all waited and I heard Ribbon sob suddenly, and her hand tightened in mine.

Presently the boiler exploded.

It wasn't what I'd expected. I'd expected a boom and a flash and a giant concussion shaking the ground and bringing the slates down from the cottage roof opposite; I'd expected something enormous and spectacular.

Instead there was a sharp *crack*! followed by a continuous rushing roar like the sound at the bottom of a huge waterfall. Instantly the road filled with a great cloud of steam, roiling and billowing and rolling down the hill towards us. The crowd broke and ran; and Ribbon and I ran with them, still clutching hands. After a while we stopped and looked back, and everything seemed to be over. Sheepishly, laughing nervously, the crowd climbed the hill again.

The steam had almost completely dispersed; a few wisps arose from the boiler. There was no sign of damage from this distance and Mestler still sat at the controls. A thrill of horror trickled down my back at the normality of it all—and when I heard the chuff-chuff-chuff of beating exhaust I think I yelped with terror. "He's started her up," a woman was repeating, over and over. "He's started her up." The crowd hesitated, then Strongarm strode forward.

"It's only another truck, men!" he shouted. "It's coming from the cannery!"

It was strange the way nobody mentioned the dead man at the controls. We crowded around the rear of the truck and a few men climbed on top and started untying the canvas, exclaiming that there was something there, under the covers. My eyes kept straying to the gently steaming Mestler and I felt somehow we ought to ask his permission; it wasn't right to loot a dead man's vehicle. Then he stirred as the men bounced about on the truck and his head flopped over and I saw his face... He must have died very quickly, to be still sitting in the same position.

The canvas was thrown back amid shouts of triumph. The sides and back of the truck clattered down. Large black pieces of machinery stood revealed on the platform. "Steam guns!" somebody yelled. It's our steam guns, men! We'll be safe from the Astan ships, now!"

Strongarm climbed to the platform and held up his hand to quiet the cheering. "Sure they're steam guns," he shouted. "But they weren't meant for us. I want you to remember what Mestler said down at the fishmarket only a short while ago. He told us there'd been a delay, that the guns wouldn't be here for days yet. So—I wonder who these guns were meant for? These guns, slipping through the town on a truck that's supposed to be empty."

"The cannery!" a man shouted. "By Phu, they're looking after themselves before the town!"

"That's about the way it is," said Strongarm when the howls of disgust had subsided. "They've moved Parliament down to the new cannery, and Parliament must be protected, and to Rax with Pallahaxi. That's the way the Parls think. But Mestler couldn't face the guilt. He couldn't face what we'd do to him when we found out. So he killed himself. If that isn't proof of Parliament's guilt I don't know what is. Well," he slapped the long barrel of one of the guns, "they needn't feel guilty about these. We'll set them up on the breakwater!"

"You know, all the stuff's not there," I said to Ribbon. "Each gun needs a furnace and a boiler. They're useless by themselves."

She looked at me and said something quite perceptive, for Ribbon. "We need *guns*, Drove. The furnaces and boilers are *quite* superfluous, my darling."

I grinned and, hearing the rumble of the approaching truck, stepped out and looked up the hill. The driver had shut off the throttle on seeing the crowd, and the vehicle was coasting slowly towards us.

"Maybe we ought to take a look at him, too," said Strongarm. He jumped down from the platform of the truck and stepped into the middle of the road, holding up his huge arms. The truck stopped a few paces away and the driver looked nervously out.

"What's happened? What's going on?"

"Just a little accident," Strongarm informed him, "Now, man. What do you carry in your truck?"

The driver's tongue passed over his lips. "Uh, canned goods, of course. What the freezing Rax do you expect from a cannery? It's canned fish for the towns inland." We were all crowding around now; the driver's eyes kept straying to the guns on the back of the other truck.

"Right now a can of fish would suit me fine," said Strongarm. He swung himself on to the rear of the truck and tore aside the canvas. "What a pity," he said quietly. "You seem to have sold it all. The truck's empty." He dropped down beside the cab and seized the terrified driver in his giant hands. "The truck's empty you freezing liar!"

"I... I swear they told me it was full."

Grope was there, shaking with fear. "And they told me mine was empty, the freezers!" he wailed. "We've been tricked by the Parls!"

"Oh, shut up," snapped Strongarm, disgusted. "Any fool driver can tell whether his truck's full or empty, just by the feel of it. You two are in the pay of the Parls and you've become Parls yourselves. Tie them up, somebody, and take them to the temple. I'll talk to them later. Now, let's get these guns loaded on to this truck. It's bad economics for it to go empty, in these difficult times..."

Later, as the guns were driven down to the breakwater, Strongarm, Ribbon and I stood beside the wrecked truck of Grope. The body of Mestler had been removed. Strongarm was gazing up the hill, where the road disappeared over the skyline before winding down to the new cannery. The sun was bright and constant, high and fierce as it had been for days.

"They pretend they're looking after our interests," he said quietly. "But all the time they're building up their own little fortress, scared like drivets in a burrow. I wonder if the same thing's happening in Asta. I wonder if all the bastards are sitting pretty while the good guys are killing one another off. Hey..." An expression of slow joy spread over his face. "Wouldn't it be great if we could make our own peace with the Astan army when it reaches here, then everybody could go home happy and leave the Parls sitting alone in their little fort, bristling with guns and nobody to shoot..."

SIXTEEN

EVENTS WERE NOW moving so fast that I was losing track of standard nights and days while the blazing furnace of the sun Phu circled overhead and the grume reached its peak. The Golden Grummet was open for business continuously and Girth, Annlee, Browneyes and myself often worked in shifts, and sometimes all at once when trade was at its height. From time to time one or other of us would creep away, exhausted, and collapse into bed to sleep for several hours before going back on duty again. Browneyes and I never took advantage of the proximity of our rooms; we were too tired even for love.

Once when I passed her room I heard a sound and puzzled, because I'd just left her down in the bar. The rooms were all occupied these days; Parls and other refugees were arriving from all over Erto, converging on the focal point of Pallahaxi. It was quite likely that one of these itinerants had gone into the wrong room. Nervous about some oaf lying in wait for my girl, I tapped on the door and, after a moment, entered.

Browneyes' mother was lying on the bed, crying. I was about to leave when she called out softly, so I went and stood beside her bed, feeling very uncomfortable.

"What's the matter, Annlee?" I asked.

She looked at me blankly, her eyes streaming; then she reached out and took my hand. Her grip was cold; she was shivering even in that hot room. I wasn't sure, even then, that she was fully aware of who I was. I detached myself and pulled some blankets over her, and left her there. Some time later she was down in the bar again, serving drinks and laughing and arguing politics with the customers as though everything was all right, as though it had always been all right.

A period came when the customers were few and Girth suggested to Browneyes, "Why don't you and Drove take a break, go for a sail or a walk or something?" He stared into his daughter's face anxiously. "You look pale, girl. You need the sun on you. Your mother and I can look after the place now."

"Are you sure that's all right, father?" asked Browneyes, smiling at me.

"Get along, you two," laughed Annlee. "Before Girth changes his mind. Oh... and keep away from the far side of town, will you?"

"Why's that?"

"The Parls say they're going to collect the guns today," said Girth grimly. "I wonder if they have the nerve. That's why nobody's here. They're all over at the breakwater."

We rigged the skimmer in silence; I know we were both thinking about Silverjack. Although a handful of men still worked among the boats on the slipway, somehow the place seemed empty without its owner's hairy figure and erratic personality. I wondered who the yard belonged to now; whether Silverjack had any relatives to take the business over. There was a feeling of slow anger within me as I thought of the man swimming to land, having done his utmost to bring the *Ysabel* to dock, only for the Parls on the quay to... what? Did they shoot him, as he swam towards them?

Then the slow current would have carried him around Finger Point and they would assume the scavengers or grume-riders would dispose of the body. It was probably gone by now. On the other hand, with the fall of the tide it might still be stranded on the rocks under the cliff, lying broken, with the incriminating springrifle bolt still lodged in the body to give the lie to the Parls' story of his being 'lost' in the disaster.

Even that word annoyed me; what did they mean, 'lost'? Nobody was lost from the *Ysabel*. Those who died were trapped below decks and blown to pieces when the boilers went. We knew what happened to them; they were eaten by grummets. 'Lost' was a genteel and optimistic euphemism worthy only of my mother, implying that one day they might be found again, and everything would be all right.

"Listen, are you sure you want to go out, Drove?" asked Browneyes anxiously.

"I'm sorry. I was thinking, that's all." The sail was filling with the light breeze. "Let's go," I said, and we scrambled in and pushed off. The water was like glue and the sailing slow in the sheltered harbour. Now that we were afloat, my dark mood began to improve. I found myself watching Browneyes in the bows and this had the effect of making me feel better still. Large numbers of skimmers rode at anchor, the ropes and chains dripping long slow drops as they rose and fell on the viscid surface. Most fishermen had stayed in town to watch events when the Parls arrived. I hoped there wouldn't be trouble.

We skidded into the outer harbour on a freshening breeze and the crowd on the breakwater came into view. Most of the town must have been there; people stood in groups around the three large guns which had been set up along the side of the tramway track, long barrels pointed bravely out to sea. Snowy grummets perched on the black iron, disputing territory with wings outspread. The birds had no fear of the crowds.

Several people waved and I headed closer in, sliding near the causeway of rocks on which the breakwater was built. "When are the Parls coming?" I shouted.

"Soon." We could recognize individual faces now; I saw Ribbon and her father. There was no sign of Wolff. Ribbon waved to us frantically, grinning and shouting. We shouted back and sailed on. Browneyes was watching me speculatively and I felt a twinge of apprehension.

"It happened again, didn't it, Drove?" she said obscurely, but confident that I knew what she meant.

"Uh?"

"I mean that you and she were involved in that truck explosion up the new cannery road and somehow I wasn't there."

"Browneyes, I couldn't help that. I love you."

Her eyes softened. "I know. But I still have this awful feeling that if I go on missing things, then in the end I'll miss out on you. That won't happen, will it, Drove?"

"Never," I said, wondering why I felt so guilty.

"Keep going, otherwise she'll want to come with us." Indeed, Ribbon was strolling along the breakwater parallel with our course, smiling down at us. "She's changed, too." said Browneyes. "She's different recently, not so bossy. She's nicer... why is she so freezing nice?" wailed Browneyes quietly in sudden despair, gazing up at the undeniably beautiful young girl who walked so assuredly above us.

"She's growing up and becoming more sensible," I said. "It's happening to all of us. We'll none of us be the same after this summer... and in a way it scares me. I feel as though I've lost such a lot, so quickly. I've gained a lot, too," I added hastily.

A buzz of comment and speculation from the break-water saved me from an awkward situation. Browneyes lowered the sail and the little craft came to an almost instantaneous halt on the sticky surface. We waited, watching the curve on the road around the far side of the harbour. Beside us there was a commotion. A huge silver fish, long and sinuous, had been writhing on the surface for a short while and the grummets now judged it safe to attack. They wheeled about us in a screaming flock, diving at the fish and slashing it with their sharp talons until one approached too close to the head. The longfish snapped, obtained a grip on the flapping white pinions and, with a gigantic plunging, succeeded in forcing itself beneath the water, dragging the grummet after it. A few pale feathers drifted on the surface which had immediately become still. Blood floated in streaks and pools, not dispersing.

Three steam trucks puffed their way around the harbour road, whistling ceaselessly to clear the onlookers from their path. Their platforms were packed with uniformed men; the scarlet of the military police in the lead truck being followed by the more drab hues of the cannery guards in the following two. The trucks halted at the shoulder of the breakwater near the beached deep-hulls and the troops jumped down. They carried spring-rifles at the ready. "I do hope nobody tries anything silly," said Browneyes. "I don't like the look of those men. I feel as though they *want* to use their guns, like that time at the new cannery."

The onlookers were shouting and waving their fists, but Strongarm's voice could be heard calling for sanity. The troops had formed into a body and were marching along the breakwater in step, the trucks puffing slowly behind. Only one man barred their path, breaking from the grip of his comrades and running in front of the soldiers. I didn't quite see what happened. Suddenly he was not visible from my low viewpoint, while the soldiers marched relentlessly on. They halted at the first gun and waited while the truck drew alongside. Another column of smoke rose beyond the houses; soon the tramway locomotive trundled into sight, pushing a mobile crane. The crane platform was crowded with scarlet uniforms.

In a comparatively short time the guns were loaded, the troops climbed up after them and the trucks moved away, pursued by futile jeers and epithets. Strongarm stood above us; his head was bowed and his shoulders slumped. Ribbon went up to him, put her arm around him, standing on tiptoe and whispering in his ear. He grinned at her miserably, put his huge arm around her shoulder and together they walked away.

"Listen, Drove..." said Browneyes unhappily. "I'm sorry I said all those stupid things about Ribbon. I do like her, really."

By the time we'd rounded the lighthouse and were beating up the seaward side of the breakwater against the westerly breeze, the crowds had dispersed. The guns, for just three days symbols of Pallahaxi's determination to defend itself, to thumb its nose at authority, to establish independence, were gone. I was reminded of the time my father had confined me to the cottage following the fracas at the Golden Grummet.

Browneyes and I were in subdued mood. The sun was hot and the weather heavy and humid. Although the grummets had efficiently cleared the surface of the ocean of small fish, the bigger ones were now being forced to the top and lay all around us, struggling feebly or frantically according to how long the death throes had been in progress. Assorted debris had floated up from the bottom; waterlogged and decayed pieces of timber, thick weed, scum. The ocean stank.

"Maybe it wasn't such a good idea to come for a sail after all," Browneyes said. "We could always turn back and go for a walk instead. It's not nice out here, today."

"Let's go just a bit further," I said. "It might not be so bad off the Point. The tide sweeps round there. What we're getting here is the muck from the whole area." I had something in mind, but I didn't want to upset Browneyes. I wanted to see if the body was still under the cliff and, if it was, I wanted to establish the cause of death...

Browneyes was regarding the water unhappily and I could tell her thoughts were running on similar lines to mine. If the body had not been left behind with the tide, then it might well be floating in our vicinity. Every time we bumped into a piece of flotsam she started and peered apprehensively over the side.

"Drove," she said suddenly, looking out to sea, "I think there are grume-riders about." She pointed. A flurry of white showed near the horizon.

"Probably grummets," I tried to reassure her. "Anyway, we'll keep close in to the shore. We can always jump on to the rocks if anything happens." I eased the boat in under the cliffs.

We passed the place where we'd seen the body, but there was no sign of it. A large black fish floated nearby, belly up; a grummet had laid claim to the carcass and stood with talons locked into the gleaming flesh, watching us with a jealous eye. Soon Browneyes relaxed in visible relief as the water began to clear and we moved around Finger Point. "He's gone," she said with a long sigh as though she'd been holding her breath for minutes. "He's gone, gone, gone."

"The Parls killed him. I tackled Mestler and he wouldn't say anything, but I could tell. They must have shot him just after we saw him swimming to land. I suppose they had no further purpose for him, the freezers."

"Yes, well please don't talk about it, Drove. Look, do you like my dress?"

I had to smile at the naive switch. "Yes, but what happened to the yellow pullover?"

"Oh..." she coloured. "Mother said I mustn't wear it. She said it was... too small, you see. It *was* too small, really."

"Too sexy, she meant. She was frightened I'd... uh..." I broke off in confusion, having got myself into deep water.

"Look, there's the new quay," said Browneyes conversationally. "Do you think they'll be using it much, now that the *Ysabel*'s sunk?"

"I expect so. They wouldn't have built it just for one ship. Fishing boats have been offloading here... Rax. Look out!"

A grume-rider had been sitting on a rock, sunning itself. As it caught sight of our skimmer its head came up with a snort and it slid into the water, some fifty paces away. Accelerating rapidly on flailing limbs it literally bounded across the dense surface towards us.

"Lie down, Drove!" said Browneyes urgently.

My mouth dry with fear I obeyed, sliding down until I was lying in the bottom of the skimmer. Browneyes did likewise, crawling beside me, watching me quietly with anxious eyes. Out of the breeze the sun became hot on my clothes and I was sweating, though not entirely due to the heat.

The skimmer shook as the grume-rider shook it squarely. There was a bark of rage. Water rained about us in oily drops as the creature dashed itself against the thin hull in snorting, baffled anger. Then for a moment all was still and we held our breath, listening to the grume-rider panting harshly.

The boat tilted slightly and a shadow fell across us. I edged away, huddling closer to Browneyes as a blunt head appeared above the gunwale, turning this way and that, myopically scanning the interior with deceptively gentle eyes. The creature's breath filled the boat with the stench of fish and I swallowed carefully, quietly. For a long while the animal and I looked at each other.

With a disgusted snort the black head withdrew and the boat shook to a sharp, decisive slap as the grume-rider pushed himself off and skittered away. We lay there, breathing as quietly as we could while the sail hung limp, the heat intensified and it became evident that the light breeze had died entirely. At last I eased myself into a sitting position and risked a look over the gunwale.

The sea lay flat like a mirror. The lone grume-rider disported himself about a hundred paces away, flinging slow drops as he worried at a carcase and drove off diving grummets with snarls of fury. Browneyes hoisted herself beside me, careful not to attract the grume-rider's attention by too sudden a movement. "What shall we do, Drove?" she whispered. "If we try to paddle for the wharf he'll see us."

I looked towards the land, judging the distance. "We'll have to do something quickly," I said. "We're drifting further away." I took a quick look around the ocean, which had turned a dull grey as the sun was temporarily obscured by mists. Nearby, there was a large area of sea which seemed darker than the rest. Further away, near the entance to the estuary, there were long ripples in the flatness, like surf, like a solid tidal wave coming in our direction. "What's that?" I asked.

There was a tremor in Browneyes' voice. "That's... that's grume-riders, Drove. A whole pack of them; that's the way they usually work. This one here must be a rogue."

"Uh... what will they do?"

"They'll just swamp us... it happened last year, a fisherman was caught by a pack of grume-riders. They jump into the boat and they..."

There was no need for her to elaborate; I could visualize that horde of powerful brutes, each one as big as a man, converging on our tiny skimmer, bounding over the low gunwales...

I found I was watching the dark area of sea, close to port. Great sluggish bubbles were rising and bursting as though the very ocean was belching with disgust at the filth which covered its skin.

Browneyes was talking quietly beside me. "...We don't have very much time, Drove. I wish... I wish we hadn't wasted so very much time getting to know each other. Please kiss me, quickly."

I bent over and kissed her long and hard, and she clung to me and cried against my shoulder while I

watched the grume-riders racing towards us in a vora-
cious pack. I took the paddle from the bottom of the boat
and hefted it in my hand; it was all we had and there
was no point in dying before we had to. I'd never been
so scared in my life and yet I was still thinking of
Browneyes and how the freezing grume-riders would
have to kill me before they got her...

The nearby rider paused in its feasting, lifted its
head as it floated high on the buoyant water. It regarded
the approaching pack, then, turning, raced away west-
wards out to sea, flippers flailing, streaming a trail of
spray. I glanced towards the land; it was too far off now.
The pack would be upon us before we reached the
wharf.

Browneyes stiffened in my arms; she had turned
away and was staring down at the water. "Look!" she
gasped. "Oh, Drove, look!"

The dark shadow below the surface was taking
shape, becoming firm, the outlines sharp and distinct.
More bubbles rose and burst, smelling of damp timber,
of rope and tar. I stared over the side, my eyes focused
and I could see decks, broken spars, hatches, all swimming slowly towards me out of the depths of the Pallahaxi Trench. It was an eerie sight and I forgot the
danger, and the grume-riders, and shivered from sheer
superstition as the grume lifted the *Ysabel* from the
ocean bed...

The jagged end of a shattered mast broke the surface
twenty paces away, disembodied, cut off from the
wreckage below by the intervening plane of silver. But
soon the dripping black wheelhouse emerged also,
shapeless and with windows smashed but still recogniz-
able. The hatch covers rose into view, moaning softly as
the viscous water reluctantly drained away and allowed

fresh air to enter the holds. Soon the entire deck was visible, streaming water like ponderous mercury.

I thrust the paddle into the water and pushed, driving the skimmer across the short intervening distance while the grume-riders bounded closer and I could hear their barks of hunger. They had seen us; their line was converging as they closed ranks for the kill. Then the skimmer bumped against the heavy timbers of the *Ysabel* and I held on while Browneyes scrambled on to the deck. I followed, still holding the paddle; but in my haste I slipped, felt the skimmer slide away from under me as I fell towards the water and my head smashed into the black hull in a burst of light and darkness...

My fingers were clutching hardness, digging in as I dragged myself forwards and upwards, still semi-conscious and impelled by dread of the predators who by now must be almost upon me; how long had I been unconscious, how long...? I raised my head as I struggled on and I saw a vision of Browneyes against the brightness of the sky, standing astride me with paddle upraised, smashing, smashing at the leaping forms around us.

I crawled on and the deck was beginning to take shape beneath me now. I could feel it heaving as the grume buoyed it up slowly, and I could hear Browneyes now, screaming in breathless desperation as she flailed away with the paddle, "Get away from him, you freezers, get *away* from him, get *away* from him..."

I stood, staggering, fighting to clear the fog from my brain and eyes; then I stepped forward and gently took the paddle from my Browneyes as she thrashed at the inert forms, mouthing wordlessly, her eyes empty. I rolled three bodies over the edge; the water lay at least two paces below us now; they struck with a sullen splash. The grume-riders closed in instantly, tearing, devouring with low snuffling sounds. Soon, they raced away southwards.

Browneyes was pressing her hands to the sides of her face, beginning to think again, beginning to tremble. She was cut around the legs and shoulder and her pretty dress had been torn half off and hung in tatters around her waist. I put my arm around her, helped her to a hatch and sat her down; then I tore off the remains of my shirt, damped it and began to bathe her wounds as carefully as I could. She had a deep cut on her shoulder which oozed blood but her sweet breasts were unharmed and I kissed them gently as I wiped them clean. I hesitated then, but decided there were things more important than modesty and I could see blood near her waist, so I stood her up and eased the remains of the clothes from her. She had a slight cut on her hip, so I bathed that and kissed it, and washed the rest of her off while she began to smile and stroke my hair as I knelt before her.

"Now you," she said urgently, so I got undressed and she washed me down, slowly and very thoroughly. I didn't notice whether I was injured or not. She stepped back and looked at me long and frankly, then grinned.

"Who said nothing ever happened to us?" she said.

SEVENTEEN

THE BROKEN MASTS and twisted funnels were dripping slime and festooned with weed so we deduced that they had been embedded in the sea bottom, anchoring the *Ysabel* while the grume intensified. Then, at last, they had

dragged free and with the loss of most of the deck cargo
the ship had risen fast, righting herself as she neared the
surface.

Neither of us was in a hurry to report the news back
to Pallahaxi.

We lay on the deck for a while to recover, while the
hot sun dried our wounds and Browneyes looked like a
beautiful piece of jewellery as she sparkled with crystals.
It seemed a waste to put our clothes back on and there
were no boats in sight, so we wandered about the decks
which were themselves beginning to glitter as the waterlogged timbers dried out and we looked at the machinery, the remains of the deck cargo, but mostly at each
other.

We managed to open the wheelhouse door, dragged
out a bundle of wet canvas and arranged it on the deck,
folded over several times like a bed. As the slow steam
began to rise I looked at Browneyes and there was a serious, almost desperate expression on her glowing face
as she stared back at me, her gaze travelling over my
body in a searching, hungry way that made me feel shy.
Then suddenly she chuckled and grabbed hold of me
and we hugged wildly and joyfully while the crystals
rained from our bodies and we laughed like idiots.

I've often thought, since, how lucky we were that we
loved each other so much. Otherwise it might have been
awkward, because neither of us really knew what to do.
We struggled into the folds of the warm, wet sail still
laughing, wriggling as the material clung to us, clumsy
because we didn't want to let go of each other; we wanted to touch each other as much and as thoroughly as we
could. There was a moment's pause when we found that
we were lying outstretched, naked and closer than we'd
ever been before, and there was nothing to stop us doing

this wonderful, secret thing that adults did, except our own ignorance.

Then I kissed Browneyes' salty soft lips and found that I was lying on top of her, and she under me, her legs parting and her hips meeting me; I thrust down on her because it was something I just *had* to do—and I saw her wince, so I stopped quickly and I could have cried because I'd hurt her.

"Please, darling Drove. Go on," she whispered, smiling as I saw a tear start at the corner of her eye; so I did, and suddenly she was warm and soft and beautiful and tingling, and everything was going to be all right. Soon our movements grew frantic and the whole thing was happening independently from my mind; there was no way I could influence events, it was happening, happening. Browneyes was moaning "Drove, Drove, ooh..." and her eyes were fierce as they stared into mine and we couldn't get close enough, close enough as the frightening wonderful explosion came, and came, and came, and... came...

Later the sun was still there, still overhead, so there was no way of telling how long we'd been lying there. I yawned and stretched, and felt Browneyes stir beside me. I stroked her hip and kissed her; her eyes opened, she smiled and moved against me. "Drove...?"

"Listen, I think we ought to get going. There's stuff on this ship that they'll need in the town." Two steam guns still remained of the deck cargo, and no doubt the holds held further war supplies which Pallahaxi might require very soon.

"Oh, Rax. I want you to love me again, Drove. Again and again and again. I don't ever want to leave here. Hey, do you know what?" Her pout changed to a grin. "You're going to have to marry me now, Drove. I'm going to tell my parents how you took advantage of me, and you'll have to marry me. And then we'll love each other every night, for always. We'll sleep in the bed the Regent slept in."

"Browneyes, you wouldn't tell your parents, would you?"

"I will if you don't make love to me right now."

I crawled out of the improvised bed quickly, otherwise I'd never have got out. Her grasping little hands followed me all the way and at one point I almost turned back, but I managed to free myself, and stood. "Come on," I said.

She stared at me mutinously. "I can tell you want to, you can't fool me."

"Browneyes, darling, of course I want to. But don't you see? Now we have the chance to end this dispute between the town and the Parls. We've got to tell them as soon as possible, before anyone else gets hurt. Afterwards, I'll come along to your room while your parents are working. Right?"

"You'd better." She climbed to her feet and put on the remains of her dress, slowly, grinning mischievously at me all the time.

"Oh, for Phu's sake." I'd dressed quickly, now I seized Browneyes and adjusted her dress where she had deliberately left one small breast uncovered to drive me mad. It occurred to me that it was sixty days since I'd arrived in Pallahaxi and Browneyes and I had met again. It was difficult to reconcile the shy little girl in dirty clothes on the shipwreck beach with this seductive young siren who realized fully the power her loveliness had over me. I wondered if I'd grown up as quickly as she—and I thought: maybe I had.

I was now able to think in terms of larger issues, of

the future of my environment, of the reality of war. Sixty days ago I would never have thought of hurrying back to report the surfacing of a sunken ship to the authorities; I would have let them find out for themselves, while I played slingball or raced drivets.

We climbed into the skimmer and pushed off from the glittering hull of the *Ysabel*. The breeze had freshened again and the sail filled, and soon we were sliding around Finger Point with the breakwater and Pallahaxi before us. Although there was no sign of grume-riders, I kept close to the shore. I looked back once, to see the *Ysabel* floating, scintillating on the grume like a frosted cake. I wondered how long she would stay there; the grume would be waning in a few standard days, she would lose her precarious buoyancy and descend to the bottom of the Pallahaxi Trench again. Before that happened she could be offloaded and even beached—although it was unlikely that it would be economical to repair her; the explosion of the boilers had ripped her bottom out.

Eventually we reached the harbour and sailed up to the slipway of the late Silverjack's yard. We hauled the skimmer out of the water, unshipped the mast and sail and stowed them in a corner of the boathouse. Then, feeling conspicuous in our ragged clothing—and quite positive that any fool could see we'd been making love—we walked along the quay.

Ribbon and Wolff were sitting on the plinth which forms the base of the monument, looking bored and throwing bits of bread to the newspigeons. The little birds were understandably nervous and kept fluttering away whenever the huge shadow of a grummet passed overhead. Information from the battlefront had been spasmodic recently due to the number of newspigeons which were taken by grummets before they could reach Pallahaxi message post. The few items of news which had got through had not been encouraging—in fact it had served to reinforce my view that sometimes it is better to remain ignorant.

Ribbon took one look at us and she knew. She smiled secretively and said "You two look as though you've been enjoying yourselves, huh? Sometime you must tell me your secret, Browneyes. But right now you ought to get some clothes on. People are looking at you."

I swung around guiltily, thinking that maybe Browneyes' breast had popped out again, but she was quite decent. I could see what Ribbon meant, though. My girl was eyecatching, glowing as she stood there in her rags. Her skin seemed to have gained a new dimension, not only due to the grume crystals, while her lovely face radiated a serenity and contented joy just one glorious step short of total smugness. I couldn't help but stare at her as she grinned at us from her fortress of love, and I heard Ribbon chuckle ruefully.

Meanwhile Wolff was tossing crumbs to the birds, oblivious. "Look, do we have to sit here all freezing day?" he complained.

"Oh, shut up, you," snapped Ribbon, then resumed her admiring scrutiny of Browneyes. "Well, what have you been doing?" she asked. "I mean, what *else* have you been doing?"

"Ribbon, we must see your father quickly," I said. "The *Ysabel* has surfaced again."

"Oh... right." Ribbon stood quickly. She didn't seem particularly surprised; I suppose this was a fairly common phenomenon along the coast. "He's up at the temple, I think. I'll come with you. Is there anything left worth salvaging?"

"A couple of guns still on the deck. I expect there's still plenty in the holds, even though there's that freezing great hole in the bottom. Enough to give us some sort of protection if the Astan men-of-war come close again."

"If the Parls let us keep the stuff," said Ribbon thoughtfully.

"They wouldn't dare to take it away from us, not this time. They said it was meant for the town, remember?"

"After it was lost they said that," said Ribbon significantly. I hoped her father didn't share her cynicism, or my hopes of a reconciliation between the town and the Parls would get nowhere.

Browneyes, Ribbon and I made our way up the main street to the temple, followed after an interval by Wolff; I imagined he was ashamed of being seen with us in our present state of undress, but didn't want to miss out on any developments. Browneyes had hardly uttered a word since we'd stepped ashore; all she could do was smile quietly to herself and radiate a happiness which shouted at everyone who looked at her—and everyone did, as we walked through the main street of Pallahaxi. And the way she clung on to my hand told them who was responsible... I wondered how I was going to face her parents.

An unpleasant scene met us at the temple; Strongarm was questioning the truck drivers—Grope and the other man—with scant attention to the niceties. "All right, you freezers!" he was shouting. "Now tell me this. If they're not shipping the fish out, then what the freezing Rax are they doing with it? Eating it?" He towered over them as they lay bound on the floor.

Grope whimpered, "I don't know, honestly I don't

know... all I did was drive and ask no questions." He had twisted one of his strange, two-pronged hands free from his bonds and was holding it out, as though to ward off another in a long series of kicks.

"Father!" called Ribbon and Strongarm turned away instantly, his face transformed as he saw his daughter. I thought to myself—as I had thought before—it *is* possible for parents and children to love one another; where did I lose out? Then Strongarm saw Browneyes and me, and his warm smile turned to ordinary friendliness, which was good to see in an adult, anyway. "Drove and Browneyes have something important to tell you," Ribbon said.

"Congratulations," murmured Strongarm dryly, staring fascinated at Browneyes, as though he'd never seen her before. "You're a lucky freezer, Drove."

I had to laugh and Browneyes didn't even blush. "It's not that, Strongarm," I said. "We were out over the Trench in my skimmer, and the *Ysabel* came up." I described the event.

"You say she's still there?" he said before I'd finished. "She was floating high?"

"She'll float higher when you take those guns off the deck."

"And we shall... and we shall." He was pacing about, thinking hard. "Just as soon as I can round up some men and boats. There's my skimmer, and poor old Silverjack has one at his yard. And Bordin, and Bighead... four boats should be enough. Only two guns left, you say? That's a pity..." He addressed the prisoners. "It'll be a long time before I get back, so you'll have plenty of time to think. And remember this. When the troops came to take back those guns today, they didn't bother to collect you two at the same time. Just think of that, when you're trying to decide whose side you're on."

"Do you know where my father is?" I asked Strongarm.

His eyes went cold. "He was seen passing through the town in the direction of the new cannery a short while ago. He had the man Thrawn with him. What do you want him for?"

"Well, to tell him about the *Ysabel*, of course. There were no Parls on the new wharf to see her. I don't suppose they know she's surfaced yet." I was beginning to think I'd made a mistake in telling Strongarm my intentions.

"Can't you let them find out by themselves?"

"Strongarm, can't you see? This is the chance for the Parls and the town to get together. They promised the guns and here they are—our guns, not guns they can say we stole. They can help us unload the *Ysabel* and set up the guns, and train us how to use them. We can't go on fighting each other like this, with the Astans only just over the hills!"

He watched me as I spoke; and when I'd finished he shook his head. "I like your sentiments, Drove, but I don't share your trust in the Parls. Never mind; we'll see. You go along and tell your father— but I'd rather my daughter didn't go with you. I can see us all having a freezing big battle around the *Ysabel*."

We borrowed a loxcart, and Browneyes and I set off up the hill out of town. The animal was slow and reluctant at first, but a lorin saw our problem, dropped out of a nearby tree and took the lox in hand, trotting alongside the shambling beast and encouraging it. So we reached the top and the river valley lay below us.

The estuary was almost completely dried out, a streak of brown mud across the fields and open land; the river ran as a glittering thread through the mudflats. A single trail of smoke rose from the cannery buildings; I noticed several new buildings since I had last seen the restricted area. A row of trucks stood idle near the gate and the dry bed of the estuary was littered with beached skimmers and deep-hulls. The cannery looked asleep, almost abandoned.

The lorin left us at this point, running off among the sticklebushes of the hillside in the direction of a number of holes in the face of the escarpment. The lox ambled on contentedly. There was a movement far below as a guard emerged from his hut and threw the gate open. A truck fountained steam and the workers came pouring from the largest building, their shift over. They piled into trailers attached to the truck and the whole train moved away with a shrill whistle, climbing the hill towards us. The sudden activity was a curious incongruity in the timeless quietude of the scene.

"Do you still love me, darling?" asked Browneyes unexpectedly.

I stared at her. "Why do you ask that? Of course I do."

"Oh..." she smiled happily. "I just wanted to hear you say it. After all, it's just possible you've changed your mind. My mother told me men often change their minds, once they've... uh... you know, *seduced* a girl..."

We were already sitting very close in the loxcart but now I moved closer still, finding that if I reached my arm further around her, I could cup her breast through a tear in the dress. "Just remember who did the seducing," I said.

At this point the train climbed past us and the homeward-bound Pallahaxi workers waved and whistled as they passed. I left my hand where it was, feeling reckless. There would be talk in the Golden Grummet later on, I thought.

Finally we drew up at the cannery gate and dismounted. The guard approached, staring suspiciously through the wire. "We must see Alika-Burt. Will you tell him we're here?" I requested importantly. "I'm his son Drove and this is Pallahaxi-Browneyes, my girlfriend."

If I had expected the guard to spring to attention at this revelation I was disappointed. He mumbled something and departed; then, much later, returned and opened the gate with a clattering of bolts. "Follow me," he said curtly, locking the gate behind us. He then strode off at speed.

I had little time to take in my surroundings as Browneyes and I panted at his heels. There were large boxes everywhere, and even larger objects covered with sheets. The cannery workers who lived in Pallahaxi had naturally been questioned many times as to the nature of the new cannery, but they had not been helpful. So far as they could tell, it was much the same as the old cannery; although the machinery was more modern the end product was the same. Remembering the incident of the empty truck, I had time briefly to wonder what they *did* with the end product. The buildings were more complex than I had realized; when looking down on this place from the hillside I had never received a true impression of its size. There were catwalks above and stairways disappearing into the grounds; tanks marked 'distil', tanks marked 'water', green doors and yellow doors and blue doors.

It was a yellow door which the guard flung open. He stepped aside and motioned us to enter. We found ourselves in a small room with one window, a desk and chair, a newspigeon cage and a tall rack of shelves.

There was little else of note in the room except my father, who sat in the chair regarding us with incredulous fury.

"I trust you have an explanation for this," he said at last, in a voice of infinite menace.

"Of course, father. I wouldn't have come unless it was important." Simple, idealistic fool that I was, I still thought it was important to stop the incipient civil war. "You see, Browneyes and I—"

But father had leaped to his feet in a classic display of temper. "Do you realize that you've probably made me the laughing-stock of this entire operation, slinking in here half-naked with that trollop hanging on to you? And you dare to mention her name in my presence? You even dare to bring her into my presence, parading herself for everyone to see, and her no more than a child? By Phu, I never thought the day would come..."

"—around Finger Point," I was meanwhile continuing doggedly, "and while they were attacking us the *Ysabel* floated up on the grume. We managed to get the skimmer alongside and BROWNEYES SAVED MY LIFE and after a while we took a look at—"

"You said what?"

"I said Browneyes saved my life. Browneyes."

"Are you trying to tell me the *Ysabel*'s floating out there?"

"That's right. I've already told them in the town and they're organizing a salvage party right now."

"You've told them *what*?"

"I said I've already told them in—"

"I know what you said. I know what you said." He was suddenly silent, staring at me with wide eyes and it took a moment for me to realize that he was frightened, deathly frightened of something I'd said. He looked old, almost *dying*, in the way Aunt Zu had while she was stripping the clothes off me, in the way Horlox-Mestler had when he walked to his death in the steam. There was a shivering in my stomach as it dawned on me that this was not merely the usual battle between us. This time something had gone wrong, terribly wrong. "Wait here," he said at last. "Just wait right here, you two." He almost ran from the room, slamming the door behind him.

Browneyes was staring at me and she looked frightened too.

"He's just a fool," I said. "I'm sorry he called you all those things, my darling."

"Something's wrong, Drove. I don't think... I don't think those guns were meant for the town at all. I think Ribbon's father was right; they wanted them here. But this time your father knows Pallahaxi will fight to keep them."

"Rax. Just tell me why I didn't keep my nose out of it, Browneyes."

"Because you were hoping you could make it up with your father, that's why. You thought he would be pleased and you wanted him to be pleased. I know you hate your father, Drove—but you don't *want* to hate him."

The door banged open at this moment and two guards came in, big and bristling. "You, come with us," one said to Browneyes, catching hold of her arm.

"Take your filthy hands off her!" I yelled. I jumped for him but the other guard caught me, pinning my arms behind my back. I kicked out frantically, but one man held me while the other was out of range, dragging Browneyes through the doorway. She screamed and twisted in his grasp but he tightened his arm around her waist and seized her thrashing fists in his other hand. Then they were gone, and I fought my guard hopelessly for a while. He merely chuckled, twisting my arm until the shoulder cracked.

At last the other guard returned. "Right, you can let him go," he said breathlessly. I ran to the door.

There was nobody outside. There were buildings with doors; all shut, all silent. Beyond them I could see the wire fence. Above, the sun blazed down casting black shadows among the dazzling brightness.

"Where is she?" I shouted. "What have you done with her?"

The two guards were walking away; I ran after them, grabbing their arms. They shook me off, walking on.

Then faintly I heard her call. "Drove! Drove!" I stared in the direction from which her voice came, but at first could see nothing. I moved past a small shed.

Then I saw her running, along by the fence, jumping ditches as she looked in my direction. She saw me and stopped, holding out her arms and crying, while I ran towards her.

I hesitated, looked towards the locked gate where the guard stood watching, grinning. Then I turned back to Browneyes and I think I was crying too. "What have they done to us, my darling?" I mumbled. "What have the freezers done to us?"

She was outside the fence and I was inside.

One of us was a prisoner.

EIGHTEEN

THE FENCE WAS at least five paces high and strongly made of wire mesh; all Browneyes and I could do was touch fingers. We did this for some time, gazing at each other and saying very little; realizing, I think, that there was little point in speculation. The authorities, the adult world, had separated us with the same impersonal finality that I employed when separating a pair of pet drivets whom I didn't want to mate. As my girl and I stood there, I knew for the first time just how much of the poor compulsive animal there was in me—despite my fine thoughts recently. All that crap about changing attitudes, burgeoning adulthood, peaking intelligence—all that was meaningless, irrelevant beside the desolation of being parted from my female.

We walked along to the gate, once, and tried reasoning with the guard; but like all of his kind he merely stated that he had his orders.

"Whose orders?" I shouted at him. "Who gave you those freezing orders?"

There may have been sympathy in his eyes, there may not. I don't know. He just said, "Your father's orders, Alika-Drove."

Browneyes looked so alone out there. There was not a living soul in sight; just the Yellow Mountains in the distance, then the trees, the fields, the hills, the open land. Nearby were vast heaps of excavated dirt, the ground scarred by trucks and loxcarts, trampled flat and bare of grass. There stood Browneyes, less than a pace away, sad and crying and caressing my fingertips, pathetic in her ragged dress with all the glow and excitement of new womanmhood gone. She looked like a hurt child, which she was, and my mind and body ached for love of her.

Then the two guards came and told me that my father would see me now. They took my arms and led me away; I watched Browneyes over my shoulder until a building cut her off from me.

They took me down steps and through a series of doors, along corridors where distil lamps burned evenly from their brackets. Eventually they knocked on yet another door and waited.

It was opened by my mother. I walked past her and found myself in an ordinary room, like the room in any house—except that there was no window. There was a table and chairs and all the usual furniture, all the usual litter of newspapers and food containers and ornaments and things that make a home; the only unusual factor was that all this should be here, under the cannery.

My mother was smiling at me. "Sit down, Drove," she said, and I obeyed automatically. "This is our new home. Do you like it, dear?"

I gazed around and saw the war map on the far wall. The Astan flags were very close, a tight ring around the coastal region of which Pallahaxi was the centre. Mother followed my eyes and her smile widened. "But they won't get us here, Drove dear. We're safe down here. Nobody can get us."

"What the freezing Rax are you talking about, mother? What about the town? What about the people in Pallahaxi? What's this all about?"

"There's room for them, is there? Some will perish. The good will be saved."

She was talking strangely, even for her. "That wire isn't going to stop the Astans, mother," I said.

Still with that crazy look on her face she said, "Ah, but we have guns, lots and lots of guns. Oh, lots and lots and lots."

"I'm getting out of here," I muttered, making for the door with one eye on mother. She made no attempt to stop me, but as I reached the door it swung open and father hurried in.

"There you are," he said briefly. "Right, get this straight. Your room is through that door, that's where you sleep. Otherwise you're free to go where you like inside the wire, so long as you don't go through the green doors or the red doors. Just keep out of everybody's way, that's all. Any funny business and I'll have you confined to quarters. This is a military establishment, you understand?"

"I thought it was the new seat of Government. Whom are we governing?"

"You will meet all the Members in due course and you will be polite to them."

"Certainly, father. And you will let Browneyes in?"

His impatience quickly turned to petulance. "I will not bargain with you, Drove! Just who exactly do you think you are? That girl stays outside, where she belongs!"

"Right." I walked past him to the door. "Then just tell the guards to let me out, will you?"

"Oh, Phu... Oh, Phu..." mother whined.

Father seized my arm in his rough grip. "Now listen to me, Drove, and save the arguments until later, when there's time. I'll just tell you straight that there's two types of people in this world as it is now—the winners and the losers. It's as simple as that. And so far as I'm concerned it is my duty to ensure that the members of my family are on the winning side. Don't you understand, I'm doing it for your sake?"

"After all," whimpered mother, "you must have some consideration, Drove. Think how it would reflect on your father's position if you went over to the—"

"Shut up!" yelled father, and I thought for a moment he was going to hit her. His face was livid and his mouth twisted; then quite suddenly he deflated, drew away from us and sat down. I stared at him. He looked normal, only more so. When he spoke, it was quietly. "One day I'll find out why everything I try to do is countered with opposition or stupidity or misunderstanding," he said. "I am insisting you stay with us, Drove, because I know that otherwise you will die, and I don't want my son to die—do you believe that? And as for you, Fayette, I'd like you to remember that this place is now full of Members and compared with the average status I am a pretty small fish. And Drove, space is limited here as you can imagine, and everyone has friends or relatives they'd like to bring inside the wire, but they can't—and as I am a small fish, you will appreciate that there is no way I can bring your, uh, girlfriend inside. Now," he said softly, regarding each of us in turn with only a little twitch at the corner of his mouth to indicate that he walked a hairsbreadth from total breakdown, "I'd like you both to tell me that you understand my viewpoint."

"When I think how I've worked and slaved for that boy—"

"Come with me, Drove," said father with a bright smile, taking my arm quite gently but almost running me from the room and down the corridor. We went through doors, climbed stairs and emerged into daylight. The sun was gone; the air was misty but still very warm; my clothes began to stick to me. I immediately looked around for Browneyes and saw her, sitting for-lornly on the ground beyond the wire.

Father was sniffing the air. "It looks as though the drench is coming," he said cheerfully. "By Phu, it really looks as though the drench is coming. I must tell the Members. I must tell the Members. Do you remember that drench two years ago, Drove, when the basement flooded and your drivets drowned? They could swim, but the water rose past the roof of their cage. There's a lesson for all of us in that, Drove. A lesson, oh yes..."

I was edging away, scared sick. He followed me, babbling on. "That's your girl over there, is it, Drove? Pretty little thing. Pretty little... let's go over and talk to her. Shame, her sitting all alone like that. I remember your mother..." Suddenly he stopped and stood quite still, staring southwards. I followed his gaze uneasily but could see nothing out of the ordinary, merely the high trees of Finger Point and the tiny figures of lorin. When I turned back he was looking at Browneyes again. "Come on," he said, walking briskly towards her.

She was watching us hopefully, but her face fell when I shook my head.

Father said, "Young lady, I've been rude to you and I'm very sorry. I hope you'll find it in you to forgive me for what I said, and for having to take Drove away from you like this." He spoke steadily and normally—and sin-cerely. "Believe me I have the best of reasons."

Browneyes looked up at him, her eyes swimming. "I'm not bothered about what you called me, I've been c-called names before... b-but I'll never forgive you for taking Drove away, it's the worst thing anybody's ever done to me in all of my life and I think you must be a very evil man."

He sighed, absently watching the Pallahaxi road where a huge crowd of people had appeared, swarming over the brow of the hill and descending towards us. "I think your father will be here soon," he said. "It would be best if you went back with him. And please believe me, I really am sorry. Come along to the gate, both of you."

He was back in control of himself. "Fetch Zeldon-Thrawn and Juba-Liptel," he snapped to the guard. "And alert the troops. Hurry, now!" The guard left at a run; I think he'd been asleep in his hut and had failed to notice the oncoming horde. Father turned and looked thoughtfully up the hill again.

Browneyes was outside the gate and I was inside, but only the heavy bolts separated us. I walked to the gate and began to tug at the bottom bolt. My father pulled me away bodily, but without undue violence.

"Just let me out of here, you freezer!" I yelled, struggling. "It makes no difference to you whether I'm inside or outside!"

I felt him tense. "Didn't you listen either, Drove?" he said quietly, and released me. For a wild moment I thought he was going to let me out, but as I stepped forward to the gate there were guards and troops all around. They stood with springrifles cocked, rapidly shuffling themselves into a spaced line inside the fence. I heard a hiss and a rumble, and a mobile steam gun was wheeled into position beside the gate, barrel poking through a small hole in the wire mesh. I saw troops stripping the covers from the long line of rectangular objects we had seen—so very long ago—from the other side of the river; these too proved to be steam guns, equally spaced around the entire perimeter of the large compound. More troops emerged from the buildings, wheeling portable boilers from which steam rose.

I whirled round on my father, staring at him. "What's going on?" I shouted. "Those are Pallahaxi people coming! For Phu's sake, who are we *against*?"

"We are against anyone who wants to kill us," he said, then walked among the guards, giving orders. I saw Zeldon-Thrawn and another man whom I took to be Juba-Liptel talking nearby, eyeing the rapidly approaching mob. After a moment Thrawn raised a hailing funnel to his lips.

"All right," he boomed. "That's close enough!"

The main body of the crowd hesitated some distance off but the large figure of Strongarm continued to stride forward. After a brief struggle Ribbon detached herself from restraining hands and ran after him.

I stepped up to my father who was standing beside a phalanx of guards. He glanced at me expressionlessly. "If your men shoot them," I said, "I will kill you, father, the very first chance I get."

He looked back towards the Pallahaxi people. "You're overwrought, Drove," he said indifferently. "It would be best if you went back down with your mother."

Strongarm halted at the gate, unharmed. He looked down in some annoyance on finding Ribbon panting beside him, then said loudly, "Who's in charge here?"

"I am," said Zeldon-Thrawn.

Strongarm paused, then said. "Perhaps you'll tell us who you intend to use those guns against. It was my understanding that our enemies are the Astans. But the guns seem to be pointed at us." And Thrawn, too, had that look on his face; that look of death. "Don't play with me, Pallahaxi-Strongarm," he snapped. "We both know the reason for this charade. Now say it, man. Say it!"

Strongarm gripped the fence with his hands and I saw his fingers whiten with the pressure. "All right," he said in controlled tones. "We've been aboard the *Ysabel*. Its cargo was guns and munitions for the defence of Pallahaxi, you said. So tell us this. Why was all that stuff on board made in Asta, man? Guns and shot and supplies, canned goods and distil, all made in Asta! Why is Parliament trading with the enemy?" His voice rose to a roar. "Whose side are you on?"

Thrawn was silent as Strongarm, losing control, shook the wires impotently. At last Ribbon got his hands away; he turned and looked at her blankly, then nodded as she whispered something to him. Ribbon next spoke to Browneyes who shook her head violently, crying. Then Strongarm took Browneyes firmly by the arm and the three of them made their way back to the main body of the townsfolk. Browneyes was looking over her shoulder all the way, stumbling as Strongarm pulled her along.

I heard a guard say to my father, "Shall we open fire now, Alika-Burt?"

And my father said, "Don't bother. They're already dead."

Much later they came again. The rain was beginning to fall steadily now, and it was becoming colder. Little pockets of mist swirled about, rising from the river. We watched them come down the hill from Pallahaxi; and there was steam trailing above their heads. They dispersed before they came within range of our guns and took up positions among the fields and ditches and swamps, but still the steam rose from their two guns and the Parls were able to pinpoint them and send a fusillade of shots in reply to each lone ball from Pallahaxi. Once they rushed the fence under cover of one of the new short nights, but were beaten off under the light of distil flares and left many dead. For a long time I couldn't go near that side of the compound for fear I would recognize one of the bodies. Then, one morning, they had all been removed.

I spent most of the time pacing about the compound looking out at the world and hoping to get a glimpse of Browneyes but the townsfolk rarely showed themselves now, and probably would not allow her to approach the fence. I examined the guns and other equipment around the cannery and found that a considerable amount was of Astan origin. I asked my father and Zeldon-Thrawn about this but they were uncommunicative; which served to reinforce my suspicion that Strongarm was right; that, incredibly, the Erto Parliament had concluded some sort of pact with Asta. Maybe, I thought, the war was over.

Despite the fact that people constantly referred to the Members and their Regent, I never saw them; apart from Zeldon-Thrawn. I began to doubt their presence and the feeling grew that somehow we were in a little closed world of our own, a purposeless world consisting solely of the troops, the guards, my parents, Thrawn, Liptel and the administrative staff and families. I kept asking myself: what are we doing here? Why are we fighting?

Nobody would tell me; they were all too busy, too nervous, until one day after a long lull in the gunfire Zeldon-Thrawn asked me into his office.

"I understood from Horlox-Mestler before he died that you have a working knowledge of our solar system, Drove," he said pleasantly as I sat and glowered at him. "I hope you don't mind if I continue where he left off. It's important that you know. It might explain a lot to you—and it might help explain the position of us in the cannery. You have to live with us, and you'll find it easier not to hate us. You might even be able to help."

"Uh."

"Now." He took a charcoal stick and drew a diagram similar to the one Mestler had produced, but smaller, leaving a great deal of blank paper. "You are already familiar with our world's passage on an elliptical orbit around the sun Phu. This is a proven fact although, until not many years ago, it was assumed that Phu revolved around us in a double helix." He chuckled. "I still find that a fascinating concept. However... in recent years a great deal of theoretical work was performed by our astronomers and, although they could explain the orbit as being in the nature of things, there were two factors which disturbed them.

"Firstly it would be logical to assume that our world was originally a part of Phu which broke off, or was spun off. But if this was so—then why does our planet revolve on its axis at *right* angles to its orbital path? Logically it ought to spin on the same plane, or very nearly so.

"And secondly, unexplained perturbations were discovered in the orbit."

He paused and sipped from a mug, regarding me thoughtfully. "Do these points strike you as interesting, Drove? They ought to. They interested our astronomers, and they resulted in certain further theories.

"The first theory postulated that at some time in the distant past, there was no relationship between our world and the sun Phu. We were not part of our sun. We had come from elsewhere; we had wandered through space and been captured.

"The second theory quickly became proven fact. The

perturbations in our orbit were caused by the giant planet Rax.

"And with the invention of the telescope, the two theories became one fact. It was found that Rax revolves on its axis on the same plane as ourselves. Rax and ourselves were once part of the same system—in fact we may even have been a part of Rax itself—and the sun Phu was the outsider..."

He allowed this to sink in. At last I said, "Are you saying that all this nonsense about the Great Lox Phu dragging us from the clutches of the ice-devil Rax is true? That Phu pulled us out of an orbit around Rax?" It was a disappointing thing to hear; it was as though my mother was proved right.

"It's true, but it's only half the story. It's a two-sided arrangement you see...

"Now the time has come for Rax to pull us back."

There was a long silence and I was shivering despite the warmth of the room, shivering in imagination of Rax cold in the sky, year after year with Phu a tiny point among the stars. Perpetual darkness, perpetual cold. This was the end of the world. Was this the end of the world?

"How many years?" I whispered. "How many years before we see Phu again?"

"Not many, comparatively." He hesitated. "Forty, they calculate. We have the food, the fuel—even though we lost a whole shipment of distil in the *Ysabel*. For the first time, civilization will continue... through us."

"But what about everybody else?" In fact I was thinking only of Browneyes. My Browneyes, dying a terrible death of cold while all the Parls, including myself, sat warm and snug underground.

I was conscious that I was talking, that Thrawn was

answering, that before long I was raving, trembling, that my voice was hoarse and my face wet with tears. After a while there seemed nothing more to say, no other way to say it. I tried to control myself, thinking: somehow I'll get out of here—or get Browneyes in here... Thrawn sat there, waiting patiently and sympathetically for me to recover. At last I said, "The war with Asta was all a pretence, then?" My voice was still shaky.

He said quietly, "No, the war is genuine; it happened, and while it was in progress certain astronomical facts came to light, certain calculations were made quite coincidentally. It then seemed more convenient to allow the war to continue, that's all."

"By Phu, I'm sure it did!" I was beginning to lose control again. "It allows you to take security measures like fortifying this place against your own people, while Astans and Ertons wipe each other out. And my father... he knew this, all the time... Don't you have any thought for the men who died in your fake war, who are still dying?"

"They will die in any case. They'll be happier, dying for a cause... Listen, Drove, I understand how you feel," he said reasonably. "I'm telling you all this because I feel you may be the one person capable of making Strongarm listen to reason. I want him to call off his men. Even you must admit that they gain nothing by attacking us."

"Get frozen, Thrawn," I said harshly. "The more Parls they take with them, the happier I'll be. And so will they; like you said, it's better to die for a cause."

"That's a negative attitude, Drove. Causes don't make sense any longer."

"And what about little Squint, and Silverjack? I suppose you killed them too?"

He sighed. "I want you to understand that you're one of us, one of the winners, whether you like it or not. In different ways Squint and Silverjack endangered our plans by discovering the nature of our operations, so they had to be eliminated. I wasn't here at the time, but if I'd been Horlox-Mestler, I'd have been forced to take the same steps. The whole operation could have been defeated if the public had discovered our purpose too soon—and that applies to the shelter complex on the Astan coast, too."

"That follows," I said bitterly. "The Astans have their own twin set-up. I suppose you've been exchanging vital supples during the curfew. Just as a matter of interest, is it the Astan public who occupy their shelter, or their Government?"

"Don't be stupid, Alika-Drove," he said tiredly. "If you don't propose to help, then just get out of my sight, will you?"

Some days later the townsfolk attacked again, this time with greater force and with more weapons. I was not allowed out of doors during the heaviest of exchanges, but I saw enough to realize that the Astan army—what was left of it after the bitter fighting across Erto—had joined forces with Strongarm and his men. This, of course, was what Zeldon-Thrawn had been afraid of. The battle lasted several days until gunfire became sporadic and eventually ceased with the Parls' defences unbreached. I tried to feel satisfied that we'd lost a large number of troops, but found that I wasn't made that way—besides, the Members and the Regent still sat in their holes below, unscathed.

"Now you understand why we had to fortify this place," said Thrawn afterwards. "The Astans and Pallahaxi concluded a pact which would logically mean

217

peace. But no, they had to find someone to attack—and what better target than us? And what did it profit them? What would they have gained if they had killed us? Work that one out, but don't bother to tell me the answer. I know already. I also know it's just possible you might have saved a lot of lives..."

NINTEEN

AS THE DAYS went by we saw little of the people of Pallahaxi; the mists thickened and the drench intensified to a steady, chill downpour. Visibility was reduced to about fifty paces. This would have been the ideal time for the men of Pallahaxi to rush the fence, and those in charge of defences sensed this; for many days guards were positioned close together around the perimeter, but no attack came. In a way this was not surprising. In this inclement weather the very thought of injury was terrifying—to lie there bleeding on the wet ground while the cold ate into a man's body, bringing the long madness before the merciful intervention of death... The guards wore thick furs, and each man carried hot bricks which were renewed at frequent intervals.

I spent most of my time in the troops' and guards' quarters, only visiting my room for the purpose of sleeping. I found it difficult to speak to my father now that I was aware of the lies he had been telling me ever since we came to Pallahaxi, and even before. I realized why he had flown into such quick rages whenever I had doubted him. He must have been alarmed when I questioned the veracity of the news bulletins, or the war itself. I wondered how much mother had known.

The shelter complex was much larger than I had at first realized, and although there were many forbidden areas I soon gained a rough knowledge of the general layout. The cannery plant was now abandoned, its purpose fulfilled, its produce stowed away.

There were four levels underground. Nearest the surface were the quarters of the guards and troops; virtually an all-male level apart from a few nurses and cooks. In the next level down were the general body of the Parls—the administrative staff and their families including my mother and father. There were many Astans among these people and I remembered bitterly my feelings of patriotism when Wolff, Ribbon, Squint and I had thought we were chasing a spy...

Below this—and here the restricted areas began— lived the Members and their families, some two hundred people. I rarely saw them, and they never ventured above ground—which was hardly surprising in view of the rapidly worsening weather. Probably Zeldon-Thrawn was the only member I ever spoke to, and after a while even he was seldom seen in the Administrative level, having apparently handed over most of the responsibility for defence to my father. I understood that there was yet another level below all these which housed the Regent and his entourage—but further details were not available.

The doors giving access to these levels were colour-coded, and all levels had independent access to the open air. Yellow doors were for use by everybody, blue for administrative officials and above, green for Members and above, and red—I only knew of two such doors— for the Regent and his courtiers only.

Sometimes the shelter complex, when viewed in the abstract, seemed to be a microcosm of the outside world as I had once known it...

A few more questions were answered; the guards and troops were my main sources of information. Squint had crossed the river, as we thought, and had been pointlessly shot by a guard who mistook him for an animal as he was darting for cover; nobody knew whether or not he had discovered the true nature of the cannery, despite what Thrawn had said.

But Silverjack had. Silverjack had identified Astan items in the *Ysabel*'s cargo...

Eventually the outside world entered our awareness again. One day there was a shout from a guard which brought the troops out at a run. I followed the exodus but was at first unable to discover the cause of the excitement due to the milling crowd, but suddenly I caught sight of figures beyond the wire. I ran across with my thoughts shouting Browneyes! but she was not there. About fifteen figures stood in the swirling mist, apparitions from a world some of us had almost forgotten, staring at us wordlessly. My father stood among the troops. I waited resignedly for him to give the order to shoot, but he too seemed to have been affected by the general atmosphere of inexplicable delight. After the first shock of surprise the troops were calling out to the newcomers, asking for news of acquaintances, laughing and shouting meaninglessly and slapping one another on the back while the strangers stared enigmatically through the wire.

Then the silent group began to pull rolls of canvas, ropes and poles from their back packs and soon had set up crude tents. Two more men arrived, dragging a handcart piled high with logs. Later there was a large fire burning and the men huddled around it, their faces crimson in the flickering glow as the warmth drove the naked fear from their eyes and they were able to think and speak to each other and, finally, to us. I wondered what kind of men they were, to leave the comparable comfort of Pallahaxi's stone houses for the risk of insanity and death in their present miserable surroundings. The troops threw items of food over the wire to them; I saw my father watching, tight-lipped.

As time went by their numbers increased and the camp assumed the proportions of a small village. Orders were issued forbidding the troops to throw food or fuel to the Campers, as they were called.

In due course most of the familiar faces from Pallahaxi joined the Campers and one wonderful sad day Browneyes arrived and we managed to kiss, awkwardly and painfully, through the wire. She said her parents would be arriving soon; Strongarm was already there, and Ribbon and Una and most of the others. Later the same day Wolff and his parents arrived; they did not join the main body of the Campers but stood near the gate, shouting and rattling the wire.

"What do you want?" I heard my father ask.

"Well, we want in, of course. You know me, Alika-Burt. I work for the Government. I demand you let me in." Wolff's father's voice rose nervously at the sight of my father's unchanging expression.

"You're too late," father said. "Nobody is permitted to enter. All available accommodation is taken." He spoke woodenly.

Wolff's mother began to speak rapidly. "Look, Burt, we have a right to come in. That's the only reason Klegg works for the Government, so he'll be looked after in times like this. It's not easy being a Parl's wife, I can tell you, with all the nastiness I have to face from the general public in the stores..."

I noticed Ribbon had wandered over to them; suddenly she spoke. "Don't you let them in, Alika-Burt. They're a bunch of snobby freezers." I hadn't really noticed Ribbon before; I'd been so occupied with Browneyes arrival. Now, looking at her, I had a shock. She was thinner, the planes of her face angular and almost old-looking, and she looked dirty.

"It's a shame," said Browneyes later as Wolff's family departed screaming threats into the mist and Ribbon sloped back to her father's tent. "She seems to have gone, you know, *common*." She regarded me anxiously as knowingly she used one of my mother's favourite words. "Honestly I don't like to put it like that, Drove— but that's the way she is. She seems to have gone all hard and nasty, and I can't get along with her any more."

Browneyes father, Girth, came striding up to the wire the following morning. This was the first time he'd seen the camp; he was a late-comer. He seized Browneyes by the arm, none too gently. "You come away from that freezer, my girl!"

"B-but it's Drove!"

"He's a freezing Parl and I won't have you associating with him!"

I stared at him. We'd always gotten along well together in the past and I couldn't understand what had come over him. His face was grim and haggard.

"Father, he can't help being on the other side!" cried Browneyes. "They won't let him out!"

"Yes, and I don't suppose he tries too hard. He has warmth and food for forty years or more inside there, so why should he want to leave?" This was the first time I'd heard that the public was aware of the true situation and I wondered how they'd found out. Not that it mattered.

222

It was hardly the sort of intelligence that could be kept secret for long.

Now he was tugging at her arm while she clung on to the wire, crying, "Let me go, father! You've never been like this before. Please fetch mother, she'll tell you. She won't let you..."

Momentarily he relaxed his grip, face bitter. "Your mother's dead," he said coldly. "She died last night. She... she took her own life."

"Oh..." Browneyes' fingers sought mine through the wire; her eyes were streaming and I desperately wanted to hold her, to comfort her.

"So come with me. I hold the Parls responsible for your mother's death and I'll not allow you to hang around here like this. You're a traitor to your own people! What they must think of you I don't know!"

Browneyes had closed her eyes as for a long time she hung on to the wire with both hands. I saw tears trickle out from under her lashes, then suddenly she tensed and swung around, facing her father, releasing the fence and snatching her arm from his grasp.

"Now listen to me," she said shakily. "And look around at what you call my own people. Over there is Strongarm talking to the Astan general, and not so many days ago they'd have killed each other on sight, because Parliament told them to. See further along there? That's Ribbon flirting with the Parl soldiers through the wire. Soon they may have to shoot her, because Parliament tells them to. All among these tents and huts are people being friendly because right now nobody's telling them to hate each other, even though we're all going to die soon. And in the middle of all this is *you*, father, telling me to hate my Drove and using poor mother as an excuse. Now get away from us, please."

Girth stared at her, shrugged and turned away, moving off among the campers. I don't know if he'd heard half of what Browneyes said; and if he had, I don't suppose he'd understood. He had merely found the opposition too great, too much to fight, on top of everything else. Browneyes looked after him and I heard her whisper, "Sorry, father..."

In the days that followed Browneyes often asked me about life in the shelter and, being Browneyes, her main concern was that I would find some irresistibly attractive girl down there and she would lose what little of me she had left.

"There are some girls down there among the administrative families," I admitted, "but I don't speak to them much. I don't want to be, uh, *classed* with them, I reckon. Before you came here I used to spend most of my time with the soldiers, playing cards."

She glanced along the wire to where Ribbon, as usual, was chatting through the fence with the troops. "I don't understand it," she said. "What happens when it gets *really* cold, and we're... we're all gone, and the soldiers have nothing to guard. Do they just sit there, all those men, in their shelter for forty years?"

Strongarm approached at this point, overhearing the last words. "Of course they don't," he said quietly. "I don't know just how big the storehouses are in that complex, but I do know there are about six hundred Members and Parls and their families—and there must be at least an equal number of troops. Who will have served their purpose, once we're dead and out of here..."

I didn't want to think about that. "Why are you all out here, Strongarm?" I asked. "Why doesn't everybody go back to Pallahaxi? It would be much warmer there, in the houses."

He smiled. "That's what I kept asking myself, when people were drifting out here and setting up camp. I'd ask them why they were going, and do you know what they'd say? They'd say: well, there's not much point in staying here, is there? So after a while I came along myself, and now I know. When you know you're going to die but you can see life somewhere else, then you want to huddle up against it, in the hope that a little bit might rub off on you."

And so the drench went on, and the days grew shorter and the rain turned to snow. Browneyes and I built ourselves a small hutch against the wire and we would sit in it by the hour, gazing at each other and touching fingers through the mesh, warmed by the glow of a Government heater. We would reminisce together like old people, alhough we had so little to reminisce about. There were no secrets between us, no recriminations over the disparity in our present situations. We knew we'd have been together if we'd had the chance, and we knew we'd never get that chance in the future, so we talked about the past, and tortured ourselves with quiet, intimate reminiscences about the only time we'd made love.

Outside, the tide rose and the estuary filled again and the beached boats, unattended, floated and went drifting out to sea on the current. There were a few cases of compulsive running among the Campers as their fires began to burn low and fear prevented them from scavenging for more fuel in the deepening snow. Often as Browneyes and I sat in our divided hut we would hear the scream as the cold reached into a mind and planted madness there, and the poor body began to run instinctively to fight away the chill. Almost inevitably exhaustion and collapse came before the pumping blood could restore a measure of warmth and sanity—and so there would be one less mouth to feed.

Perhaps the saddest thing was the disintegration of Ribbon. In the loss of all her material possessions, her pretty clothes—even, tragically, her pretty face—she resorted to her last characteristic, the only tiny bit of Ribbon she had left; her sex.

In the later days her father rarely mentioned her, and I spoke to her only once. She asked me to come to the other side of the compound, beyond the gate where the fence met the river. My heart sank as we halted at the water and she gave me a coquettish look through the wire.

"I've just got to get inside, Drove," she said. "You must help me. Your father has the keys to the gate."

"Listen," I mumbled, avoiding her eyes. "Don't be silly, Ribbon. There are guards at the gate all the time, even if I could get hold of the key, which I couldn't."

"Oh, the guards," she said airily. "Don't bother about the guards. I can always get past them. They'd do anything for me—there's hardly a woman in the place. I don't think you quite realize the power a woman has in this sort of situation, Drove."

"Please don't talk like that, Ribbon."

"They say they can hide me in their quarters and nobody would even know I was there. After all, you'd like me to be inside there with you, hey, Drove? You once told me you thought I was pretty, and I could be very nice to you, you know. You'd like that, wouldn't you? You always did want to make love to me, didn't you, Drove?" She smiled horribly; it was like a nightmare.

"Ribbon, I can't stand hearing this. I can't help you. I'm sorry." I began to walk away. I wanted to be sick.

Her voice grew harsh and strident. "You stinking

freezer, you're a Parl just like the rest of them! Well, I'll tell you this, Alika-Drove. I want to live and I have as much right to live as you and if I have to *abase* myself to stay alive then by Rax I'll do it!" She laughed, a cackle like an old crone. "You don't think I *wanted* to sleep with you, surely? Rax, the very *thought* disgusts me; you men, you're all the same, filthy beasts. *Beasts!* And your ego! What in the world made you think I *wanted* you, I'll never know!"

I had to say it, for the sake of the past, for the sake of truth. I walked back to her and said, "Ribbon, I never said you wanted me. For a long time *I* wanted *you*, because I always loved you, just a little. I'd like things to stay like that."

For just a moment her eyes softened and the old Ribbon looked out through them; but instantly the ice-devil was back, twisting her thoughts. "Love?" she shrilled. "You don't know what love is and neither does that little prig Browneyes. Love doesn't exist—we were just kidding ourselves. The only real thing is this!" She waved her arm extravagantly, indicating the cannery, the fence, and the drifting, settling snow.

There was only one way out and I took it. I walked away quickly, leaving her screaming at the wire. Her words had struck at my very existence and when I crept back into the little shack by the fence, I was almost surprised to see my Browneyes there on the other side, loving me, showing me that love still existed, assuring me that it would always exist.

TWENTY

DAYS WENT BY. The snow dwindled to a sprinkle and eventually stopped. The sky cleared and the stars reappeared at night, hard and glittering coldly. The sun Phu was small, smaller than I'd ever seen it before and hardly able to warm the frosty air even at noon, although still providing light enough to distinguish day from night. I wondered just how bright the days would be when our world was firmly in the clutches of Rax—not that I would ever be able to see those days, since the entrances to the complex would long since have been sealed to keep the warmth in, down below. I would have asked Thrawn, but I hadn't seen him for a long time; and my father's knowledge of astronomy was slight.

With the cessation of the snow and the clearing of the air it was now possible to see as far as the Yellow Mountains again—although they were now white, and would remain so for forty years. Nearby, the obo trees on Finger Point had become visible as silver pyramids against the pale blue of the sky. Anemone trees stood motionless among them. It was a desolate landscape; the only signs of life were a few lorin who could occasionally be seen moving dark against the snow of the escarpment where their deep burrows were—and the pathetic remnants of humanity camped outside the wire.

One day the canvas entrance to my rough hut was pulled aside and my father entered, bent double. He squatted beside me and glanced at Browneyes on the other side of the fence. Between us, the heater murmured comfortingly. "What do you want?" I asked sharply. Our shack was a private place, something between Browneyes and me, and father's presence was a desecration.

"The heater will have to go," he said briefly.

"Get frozen, father!"

"I'm sorry, Drove. I did my best for you. I even came myself instead of letting the guards take it. But there's talk in the complex; they say it's burning fuel uneconomically when we need it below. Some people were saying it was favouritism, your being allowed to use it out here. I'm afraid I'll have to take it. Build a fire, son."

"How can I build a fire inside a hut, you fool?"

"That sort of talk will get you nowhere, Drove." He seized the heater but released it instantly with a curse, licking his burned fingers. "By Phu!" he shouted, enraged and blaming me. "If you can't keep a civil tongue in your head I'll have the guards raze this hovel to the ground!" He stormed out, and shortly afterwards the guards came.

Browneyes and I built a large fire against the wire and met in the open from then on, but it wasn't the same. We were in full view of everyone and, worse, the fire attracted people. Understandably enough they would huddle around it but this made things difficult for Browneyes and me, as we were unable to converse freely any more. They would have thought us crazy, some of the things we'd been saying to each other.

Meanwhile, the situation among the Campers was worsening. Every morning there were fewer people around than the previous day; every night someone would awake chilled from their fitful sleep, and panic, and jump up and start running, and running...

The deep snow beyond the trampled area of the encampment was dotted with the trails of those for whom the effort of sustaining life in this dreadful cold had proved too much. Worse, many of the trails terminated in a visible inert heap, a constant reminder to the remaining Campers that they would all go that way, sooner or later.

Strongarm stayed, fighting off the cold by strength of will, as did his wife Una. Browneyes' father died quickly, not long after his irrational outburst at the wire; I was sorry to see him go, and Browneyes was inconsolable for several days. Ribbon died in her bed after a day of coughing and chest pains, and Browneyes cried over her, too, but I could feel little pain. I'd lost Ribbon many days before, where the fence met the river...

I felt guilty when I walked into the compound every morning after a warm night's sleep in a comfortable bed, to meet the sad wrecks beyond the wire. Often I would smuggle food to them, and an occasional small bottle of distil—for drinking; the stuff was much too precious to waste as fuel. Nevertheless, no matter what I did, I felt obscurely that I was in the wrong, and their reproachful eyes as they accepted the gifts from my warm hands reinforced this feeling. They needed me for what I brought them, yet they hated me for what I was.

Except Strongarm and Browneyes. Strongarm was the leader of the Campers and his huge form was everywhere, digging for fuel, rebuilding tents and shacks, chasing after runners and bringing them back slung over his shoulder, pummelling them and shouting reason into their numbed brains until their eyes cleared and they lived again.

And Browneyes... she never gave up; I don't think she would have started running even if an ice-devil had reached for her legs. She remained calm and beautiful, a little thinner but not too much, a small fur-clad bundle of sanity in all the madness around. Whenever I left the complex and made for the fence I would see her working; then she would look up and see me, and run towards me with a little cry of welcome, to be brought up short by the wire and stand there with arms spread, smiling love at me the way she always did.

The thought that this would end, that one morning she would inevitably be gone, gave me nightmares; and each morning as I opened the door to an even colder day, the dread within my chest would amount to physical pain which only abated when I saw her small figure run to the wire to meet me.

And at last it happened. One morning she was gone, Strongarm was gone, they were all gone. I ran to the fence, my eyes frantically searching the abandoned tents and shacks, the still smouldering fires, the multitude of tracks in the snow; but there was nobody there. I looked around for a note; thinking, maybe, they've all gone looking for fuel—but there was no word; there was nothing.

They never came back.

"They've gone back to Pallahaxi, of course." my father said. "They should never have left there in the first place. Why, with careful rationing they could last another year there, maybe two."

Mother smiled and I knew that they were both relieved that my unfortunate 'phase', as they put it, was over. "There are a lot of really nice people on our level, Drove. You've never had the chance to meet them. Of course, your father's never said anything—but it's been very *awkward* for us, your hanging around with the general public all the time. We're so glad you're back, dear."

Two days later I found a girl in our rooms, about my

own age and drinking cocha juice with my mother. Instantly I mistrusted the situation and my suspicions proved justified when mother left the room. "I must slip out for a moment, Drove," she said brightly. "You can look after Yelda while I'm away, I'm sure."

She left me staring furiously at the wretched girl who was smiling vapidly into her cocha. Facially she was reminiscent of Wolff; the resemblance did not end there, as I noticed she had no breasts. As if this were not enough, I've always detested the name Yelda since a traumatic love affair at the age of six.

The girl exposed her teeth. "What a nice person your mother is."

At least she was not scared to tackle a controversial topic. "I have a suspicion that my mother is insane," I said.

"She and I have so much in common," continued Yelda; ignoring me—or then again, maybe not. "We're both so fond of cooking and dressmaking and other things; do you know, I hardly noticed that she's so much older than I? She acts so *young*. She really does."

"To the point of childishness."

"Would you like a cup of cocha juice, Drove?"

"I detest the stuff, thanks. Only fools and women drink cocha juice."

"My, aren't you the rude one?" Yelda suddenly went on the offensive and I slumped back, beaten already. I was too sick and tired to fight. "You know, I didn't have to come here. I can leave right now, if I want to, Drove. I can tell you don't like me—I'm very quick at sizing people up. You resented me from the moment you saw me. Why?" She stared at me in toothy hostility.

"Yelda," I said with difficulty, "I'm sorry. I was trying to needle you because I felt low. And it just so happens that I don't like my mother and I don't like cocha juice, so you picked two unfortunate subjects. Let's try again, shall we?"

She was already standing, ready to leave, but now she hesitated. "Well... well, all right then. All right, if you promise to be nice. I wasn't sure about even coming here, you know, because of what everybody's been saying about you and some girl. Anyway... do you play Circlets? I noticed a Circlets board in the corner. I'm very good at Circlets. I can always beat my brother."

I seemed to have stepped back into the past. My breastless playmate was smiling happily again as she set up the counters, and soon she would start picking her nose or having to go to the washroom.

So we played Circlets and I don't know whether I enjoyed it or not, but there were short periods when I didn't think of Browneyes so it passed the time away, and there was going to be plenty of time to pass away. We talked about the children on our level and Yelda seemed to know them all; a lot of them she liked but others were just hateful, and kept pulling her hair. "But I like you, Drove," she said. "Boys are usually so rough and smelly, but you're nice. I hope you'll let me come and play with you again..."

I was still staring incredulously into space when my mother arrived back. "Where's Yelda?" she asked immediately. "I hope you weren't rude to her, Drove."

"She's in the washroom."

"Oh, good. She seems such a nice girl, don't you think? Wholesome and unspoilt. Very much the sort of person your father and I would like you to associate with."

"Look, mother, are you really serious? I mean, are you really thinking about what you're saying? Don't you know who I am?"

She smiled indulgently. "Of course, dear. And it's very nice to have you back with us. Your father and I have missed you—but then we've been very busy, this last two hundred days. Imagine that—it's only two hundred days since we left Alika. How time flies... I expect you miss your pet drivets, dear."

And she actually had me remembering, with self-recrimination, that I'd left the drivets under the seat of the motorcart ever since smuggling them out of the house at Alika. They'd probably died by the second day of the journey; it's a wonder we hadn't smelled them.

I wondered if it would be possible to play it her way, to recapture some sort of eternal childhood for her benefit, capering before her like a jester until my hair turned grey and my teeth fell out and she began to think maybe I was a little too old for short pants.

Later that evening my father arrived back at the rooms in some excitement after a multi-level meeting attended, so he said in awed tones, by the Regent. It seemed we were all going to have our names changed.

"Place of birth means nothing now," he said. "And the Members feel that the time has come to make a new start. We're all in this together, they said—so where a man comes from has no significance any more."

"That's right, Burt," said mother. "Although I always felt we were in some way... *distinguished*, coming from the capital, you know."

"We are not the only people ever to come out of Alika, Fayette," chuckled father in fine good humour. "And Alika itself is just a name now, a meaningless jumble of abandoned ruins."

I spoke carefully, feeling too tired to incur his wrath. "So what are we calling ourselves now, father?"

"Our new prefixes will be based on the level on

which we live, so that it will be possible to identify a person completely when he introduces himself. Much better; much more polite this way, I feel. Under the old system it was so easy to make a mistake as to a person's standing. So now, after the Regent, his entourage will bear the prefix 'Secondly'. The Members will be 'Thirdly'—our good friend Thrawn will be known as Thirdly-Thrawn rather than Zeldon-Thrawn. I hope you will remember that, Drove. Or should I say?" and here he laughed outright "—Fourthly-Drove."

That night as I lay in bed I found I was repeating it to myself, over and over until it became one of those obsessions which forbid sleep: Fourthly-Drove, Fourthly-Drove, Fourthly-Drove...

I awoke with a slight headache and a feeling of lassitude; and I found that I was wondering about the troops and guards, and whether they were to be known as Fifthly. My father hadn't mentioned them last night. I dressed warmly, thinking I might have a look outside; it was some time since I had been out in the cold, and the fresh air would probably make me feel better. It had been a night of strange dreams and flickering images; the room had been cold and many times I had awoken, thinking Aunt Zu was standing over me.

I climbed the stairs and paused before a yellow door. I tried the handle but it was locked. Listening, I could not hear the usual murmur of conversation from the troops' billets. I was aware of a feeling of unease and hurried back down the steps to meet my father striding along the corridor. "Drove!" he called, on seeing me. "Have you been fooling around with the doors?"

"Not me. I've only just got up."

"Strange thing... strange thing... " he murmured almost to himself. "I could have sworn Thrawn asked me to see him this morning, but the door's locked. All the green doors are locked. I can't get through to the Members; it's most inconvenient. We have important business to discuss." He shivered suddenly. "Cold, isn't it. I must check the heating."

"The troops doors are locked too," I said.

He looked discomfited. "Are they? Are they? Yes, there was something said at the meeting about that. In the interests of fuel economy, it's better if we don't have too much coming and going between levels... Perhaps someone misunderstood the resolution at the meeting. It was only the yellow doors we were talking about. Yes, that must be it." He hurried away, muttering.

I climbed the stairs; despite my wrapping of furs I shivered at a vision of Aunt Zu I had caught from my father's worried face. The memory of that terrible evening in Alika was now firmly back in my mind—and with it, something else: a question. Something to do with the meaning of fear, the meaning of legends.

The wind was strong as I shut the door behind me and stood looking at the snow and the fence. I noticed that the gate swung open, clanging with the wind. There was nobody to keep out, now. I wondered about the Great Lox.

How could a legend be so close to the truth? Who was the man who first dreamed up the notion of the Great Lox Phu dragging the world from the tentacles of the ice-devil Rax? And then suggested that one day the process might be reversed?

Surely, it could only be a man who had lived through the previous ordeal. And how had he survived, with no technology at his disposal? He couldn't have had a technology, otherwise it would have left traces—after all, the Great Freeze only lasted forty years.

I caught myself walking fast as the cold prodded at my mind with icy fingertips—and for the first time I wondered *why* I was scared of the cold. I had been told that it was an instinct. As pain warns a man against the dangers of injury, so fear warns him against freezing. But why fear? Wasn't the cold itself enough warning?

Unless it was a race memory, inherited from the minds of those people who had survived the last Great Freeze...

So then I knew I had beaten them at last, and I laughed aloud as I stood in the blinding, slashing cold. They wouldn't survive; they were too clumsy, too selfish to survive down in their artificial burrow. And even if by some miracle they did, when the sun again shone on their faces they would be old, horribly old as they crawled to the surface and wept their relief. And even their children would have lost their childhood, and would never have sailed a boat, or watched a cloud, or ridden the grume. They were the losers.

As the cold ate into me I saw the vision of a pretty girl with her foot caught, soon falling asleep, waking safe with no memory of having slept, no memory of the passage of time.

And recently, empty shacks, empty tents...

And a long time ago, a small boy waking on a doorstep fresh and happy; and while he had been sleeping he would not have breathed, neither would his heart have beaten...

Neither would he have aged.

My thoughts were failing now, but there was no fear. Dimly I saw Browneyes, still young, smiling at me under the new sun, kissing me with our love still new, very soon now because this sleep has no memory...

Presently the lorin came.